Lust Bites

Lust Bites

Kristina Lloyd
Mathilde Madden
Portia Da Costa

BLACK LACE

Black Lace books contain sexual fantasies.
In real life, always practise safe sex.

First published in 2007 by
Black Lace
Thames Wharf Studios
Rainville Rd
London W6 9HA

A catalogue record for this book is available from the British Library.

www.black-lace-books.com

http://lustbites.blogspot.com/

Typeset by SetSystems Ltd, Saffron Walden, Essex

Printed and bound by CPI Bookmarque, Croydon, CR0 4TD

The paper used in this book is a natural, recyclable product made
from wood grown in sustainable forests. The manufacturing process
conforms to the regulations of the country of origin.

ISBN 978 0 352 34153 2

Distributed in the USA by Holtzbrinck Publishers, LLC, 175 Fifth Avenue,
New York, NY 10010, USA

The Vampire's Heart
Kristina Lloyd

Prologue

In the moments before Esther's return to the world, Billy Dresner III was slouching towards the waterfront, past crumbling tenements, alleyways and whores, a stolen black Labrador trotting at his side. According to the tag, its name was Maxie. But no matter.

By the derelict warehouses of the Hudson, Billy knelt and killed the dog with a single bite. He fed in a guilty frenzy, trains rumbling in the distance, until he was snagged by a sense of movement far beyond the city and across the cold dark ocean.

Could it be?

Billy rose, face lifted to the heavens. Yes, it had to be. This was it. The moon silvered him in a seraphic glow, his shorn hair glinting, and he stared into the night, a bloodied masculine angel, hardly daring to believe.

Over 3,000 miles away, north of London's Maida Vale, a girl was born who, according to the midwife, had 'two arms, two legs, one head'. When the slippery livid child released her first roaring breath, Billy knew the world had changed.

He stood by the crumbling docks, gazing up at a hundred thousand million stars.

She was back.

Somewhere on earth, she was back. Centuries of longing were coming to a close, a prospect that filled him with happiness and dread. Tears glittered in his eyes. He blinked and let them fall, promising himself that this time he would be kind to her.

1

The icecap sparkled in the starlight, and the team was the only sign of life, six halogen headtorches shining on the snow, sledges hissing as they hauled. Doug's breath was laboured, his coughing fits hampering their progress. They were behind schedule and wouldn't reach camp for another hour.

'You OK?' checked Esther. It hardly seemed worth asking because she couldn't see his eyes. Instead, she saw only her reflection in the silver mirrors of his snow goggles.

'Fine,' said Doug, his voice hoarse. 'Stop asking, will you?'

A fur hood fringed his half-masked face and his brown beard was jewelled with frost. Esther heaved alongside him, ski-poles stabbing in the snow, saying nothing. Half a mile ahead, the other four moved as one; small colourful figures on the dusky ice. It shamed her to think they might have guessed her secret.

'Give me your warmth,' Doug had said last night. His hand had moved inside her thermals, making her whimper in response. Their breath had puffed out, freezing white in the air. She remembered his voice, gentle through gritted teeth. They mustn't be heard by the others.

'You're wet. You want it,' he'd huffed. His fingers, brutally cold at first, worked inside her. Their sleeping bags hissed as they moved on shifting layers of caribou skins and synthetics. Doug's voice scoured her senses the way his beard scoured her skin.

Even in a heated tent, it was too cold for sex. Doug was too cold for sex. Esther couldn't even be sure they liked each other any more. But she could see they were complicit in their need, hungry to stave off the threat of oblivion this boundless, moonlit world inspired.

And yes, she *had* wanted it. Still did. But she wanted it in the way an animal wants it, and that wasn't reason enough.

Imagine a place where your mind is free, where the glacial air is fresh and pure. Imagine dazzling white landscapes, polar bears and seals as you follow in the footsteps of history's great explorers. Imagine the Arctic. Imagine the challenge. Imagine everything is possible with White Sky Adventures.

This trek was no holiday. Partly sponsored, partly funded by White Sky, its purpose was to establish routes and itineraries for a new line in extreme vacations. Doug, a healthy office worker with a sense of adventure, belonged to the company's target demographic. If he struggled with the level, then it was probably too tough.

Esther had to slow to match his pace and the rhythm frustrated. Her thighs and arms wanted to push on, to work at their muscular peak, and this sluggishness dragged on her body. She would need to gain greater patience if she were to make it as an expedition leader.

Their skis hissed in the lengthening silence until, in a voice quivering with emotion, Doug said, 'My feet hurt. Can you understand that? My feet fucking hurt.'

'We'll look at them later,' said Esther, and she thought of Shackleton all those years ago, removing his boots and seeing frostbitten flesh fall from his toes, exposing bone.

You couldn't escape the stories of this place. Sometimes, it was a mythical land where ancient explorers sailed through peppermint green seas, mistaking icebergs for giant swans and narwhals for aquatic unicorns. Over the centuries, reports had come back of ghostly mountains, mock suns and nights lit with curtains of coloured phosphorescence. Sometimes it was a frozen desert, tempting men onto foolish, heroic quests. Their stories hung in the emptiness: tales of survival and loss; of horror and madness; of people on the borderline between life and death. And, of course, there were many untold stories too, stories with no one left to tell them.

'Give me your warmth,' Doug had said.

Esther cringed now to think of his hand between her thighs last night. It seemed an extraordinary intimacy when, for the most part, hands out here were hidden inside gloves. If you wanted to eat a person, it was said, first remove their hands. Hands make us human. And hadn't there been rumours of cannibalism and severed hands on Franklin's final expedition? Where might the hands go? Could there be a cache or two out here, buried under the snow, perfectly preserved?

No, it didn't do to think such things. But spend enough time on the ice and anyone's thoughts will start to warp.

'Hey!'

A voice sailed across the ice.

In the starlit gloom, Esther could make out Bird, their team leader, waving a ski pole in the air. He pointed east, directing their attention. Esther checked her wristwatch for bearings. It looked like a minor deviation, probably to investigate something unusual, most likely a dead animal. A break in the monotony was always welcome. She started to pull away from Doug, towing faster.

It would be better tonight. They would reach the mushers' cabin, an isolated timber lodge where all six would share a room. For the last three nights, they'd camped by snow walls, the team dividing themselves among four-man and two-man tents, an exercise in team-building Bird was experimenting with. Even the married couple, Margret and Johannes Kappel, were to sleep apart. Esther had spent most nights in the large tent, lying alongside Adrian, the landscape photographer, or Margret, who talked German in her sleep. She'd spent last night paired with Doug.

'I haven't slept since we got here,' he'd said bitterly just as Esther was about to drift off. He made it sound as if it were her fault and Esther, cocooned in her sleeping bag, didn't reply. He would never sleep if they started talking.

'I hate this place,' he went on, addressing the domed ceiling. 'I hate the darkness. The sun doesn't rise. There's no dawn, no new day. I hate it. It's all the same fucking endless night.'

Esther rolled onto her back and they lay there like two larval grubs. 'It'll change soon. When the sun comes, the days start getting longer really quickly.'

'It's too big,' he said. 'I can't get my head round it. Too much space.'

'I know,' murmured Esther.

'And too cold. Too cold to sleep.'

'Try,' said Esther. 'Just try to sleep.'

They lay there in silence, the amber tent faintly lit by a star-encrusted sky, shining down and glancing off the ice. Snowlight, Esther called it. She adored the ice. It thrilled and appalled, holding a serenity never far from treachery. You couldn't fathom it. Areas of Greenland were still marked 'unexplored' on maps. And even if its terrain were charted, you wouldn't know it. You could never know its heart.

'You enjoy patronising me, don't you?' whispered Doug. His breath had misted above them in apricot-tinged clouds.

Esther sighed quietly, 'Doug, please. I don't want to –'

'You enjoy it,' he accused.

His sleeping bag rustled as he edged closer, speaking

against her ear now, his breath tickling. Esther turned away, wanting to ignore him because he was being an idiot, but Doug was quick. Fabric hissed in a flurry of movement and he switched on a torch, filling the tent with the fake daybreak of halogen.

In the clear white light, Esther could see all the detail of his toffee-brown eyes, the pores on his nose and individual hairs on the edge of his beard. She recalled first meeting him at a cheap and cheerful pasta restaurant with a bunch of other people. 'Mmm, nice,' she'd thought, knowing he was slated to join the team. And 'Mmm, even nicer' when, at the end of the evening, he'd given her a goodbye peck on the cheek, his beard scratching pleasantly, his hand a light pressure on her hip.

There'd been a spark between them from the off but they'd always maintained a professional distance, even when flirting.

'If it weren't for this trip,' Doug had once teased, 'I'd make a pass at you.'

Esther had tried to convince herself their feelings would fade once they hit the ice but instead it seemed Doug's desires were being channelled in a new direction. He was becoming increasingly irritated with her. She could see he was struggling with the trek but wasn't sure how much. He might be just tetchy. Or he could be seriously losing it.

'What's wrong, Doug?' she asked. 'Why are you being like this?'

He looked down at her for a long time before declaring, 'I want you'. His voice, bold and strong, made the words sound so uncomplicated, and it stirred Esther's lust. She gazed back, confused. For that moment, she felt she might be with Doug from home, the man she liked, not Doug the team-mate who'd been behaving like a prick. This was too dangerous. They had another three weeks on the ice, and the fallout could be hell, the impact on the team disastrous. Esther wondered if Bird, noting the tensions between the two of them, had paired them in a tent hoping to solve the problem.

'Doug, please,' she said. 'Let's just sleep.'

Doug frowned then, before Esther knew what was happening, he was kissing her hard, his bristles crushing into her skin as he filled her mouth with the hot slithering shock of his tongue. He clutched a fist of her long dark hair, knocking her woollen cap askew. Despite herself, Esther responded, protesting faintly as they kissed.

She could smell him, a hint of stale sweat and unwashed hair but knew she didn't smell too great either. When you bathed by frolicking half-naked in the snow, you didn't bathe too often. Their mutual grubbiness excited her. It felt primitive and abandoned, perfectly in tune with their surroundings.

Oh, why couldn't this have happened months ago? Why couldn't he have pressed her against his car and pushed his hand up her skirt? Why couldn't he have fucked her over the big table after one of their team meetings? Why couldn't they have done what she'd fantasised about and maybe they'd have got it out of their systems?

Esther pulled back. 'Doug, don't,' she whispered, her breath clouding on his face.

Again Doug ignored her and again she let him. He tugged the zipper of her sleeping bag, its metallic rasp slicing through the silence as the casing split open, revealing Esther, unpeeled in tubular underclothes.

She wriggled to tug a caribou skin over them as Doug shoved his hand down her thermals. His fingers were so cold that when he buried two inside her, Esther gasped in discomfort.

'You're wet. You want it,' he breathed, watching her expression as he roused her.

'You sod,' she whispered, closing her eyes.

'Don't you like it?' he murmured. He kissed her neck, teeth scraping and whiskers prickling.

Esther adored it, and was disappointed at how easily Doug had knocked her off balance. Christ, was she that weak? A few days in the Arctic and any man starts looking good? But no, she liked him. Not this much though. Oh, get a grip, she told herself. Think about tomorrow and the day after: six people in the middle of nowhere, team spirit splintering around their sordid little secret.

But it was difficult to stop when his fingers were so good. Physical pleasures were rare, and this was heaven, her juices spilling warmly as he masturbated her.

A spasm of willpower made her push against his chest. 'Doug, back off. We can't do this.'

He curled his fingers inside her, giving her a steady look. 'We can,' he said, and Esther began sliding towards agreement.

'You've wanted this as long as I have,' Doug went on.

'But the others,' breathed Esther.

'They don't need to know,' said Doug, and he worked his fingers with deep slow thrusts.

Esther moaned, succumbing fast. She needed badly to feel him inside her, to have his cock hammering into her soft wet warmth. She wanted to feel fleshy and vivid, and soon all she could think of was something along the lines of being hung for a sheep as a lamb.

'Oh, just fuck me,' she gasped, shoving her thermals down to her ankles.

Doug seemed surprised and a touch disappointed that she'd relented so quickly. Perhaps he'd been hoping for a fight. Puffing and grunting, he knelt up, fiddling with his underwear as Esther dropped her knees wide, her hips tipping in search of him. Doug fumbled to drape a fur over his half-bared butt. His knob nosed at her entrance then he plunged deep, his thickness prising her flesh apart, making Esther groan.

'Shhh,' he warned, because the other tent was only feet away. Bearing his weight on his arms, he slid in a series of deep deliberate strokes.

'Ah, ah,' she whimpered, doing her best to keep quiet. Increasingly urgent, their groins mashed together in a clumsy, savage fuck. Skins and fur slipped about them, nylon hissed and the flysheet flapped as they gasped and panted, bucking and frigging.

'Take it, go on,' Doug had murmured as he'd neared his peak.

Then they'd climaxed separately with hushed private shudders, eyes squeezed shut, heads turned aside. In the morning, Esther had woken with embarrassment and regret. Presumably Doug had felt the same.

He'd worn snow goggles for much of the following day, even though it was dark. 'My eyes are sore,' he'd rasped when Adrian had asked about them. 'My eyes and my feet, OK?' He broke into a fit of coughing. 'Oh, and did I mention my throat?'

He couldn't look Esther in the eye, more like. He had to hide behind big mirrored lenses, about the only place you *could* hide out here. Whenever Esther looked at him, all she got were reflections.

Bird called across the ice. 'Hey, looks like a carcass!'

The wind was gathering and snowflakes whirled in the dimness.

Esther stabbed her poles harder, heaving on her sledge, eager to join Bird as he hauled closer to the lump on the ice.

'Fox,' he said as Esther approached. 'What a beauty.'

Snowflakes flitted across the beams of their head-torches as they studied the creature, its white fur stiff with icicles, mouth sagging open, gums and yellow teeth exposed. Drifts of snow slanted against its belly, and its neck was ripped open in a meaty gash, the snow pink and pitted where blood had seeped down.

'Funny kill,' said Esther. 'What did that?'

'Dunno,' said Bird. 'Weird. It's hardly been touched.' He toed the fox with his boot. 'Not much blood either.'

'Must have been a while ago,' said Esther. 'Tracks are all covered.'

'Hmm. Maybe,' said Bird.

Johannes approached. 'My God,' he said brightly. 'Precisely in the neck! It is looking like vampire bat.'

Esther laughed, yet even as she did so she felt a sense of unease. She turned to see Doug trekking on his own, his headlamp shining in the snow-filled dusk, a lonely figure bent like a cripple and refusing to be drawn.

And she looked back at the fox, remembering another tale of two stranded explorers who'd survived for weeks by drinking each other's blood. A man and a boy, she seemed to think, stuck on the coast. Yes, they'd drunk blood from a shoe, that was it.

Halogen light danced over the dead fox. Its throat sparkled like spilt rubies, the stained snow glittering like crushed pink glass. And Esther thought of those two men gazing at a frozen ocean, the blood thick and warm in their mouths.

She screwed her eyes shut, wishing she didn't think these things. Iciness stippled her cheeks as snowflakes hit. She wished she could clear her mind and escape all the stories. Out here, they always seemed too real.

To the untrained eye, *Hope's End* was nothing but a blip on the landscape, a hump of snow in a waste of ice. A Cold War relic modelled on igloo curves, it had fallen into the hands of the vampire community when one or two significant maps had been redrawn, and one or two significant people had been killed, easy things to achieve when there are vampires in high places. Mortals might be surprised by the number of monsters at the Pentagon.

No, you wouldn't know the camp was there. Its entrance was a crevice in a bank of snow zig-zagging down to the building itself, a huge high-tech dome with comfortable living quarters, two redundant research labs, a gym, a sun room and vast amounts of storage space. Its inner walls were formed of billowing curves that had something to do with tensile architecture and insulated breeze block. Billy didn't know how it worked. All he knew was that it did; and that was thanks to the billions of dollars invested in military science.

All this sophistication at the vampires' service, and Suzanne had nearly blown it. Billy was furious. He strode down the corridor, combat boots thumping, in one hand a dead white fox, in the other a dead white hare. His muscles flexed beneath his white T-shirt and dustings of snow melted in his wake.

Why the hell did she have to turn up? For months, he and Simeon had lived alone, everything fine. Suzanne appears and it's chaos. Fucking chaos.

In the main room of the dome, a sparsely furnished arena where candles cast shadows onto curved white walls, Suzanne lay naked on a polar bear rug. Her honey-pale limbs and honey-blonde curls gleamed in the fake firelight. The polar bear was open-jawed, head fixed in a mute roar. By Suzanne's side was Renfield, their pet cat, a fluffy vampire pedigree, purring contentedly as Suzanne plucked single strands from its silvery blue fur.

Billy slung the two carcasses across the room. Streaks of blood smeared on the faux stone floor as the bodies skidded towards the rug. The cat scarpered with a yowl and the animals lay there, glassy-eyed, old blood clogging their white fur like damson jelly.

Suzanne recoiled. 'Ugh,' she cried, rolling away with her hand to her mouth. 'Oh, that's rank!'

Billy's face was impassive, his voice quietly menacing. 'It's your kill,' he said.

'Oh, take it away,' complained Suzanne. 'I'm sorry, OK? Now, take it away.'

She turned to face the fire, presenting Billy with her pert little ass, hand still clamped to her mouth. He wasn't moved in the slightest, not today.

'You need to clean up after yourself, Suzanne,' he warned.

'I forgot,' said Suzanne.

'People are trekking out there. All it takes is one stupid –'

'I know, I know,' said Suzanne. 'It won't happen again.'

'I know it won't,' said Billy. 'Because, if it does, I will chain you up in the play room. I will deny you sex and blood. And you will be so tormented you'll start wishing you were mortal.'

Billy ran his hand over his head, palm skimming his beige-blond mohawk. Broad-chested and lightly tanned, he cut a punkish military figure in khakis, tight T-shirt and scuffed army boots. Some vampires found him scary. Suzanne, damn her, wasn't one of them.

She rolled onto her back, knees flopping wide. 'Do you want to fuck?' she cooed, splaying herself with her fingers. Shadows danced on her skin, and beneath her trimmed golden pubes, her scarlet slit glinted.

'No.' Billy meant it. She was too obvious. He was already bored of her.

'Oh, c'mon, Billy Boy. There's nothing to do around here. Just a little fuck.' Suzanne squashed her breasts together and waggled a pointy, lascivious tongue at him.

Billy ignored her and went to retrieve the carcasses

just as Simeon wandered into the room, three large phials in his hand. A pallid lanky figure with bony features and long black hair, he had that air of Transylvanian nobility Billy really went for.

When Simeon spotted the carcasses, he drawled, 'Oh, must we make the place untidy?'

He flicked his head, making his black hair swing, a theatrical gesture that today irked Billy. The two men had been together centuries (though it was a bit on-off) and, having no reflections, were more familiar with each other's face than their own. 'I don't know where you end and I begin,' Simeon used to say in the nineteenth century when they were tragically in love, as was the fashion.

In some ways, those blurred boundaries would always hold true. Billy often felt he could only see himself through Simeon's eyes. 'You have the most perfect straight nose,' Simeon would say. Or, 'Your eyes are palest green with black rings around them. Weirdly bright, so intense. And yet, wow, almost translucent.' Recently, he'd declared that Billy's eyes were as wild and luminous as a husky dog's. They were always trying to describe each other's eyes. 'Violets,' Billy would say to Simeon, tonguing his eyelids closed. 'And amethysts. So fucking dangerous.'

Billy grabbed the carcasses by their hind legs. 'Your cousin's a disgrace,' he said.

'He's bullying me,' simpered Suzanne. 'Make him stop.'

The fox's tongue lolled as Billy slung it over his shoulder, carrying it with the dead hare to the snow pit outside. On his return, he found Renfield licking streaks of blood from the floor and Suzanne and Simeon each with a phial of Blud. The pool balls had been racked up on the table.

'Blud?' Simeon threw a phial to Billy. He caught it

deftly. Along its length, etched white lettering stood out against the red liquid contents. BLUD™: FOR VAMPIRES WITH A HEART.

Billy had a heart. He hadn't tasted human blood for 26 years (except once), animal blood for ten. He'd gone cold turkey the moment Esther had been reborn because he wanted to devour her. He wanted her warm blood pulsing down his throat, her heartbeat filling him with life as she expired, just as it had done the first time in a courtyard in Constantinople. She'd tasted so good then, her blood flowing so sweetly, her neck as soft as a peach.

Almost 300 years later, and her death was still the most beautiful experience he'd known. Unless he quit human feeding, she'd either be dead again in no time or he'd make her a vampire. Either way, she'd be lost to him, and neither was an act of love.

He snapped off the top of his Blud and downed it in one. He tried to repress a shudder as the liquid slipped down his throat then he dashed the phial into the fire. The flames blazed green for a brief roaring moment.

'Hmm, well,' said Simeon, offended. 'Cheers everybody.' He and Suzanne raised their phials, Suzanne taking three sugar cubes from a pewter bowl on the hearth, adding them to her Blud before drinking it through a straw.

Simeon and Suzanne drank Blud to supplement their real feeding. Pickings were slim on the ice. Sometimes Simeon went to the coast and returned with tales of polar bears and all the blubber he had to bite through. But Billy knew he fed on the Inuit. He could see the flush in his cheeks and it made him so hot. When Simeon had tasted mortals, Billy wanted to fuck his brains out.

'Yuck,' said Simeon.

'Bleurgh,' said Suzanne. 'I vote we kill those trekkers. Tonight.'

Emerald flames surged twice.

'Can't you for once drink it without complaint?' said Billy.

'Oh, for God's sake, chill,' snapped Simeon, crossing to the CDs. 'I'm sick of this, absolutely sick of it. Some little whore from your past turns up and you –'

Billy was onto him instantly, moving with preternatural speed, a blur trailing behind him. Simeon's jet black bob sliced the air, his expression stunned as Billy slammed him against a wall, forcing him into an armlock.

'Jesus!'

Simeon's right cheek was squashed to the wall and Billy whispered in his other ear, his words slow and threatening. 'Don't you ever say anything like that again. Ever.' The two vampires stayed still, breathing heavily. Nostrils flared in Simeon's big aristocratic nose and candle-light cast a silvery patch on his black hair.

'Her name's Esther,' murmured Billy. 'Say it. Say Esther.'

Simeon remained silent until he was prompted by an extra twist of his arm. 'Esther, Esther,' he said.

Billy gave him a hard shove then stalked off.

'Esther,' repeated Simeon, wriggling his shoulders and stepping away. 'Remind me why you guys never hit it off. Oh, that's right. You accidentally killed her. How could I forget?'

Billy had him up against the wall in a flash, arm twisting high again. Simeon yelped in pain.

'You've never loved,' accused Billy.

Simeon gasped in outrage. 'Hah!' he said. 'Hah! And I'm here because ... because what? Fancied a change? Got bored of humans so thought I'd up-sticks and go feed on ... on Arctic fucking lemmings? And synthetic fucking blood?'

Billy twisted his arm even higher. 'Never loved!' continued Simeon. 'Well, what am I doing in this dump? Is it because ... because I think you're kind of OK? Kinda cute? Or because I ... Ouch! God knows why ... You get off on coming here. But, you know what? I find it a pretty big deal. I hate it, hate it. I'm only doing it for you because I care. And I am actually suffering quite majorly.'

'You enjoy suffering,' hissed Billy.

'Jesus Christ, man, you are such a cunt.'

Billy slammed Simeon's body to the wall once more. His erection was thickening and he pressed it against Simeon's butt.

'It's not even the same woman,' accused Simeon. 'It was centuries ago. Ever heard the phrase time to move on?'

'It's the same soul,' breathed Billy.

'And that gets you hard, does it?'

Billy grasped a handful of Simeon's hair, pulling his head back so his throat arched. His Adam's apple made a voluptuous jut in that long stubble-flecked neck, a sight that flooded Billy with memories. 'Oh, if you were mortal.'

'And what?' challenged Simeon in a stretched, reedy voice. 'You'd do what you did to her? Love me to death? Or what you did to me? Make me a vampire, possess me and make me yours?'

Billy tugged Simeon's head back still further, his grip tightening on his hair.

'You don't give a person room to breathe,' wheezed Simeon. 'That's not love, that's suffocation.'

Billy jerked Simeon away from the wall, clasping arm and hair to frogmarch him across the room. He forced him over the pool table, pressing his head onto the turquoise baize. The white ball span away and bounced off the side cushion.

'You're jealous,' murmured Billy. He tugged Simeon's flies open, pushing down his clothes to bare his pale slender ass, wisps of dark hair fringing his crack.

Simeon's erection bounced free and Billy leant over him, wrapping his fingers around that big sturdy shaft. He wanked him gently. 'Jealous,' mocked Billy, his lips behind Simeon's ear.

Simeon lay still, breathing hard and saying nothing as Billy's fist shunted along his cock, and Billy's crotch dug into his buttocks. After a while, in a tender mannered voice, Simeon whispered, 'Yes. I'm jealous. What of it?'

A surge of respect and lust nearly knocked Billy for six. Hurriedly, he unzipped and let his pants drop to his knees. 'Get your top off,' he said in a quiet command and Simeon obliged. He groaned as Billy rubbed saliva into the puckered bud of his asshole, and worked his fingers in to open him up. Billy pumped his fingers, gazing at the shifting sinew of Simeon's back, at the wings of his shoulder blades and the way candleflame and shadow rippled over his ivory skin.

It was a perfect back. Billy withdrew and clasped his own cock, blood-hard in his fist. He loved Simeon like this: submissive after a row, horny, sluttish and spread. He spat onto his fingers, moistening himself before pushing at Simeon's ring with his fat, flushed glans.

'You fucker,' said Billy tenderly. Slowly he eased forwards, meeting the circlet of muscle, forcing himself past its resistance as Simeon exulted and cursed, fingernails clawing the turquoise cloth. Both vampires groaned deeply as Billy slid his meat into the snug silky depths of his lover's ass.

Billy held his breath, his hand against the small of Simeon's back, relishing the hot squeeze around his swollen cock.

'Oh, man,' groaned Simeon. 'You complete me.'

Billy started to fuck him with slow easy lengths. The men breathed with heavy concentration until Billy drew a sharp thumbnail across his lover's back, making

Simeon groan. Blood rose to the surface and spread onto Simeon's alabaster skin. God, it was a beautiful sight. Billy slammed harder and faster.

'Oh, man,' said Simeon, jerking himself wildly.

'Jealous,' panted Billy.

'I fucking love you,' gasped Simeon and then he shot his load.

'Ah, fuck,' muttered Billy, going at him like a jackhammer.

The sprawled cat rubbed its belly on the hearth rug, frotting itself to climax. Suzanne, legs wide, masturbated with both hands. 'I love it when you two get off with each other,' she said. 'Makes me want to feed.'

2

In the lantern-lit log cabin, Margret grinned at the camera, her flushed face dimpling. The ear flaps and tassels of her blue woollen hat hung by her cheeks, giving her the appearance of a jolly medieval Dutch woman.

'If I could have anything in this moment,' she said, 'I would be having a hot bath with bubbles.'

'A glass of beer,' said Johannes as Esther panned to him. 'And some kisses from my young and beautiful girlfriend who I am very much missing.'

Margret acted scandalised and everyone laughed, Bird squeezing his toy accordion to add to the noise.

'And some superior music,' added Johannes, wagging his finger in the air.

'He wants Wagner,' yelled Adrian.

'Hey, you want Wagner?' asked Bird. 'I could give it a go.'

'Ogh!' laughed Johannes. 'Please spare us this attempt. It is too terrible.'

Esther panned to the head of the table, the camcorder recording the coffee mugs and glasses of brandy schnapps to focus briefly on the playing cards laid out in a patience game in front of Doug.

'Dougie?' she said cheerily. 'If you could have anything right now?'

Doug glanced at the camera, brown eyes pinched, and turned quickly away. 'No,' he croaked, raising his hand to shield his face. 'Please.'

Esther flinched. Oh, what a clumsy thing to do.

Johannes clapped Doug on the back. 'Tomorrow will

be better, my good man,' he said. 'But now you must rest your foot and your throat and your mind also.'

Esther panned away, recognising how awful it must be to have a bunch of people trying to coerce you into bonhomie when you were feeling low.

'Seems Doug's a little camera shy,' she said lightly. 'Losing his voice too. Unlike Bird here, our entertainment for the evening.' Bird, a thin balding man with a big hooked nose, winked to camera. 'Bird's ambition is to make it into *Heat* magazine.'

'Ah, heat,' said Margret. 'How I would like some heat.'

Bird hoicked his foot up onto the bench. 'You hum it and I'll play it, shweetheart.'

The cabin looked similar to a sauna with its slatted log walls, bunks and benches but the temperature was only just warming up. Propane lanterns hung from the ceiling, their mantles glowing and casting glints onto saucepans and utensils hanging above the cooking area. Three small windows looked out onto the dark icecap, making the interior feel extra cosy. A couple of stoves burned steadily, the smells of coffee, food and fuel lingering in the air. They'd eaten well, a meal of mushroom and chicken pasta followed by a batch of biscuits knocked up by Bird, all topped off with glasses of brandy schnapps in honour of Margret's 32nd birthday.

'Who's for checking out the skidoos?' asked Bird. 'Take 'em for a little whiz across the ice. Make sure everything's shipshape.'

'Oh, yes,' enthused Margret. 'I would like to celebrate my birthday with a small race perhaps.'

'Cool,' said Adrian. 'Wouldn't mind doing a few long exposures as well. That sky's something else tonight.'

'Ah no,' began Johannes. 'I think I would rather stay –' He caught a warning glance from his wife and cut himself short. 'A wonderful idea. I hope we will not be getting stopped for drunk-driving.'

'Essie?' said Bird. 'Do you want to hang here with Doug?'

Bird had a clever way of making orders sound like suggestions.

'Yeah, fine.'

Doug glanced up from his card game and shot Bird a grouchy look.

The other four donned their cold-weather gear and headed for the snowmobiles, stored for trekkers' use in a rudimentary garage. With their absence, the cabin felt awkwardly quiet. The gas lanterns purred faintly and Doug's cards made a plasticky snap. Esther wrote her expedition blog, stylus-tapping her entry on her palm-top. 'The wind was strong when we broke camp this morning and Adrian's sleeping bag pad was blown away. We laughed as he tried to run after it.'

Doug broke the silence. 'I shouldn't have come,' he said, his voice dry and strained. 'I don't think I can hack it.'

He looked at Esther and his eyes, scanning nervously, seemed to demand something of her. His beard was growing out of shape already, and he had a hint of wildness in his manner. For Doug to be showing signs of instability already was a worry. It was well known the solitude of the ice could send people crazy, and anxiety, irritation and depression weren't uncommon. All that nothingness affected a person.

The Long Eye, they called it, or the thousand-mile stare. Esther had seen photos of explorers gazing right through the camera, right through the viewer. Their eyes were blank, their expressions suggesting they were seeing some incommunicable horror beyond. She'd heard of how their thoughts would warp, drifting from reality to abstraction. But in the pictures, they didn't look as if they had thoughts. They looked hollowed out, the living dead.

But this happened to people in extreme conditions,

usually Antarctica. This was a trek that had barely begun and they'd arrived, more or less, at the end of a winter-long night. The sun was coming. But it was difficult. No one knew how they'd react. If you were a person with issues, an Arctic winter would always be a problem – how do you make the darkness go away?

'Hey, don't worry,' said Esther. 'Everyone gets like this. You're probably readjusting. Today's been a slog but we'll soon –'

'No,' rasped Doug. 'I'm going to fuck it up. I know it. I'm going to fuck it up for everyone. I'm going to –'

'No, you're not. We won't let you. The only way –'

'You know what drives me mad?' Doug interrupted. 'The noise. The noise of all the crap hanging from my parka. Compass, knife, clips. Torch. Zippers. Flapping. Everything flapping. And rustling. Every step. It's all noise, noise, noise. I can still hear it. All day it's been driving me mad. It's in my head. Clanking and tinkling and rustling.' Doug slapped and brushed at his chest as if trying to dislodge insects. 'It's like some ... some horrible metal orchestra. Torture. A special torture designed to –'

'Doug, take it easy,' said Esther. 'You need to rest your throat. You're doing great, I swear. You just need a good night's –'

'Like last night? In the tent? Me and you?'

Outside, a couple of snowcats started up, engines coughing before they murmured into life. Esther wished Bird hadn't left them alone.

'Last night shouldn't have happened,' she said. 'Can we maybe try and forget –'

'Don't fuck with me, Essie.' Doug dashed his hand across the table, scattering his deck of cards. 'Just ... don't give me that shit. Don't give me regrets. Not now. Not here.' He stood briskly then crossed to stand in front of a small window, hands in his pockets.

Esther allowed a silence to pass before addressing his reflection in the glass. 'Sorry. Listen, I didn't meant to hurt you by –'

'You didn't hurt me,' said Doug. 'But don't start making out it was my fault, pretending you didn't –'

'I'm not doing that,' said Esther. 'All I'm saying is maybe we should, you know, leave it a while. It's not right. It's not us. We're on the ice. It's a weird place. Emotions get screwed up. We weren't really thinking straight last night, were we? We were stupid, so stupid. We've got weeks out here. I know it's a crappy old cliché but, well, can we just be friends? Go back to how things were?'

For a long time Doug didn't reply. A couple more snowmobiles were revved up outside and the engines grew loud before fading into the distance. They were very much alone now, the rest of the team skidding across the ice under a massive sky fluttering with a tinge of greenish phosphorescence.

'Look,' said Esther, 'if something's bugging you, talk to me or to one of the others. Don't bottle it up.' She stood to go and stand next to him then changed her mind. Instead, she cleared some space on the table and sat there looking at his back, her soft-booted feet on the bench.

'And what could you do about it?' asked Doug. His voice thinned out and broke into a brief coughing fit

Esther shrugged. 'Listen, maybe?'

Doug turned to face her, his eyes fierce and troubled. Esther wondered if that was the look he'd been concealing behind snow goggles all day.

'I've nothing to say,' he said hoarsely. 'Nothing.'

'Doug, please,' said Esther. 'Don't take it out on . . .' She trailed off, realising she was getting annoyed. She didn't want them to get into an argument.

'Take it out on you?' said Doug. 'Is that what you were

going to say? Don't take it out on me? What? Like I did last night?' He stopped to cough, wheezing till the coughs were almost silent. 'I thought you enjoyed it. I thought you liked it when I –'

'Ease up, Doug,' said Esther, her tone dark with warning anger. 'I'm not having this conversation, OK? And you need to shut up for the sake of your health.'

Doug turned to the window again, either gazing at his own reflection or out into the night. Esther couldn't tell. A long time seemed to pass. It was so quiet, nothing but the faintest ripple of gas lanterns to ease the coldness of the silence. Esther thought it was over and she might return to writing her blog. She was on the point of getting down from the table-top when Doug swung round, crossing to her with a couple of brisk paces. He stood by the bench where her feet were planted and forced her knees wide.

Esther recoiled instantly then held very still, quelling her fight or flight instinct. Doug stayed there, hands on her spread knees, examining her face, an unpleasant smile on his chapped lips.

'I should save my voice,' he rasped.

Esther returned his gaze, and after a while said, 'You should back off.'

Doug nudged her knees a fraction wider, taunting her with his defiance, the smile turning into a challenging little leer.

Out here, there was a darkness about Doug, a sense of threat that Esther found unsettling and, if she were being honest, horribly attractive. And yet even while she was attracted, she was repulsed by this faultline she saw opening up, by Doug's neediness and unpredictability.

It's this *place*, she told herself. It's not really him.

Scared yet half-aroused by his boldness, Esther was doing her best to think straight. She had two situations to consider: this immediate problem between her and

Doug plus the bigger problem of how it would impact on the team. Her priority was the team, always the team. If it weren't for them, she'd be fighting back. And it was probably a good thing she wasn't because keeping Doug calm was likely her best way forwards.

'Let's cool it, shall we?' she suggested. 'Maybe you take your hands off my knees and step back a little.' Esther was wearing thick insulating layers and she felt both protected and hampered by her clothing.

Doug gave her knees another widening nudge, still watching and smiling vaguely. Esther's heart began to bump. He wasn't backing off. She didn't know what to do or how to play it. Fear made her swallow hard. 'Dougie, please. Let's not fall out. Come on. Let's make some tea and sit down.'

It happened so fast. Doug lunged for her, a foot on the bench and then he was clambering on to the table, pushing her back. Esther cried out, wriggling away. Glass smashed, plastic mugs bounced, Esther's palm-top was sent flying.

'Doug! Get off me!'

He was above her, wild-eyed and strong, and she noticed all the different browns in his beard and the stippled hints of red. He pinned her down, big hands on her forearms as he crouched over her, his eyes lit with meanness and lust. His breathing came hard and fast, and so did hers.

Esther's face was hot, and blood was thumping in all parts of her body. She hardly knew what she was feeling most: anger or arousal.

'Come on, Essie,' he whispered harshly. 'Give up the goods. I need to rest my voice. No use talking.'

Esther shook her head. 'This isn't on, Doug. I swear I can get you pulled from this trek. I'll go to Bird. We can radio through to base. They'll get a plane sent out and that's it. You're done. All over.'

Doug's smile broadened. 'Sounds great,' he breathed. 'What time do they land?'

'Doug,' said Esther, as levelly as she could. 'Get the fuck off me.'

He pulled back slightly, taking his hands off her arms and placing them on the table. Esther was free to move but she didn't. She lay beneath his straddling crouch, suspicious of the semi-liberation he'd given her, and not quite wanting this to be over.

They locked eyes and, perhaps because Esther wasn't fighting, there was a shift in Doug's manner. Confusion flitted across his face and the hard brown glitter in his eyes melted.

He frowned. 'Essie,' he whispered. 'What's going on?'

Esther stayed silent, trusting neither his mood nor her own.

'Have I frightened you?' he asked.

Esther lowered her gaze, unable to reply. Yes, she thought, yes you have. But not in the way you think. I'm not frightened of you. I'm frightened of the way you make me feel, of the way I want you to pin me down and fuck me, careless and uncomplicated.

'Essie,' he said, and his voice was tender and frail. He tipped her chin, making her look up at him again. He had such rich eyes and the ragged beard hid his features, making him mysterious and secretive. It was Doug, and yet it wasn't. His lips were cracked and dry, and his eyes were shadowed with tiredness as if he'd spent a night on the tiles. She liked that too, liked the way he looked big and threatening but vulnerable. She wanted to take his raw lower lip between her own, run her tongue along his sores and soothe him with her moisture.

'Ess.' Doug reached to touch her face. His fingers stroked down her cheek and, because it was dangerous and they mustn't, Esther turned her face aside.

The last thing she expected to see was a pair of eyes

at the window. But there they were, green eyes peering in at them. Then they moved fast, faster than anything she knew, and they were gone, leaving only an image of a face melting down the square of glass.

Esther screamed, body jerking beneath Doug's.

Doug leapt back, palms open in surrender.

'Sorry! Sorry!' he rasped, off the table now and standing. 'Essie, sorry.'

But Esther kept screaming. They were miles from anywhere, yet something had stood and watched them. The image lingered, a pair of eyes bright with pale-green luminosity.

'There's something out there,' she breathed.

'What? What do you mean?'

Dumbstruck, Esther shook her head. No animal had eyes that vivid, and it certainly wasn't human.

'Easy,' said Doug. 'You're seeing stuff, Essie. Calm down.'

Again, Esther shook her head. 'Something's there.'

'Impossible. There's nothing there,' said Doug. 'It's this place. It ... it fucks with your head. Esther, if it helps, I know exactly how you feel.'

Hope's End was quiet, too quiet. Billy needed company. He'd done a stupid thing. It didn't do to be alone in this frame of mind. It was dangerous.

But God, she was beautiful. A strong tall woman with skin as white as snow, a rosy flush in her cheeks, dark hair tumbling past her shoulders. Until tonight, he'd never even set eyes on her incarnation as Esther, though he'd always felt, no matter what she looked like, his love for her would consume them both. Or to be less grand about it, he'd want to suck her to death.

He'd sensed her presence the moment she was born, and had vowed there and then he would quit the killing. He'd been aware of her growing up though he'd been across the Atlantic, battling his lust for blood. He'd avoided Europe for over two decades, fearing his will-power would weaken if he were near her. And that was a great shame because he and Simeon had always loved Europe. Strolling through Paris in the 1900s, jewelled canes in their hands, tails of their coats rippling behind them, was a memory Billy would treasure forever. 'So much culture,' Simeon liked to say, gesturing widely.

When Esther had started to menstruate, the surge in Billy's hunger had almost ruined him. He'd tasted her blood in the air, felt it tingle on his tongue. It had prompted him to embark on a year long spree of animal slaying, a madness that had ended with him breaking his vow in a seedy alley, guzzling on a Hispanic body-builder with a vampire he barely knew.

That had been the dark night of his soul. It could have gone either way after that. He could have given up the fight and returned to mortal feeding, becoming his violent vampire self once again. Or he could seek professional help, explore some of his 'stuff', and perhaps read a little light Buddhism.

He'd opted for the latter, for Esther's sake more than his own.

'My name's Billy and I'm a vampire.' They all had to say it. He'd struggled with a range of treatments, meditative therapy and counselling options but only with the advent of a blood substitute in the 1990s had he freed himself from the lust to inflict death. He felt morally much better for it but, Christ, it wasn't much of a life.

Billy jumped up and down, tucked his chin to his chest and ran hard on the spot.

Just say no. Blood kills. Just say no.

He feinted at the air, punching an invisible enemy, wanting the pump of adrenaline to quench his craving for more. He was a fighter in white vest and khakis, muscles glinting in the half-light, shorn head hinting at the hardness of skull, a thick squiggly vein raised on his temple.

Come on, Billy Boy! Come on, you fucker! You can do this. Fight the blood. Fight it.

But hell, maybe it was time to pack virtue in. Maybe it was fate. When Esther had lost her virginity, Billy had been ripped apart with wanting. He'd wanted to fuck and kill the world. His urge to abandon the Blud and give in to the hunger had threatened like annihilation. Hoping to keep on track, he'd exiled himself to the Arctic, far away from people and the torment of temptation. Every year since then, he'd followed winter across the globe, spending half the year in the north, the other half in the south because the lands of the midnight sun were also lands of the afternoon moon, and it was where he supposedly belonged.

And look what happens: she turns up on the ice, trekking right past his hidden shelter. It was meant to be. She was his destiny.

Or, more likely, he was hers. Oh, the poor beautiful bitch.

Simeon strolled into the white dome, looking smug, hot and skinny in his regulation black. 'So, you're back,' he said to Billy. 'Been anywhere nice?'

In front of the fire, the cat, Renfield, stretched its limbs wide and began lightly humping the hearth rug. Renfield was an Arctic vampire pedigree costing hundreds of dollars, and was the randiest, most self-sufficient, four-legged creature you were ever likely to meet.

'Where's Suzanne?' puffed Billy, jumping high on the spot.

Simeon shrugged. 'Out.'

'Out where?'

'The movies,' said Simeon. 'Then I guess she'll stop off for a Big Mac and a shake –'

'I don't trust her.'

Simeon tucked his long black bob behind an ear, exposing more of his angular jaw, more of his perfect brows and his pretty-boy loftiness. He did it on purpose. It made Billy picture him on his knees, those narrow lips tight on his cock, his silky hair in skeins around Billy's fists. And yet almost as soon as the image appeared, it morphed quickly into another: Esther's richer thicker hair in Billy's hands, Esther's sweeter softer lips on his dick, her eyes wide as he bumped the back of her throat.

Debauchery got boring after a few centuries and, relative to his usual fucks, Esther would be wholesome and shockable, hungry for corruption, just as she was the first time. The first time and the last time. His cock thickened at the memory and he fancied he'd use Simeon later in the night, fill his mouth and ass with big brutal flesh.

'Wise not to trust her,' said Simeon. 'She's vile and immoral. But man, I love her, don't you?'

'I told you to keep an eye on her. Don't let her –'

'Dude, you can't do that to women any more. They changed the rules, remember? So annoying but, hey, what can we do?'

Simeon sauntered closer to Billy, looking mischievous. He clasped his hands behind his back and cocked his head, smiling with suspicious interest.

'What?' said Billy.

Simeon kept smirking. Renfield mewed excitedly, clawing at the hearth rug and grinding so he looked like a splayed blue cat shagging a huge white bear.

'You know something, don't you?' said Billy. 'Where is she? Where's Suzanne? What's going on? Christ, I'm going to have to go fetch her, aren't I? I'm serious, if she even goes near those trekkers, I'll –'

'Um . . .' Simeon brushed a thumb against his chin, angling his face to suggest Billy had a mark there on his own chin.

Billy, self-conscious, dabbed at his lips.

'Uh, lower,' said Simeon, failing to hide his glee. 'Chin. Just there ... little, um, feather.'

Billy swiped at his face. A bloodied white feather drifted to the ground and he rubbed at his skin, furious and ashamed.

'Oh dear,' said Simeon. 'Still, you never did suit being a vegetarian. Makes you hideously grumpy.'

Billy turned on his heels, heading for the gym. 'It was just a ptarmigan,' he said. 'One worthless little bird, OK?'

Billy pulled a peg from the bench press weights.

'One worthless little bird,' echoed Simeon. 'Isn't she just?'

Johannes grunted and turned in his sleep. Doug, bending to lace his bunny boots, stiffened and listened. He didn't want to wake anyone and he waited till Johannes resumed his snoring, air whistling through his nose, before continuing. He'd been lying there with a full bladder for almost an hour and it wasn't going away.

He fixed his headtorch, closing the door softly before hurrying to the outhouse. Hell, it was so cold his dick had nearly vanished. He stood there, shivering, wishing he were back in the UK where he wasn't in permanent pain, where his throat wasn't scorched and where his toes didn't feel brittle and burnt. Daylight too. God, he ached for a sunrise. He hadn't a clue the darkness would do his head in like this. He'd been training like a maniac for this trip – months of running, cycling and weights – but, mentally, he clearly wasn't prepared.

In a few days at about noon, the sun would show its face, or rather its burning gold edge for the first time that year. Doug reckoned he'd feel better when he saw it, loads better, even though sunrise and sunset would be more or less the same, the day as short as a gnats' shag. Currently, day as they knew it consisted of the winter sky holding the colours of twilight, a rich bruise spreading around the horizon, indigo, violet and charcoal blue. The rest of the time, they were in darkness, usually starlit. Madness, but sometimes Doug could believe the sun had gone forever, died a death, and all that remained was this frozen wasteland. Sun made life. And there was no life here.

He fastened himself and was scuttling back to the cabin when a great wave of emotion snagged him. He stopped to look out over the ice, hugging his chest and beating his hands against his arms, feet stamping. How he hated it. It was a barren hellhole, sucking the energy from you. He glared at the emptiness, wanting not to be cowed, wanting to defeat it and everything it did to him.

After a while, he stopped moving and just held himself, shivering. The ice glittered with pinpricks of light. It was so beautiful, so immensely beautiful and at the same time it was terrifying. Looking at it was like looking into forever. A person could disappear entirely here.

No wonder he was freaking out. He needed to think small. Yes, that was it. Small and manageable. But small drove him crazy too, the equipment flapping on his parka, Margret's cough in the mornings, Bird's stupid accordion and the way he'd insisted on pasta when a spicy stew would have been better. Chillies. Food with hot, spicy chillies. Fire in his belly.

Doug had heard it say that out here you needed stories more than you needed food. He could almost believe it. Stories to fight the desolation, to fill the emptiness. But he wanted food too.

And Essie. Jesus Christ, but he wanted her more than ever after last night in the tent. Seeing and hearing her come had been so horny. She seemed all twisted up, half pained, half shocked, and it was such a sexy dirty sight. He should have made his move in London where everything was simpler, warmer, more civilised. Dinner, some conversation, a fuck, breakfast the next day. He imagined her wearing his bathrobe, and she looked amazing, so gentle and at home.

He was thinking better out here, alone in the dark. He needed to get a grip. He was behaving like a twat. Essie would end up hating him if he didn't wise up. Tomorrow he'd cool it, try and make it up to her. Try not too think how wet and soft she'd felt when he'd sunk into her pussy. God, even in these sub-zero temps, his dick was twitching. Time he went back into the cabin. He'd have a quick one off the wrist inside his sleeping bag. He'd be out like a light after that.

He was about to move when he heard a soft crunch on the snow. Shit. No weapon. Always carry a weapon. He had nothing.

He spun around. There was movement by the cabin. He hadn't believed Essie. Thought she was screaming to get him off her. From the shadows, a young woman skipped forwards, smiling. She was slim and beautiful, golden hair cascading around her shoulders, eyes of icy blue. And she was wearing a summer dress, lime green cotton printed with lilac dots.

Doug staggered back. It was a dream. He tried to roar but no worthwhile noise came out, only a hoarse crack and clouds of breath. He started to run, stumbling and slow in his parka and boots.

The woman's merry laughter sparkled into the night. She began to follow, frolicking alongside him. Her small breasts shook as she skipped, dancing close and spinning away. Doug heaved and gasped, feeling as if icicles were stabbing inside his throat. His lungs were ready to split. His body barely worked. He was running in slow motion, running into the emptiness, turning to look at her.

Then he fell, his body sinking in a puff of powdery snow, glacial ice beneath. The woman skipped around as he hauled himself up, her summer dress swishing, polka dots dancing. Doug hardly had any joints to move. He was all padding. Where could he run to? Infinity? He needed to get back to the cabin. He started to deviate but she headed him off, forcing him to keep going, the gleeful smile never fading from her lips.

She was wearing sandals, strappy brown sandals, and her toenails were painted red. Where was the frostbite? All Doug could do was run. He felt he might fall off the earth's edge and go spinning into forever with all the snowflakes and stars. Run and run. But it was impossible in these clothes. He was fat and bumbling. He was meat.

The colour was high in the woman's cheeks and when Doug threw a terrified glance her way, her smile opened into a huge triumphant laugh. Doug saw his death right there, caught in the moonlight that flashed on a pair of white incisors. Her throat was a velvety red cavern, and it grew bigger, trembling with her laughter, rippling with sinew, moist and stretched.

If I just keep running . . . just keep . . .

But there was nowhere to run to, and then he smelt her and he felt her. Her blonde hair snagged on his beard. Then the only thing he knew was throat, and everything went wet and red.

3

Esther used to be Selin, a servant in one of the grand wooden yalis perched on the forested banks of the Bosphorus. As the Ottoman empire dwindled, her days were spent fetching and carrying. Billy's were spent sleeping, protected from the sun in the shuttered apartments of Kasim Nadir, his mentor and vampire guide, and a man of immense cruelty.

Billy didn't yet know he was a snow vampire. Restless and alone, he'd left his home of Saxony in Eastern Europe, where he'd been a minor noble, yearning for peace and companionship. He'd had no understanding of the force that had bitten and changed him. A sailor, that was all he knew. He hadn't really clicked with the Carpathian vampires he'd met and, having learned how the Turks had suffered at the hands of Vlad the Impaler, he'd headed east, wondering if the answer lay in the land of Vlad's enemy. It would be decades before Billy understood his power, and found the vampire line to which he belonged.

Constantinople enchanted him. It was a magical city, a place of terrible beauty founded on lust, poetry and ruthlessness. Nadir, a man as brutal as the country that reared him, had been delighted to take Billy under his wing. Together, they'd stalked the city's alleyways and gardens, lurked in the shadows of mosques, or sucked on hookahs, Billy's blond hair hidden by a turban. Sometimes, they'd prowl along the river's tree-dense shoreline, feasting on victims in the dappled moonlight of leafy darkness. 'Take him,' Nadir would command. Or, 'Ignore the peasant, her skin looks coarse.'

But when Billy saw Selin, everything changed. In the twilit dusk, she sat alone by the Bosphorus, pale feet trailing in the water. Daringly, she'd pushed back her veils, revealing lush black curls, a gentle face and a slender neck of exquisite Slavic pallor. Since arriving in Turkey, Billy had seen little more of its women than their shy eyes darting above yashmaks.

'Take her,' ordered Nadir.

After watching her for several more seconds, Billy turned to Nadir. 'No,' he said, calm and clear.

It was Billy's first challenge. Nadir, as swarthy-skinned as the peasants he so disdained, cocked an eyebrow, his thin sensual lips twisting in amusement.

'Wilhelm,' he drawled. 'You are in love.'

For the next few months, it seemed the woman was always there on their night-time wanderings. Nadir had a knack of happening to pass by her as she bathed her feet; braided her hair by a window; filled a pitcher from a fountain or picked flowers from a garden. From the richness of her dress, it was clear she was a servant of some standing or a favourite in the house. Billy didn't care to imagine why.

Once, the two vampires had stood behind a marble pillar of a lantern-lit garden and had seen the girl prick herself on a rose thorn. She'd frowned, and the jewels dangling from the scarf around her head had twinkled in the soft light. Billy trained his vision on her thumb, watching her squeeze the tip to force a bead of blood to the surface. The droplet gleamed like a ruby, then Selin, lowering her yashmak, had licked it clean, her sweet little tongue darting out.

Billy's cock had pulsed harder, growing fast. He wanted to leap forward and take her, to sink his teeth into her throat, imagining how her neck would be as soft as kid leather. And at the same time he wanted to sink his cock into her cunt and fuck her until she begged for mercy. He wanted to force himself into her mouth, ramming until her eyes brimmed with tears. He wanted to corrupt her to wantonness so she'd be on her knees, veils in tatters, begging for his dick. In short, he wanted to take her beauty apart because nothing in the world was hotter than virtue and perfection debased.

'You are still saying no?' drawled Nadir, and somehow Billy was.

But Nadir was too clever for Billy. 'You're a vampire, Wilhelm, don't fight it,' he would say.

If Billy had been in control of his lusts, he could have fucked and bitten her. He longed to drink her orgasm and have her pure, private ecstasy coursing through his veins. But he didn't trust himself to quit after a nibble because he also longed to feel the last pulse of her life gliding down his throat.

'Death is life to us,' Nadir would say. 'She's nothing, just a pretty girl. If you kill her, what of it? There'll be more trinkets. You have immortality ahead of you.'

Billy began to listen and defer to Nadir as he did on all matters vampiric. They were, after all, a feeding partnership, and so it was that one dark cloudless night they decided to risk it. It would be a test of Billy's restraint. 'Feed wisely,' advised Nadir. 'She'll forget everything, then we can have her again and again. Abduct her and bring her to my apartments. I'll await you in the courtyard.'

Had Billy been more adept and less eager, he might have captured her by hypnotising her into submission. But he was impatient, horny and nervous, and when he saw her in her usual spot by the water's edge, he stole up behind her and clamped a hand to her veiled mouth. She squealed and writhed, her breath hot through the fabric, her feet thrashing in the water like caught fish. Billy was as strong as three men, and she presented him with no problems, only pleasures.

He ought to have carried her straight back to Nadir's yali but her beauty, the scent of her skin, and her struggles quite undid him. On the grassy slope, he'd tugged her yashmak free, pinned down her arms down and forced a kiss onto her lips, tasting her moans of protest and feeling her body surge and squirm. He cupped a hand between her legs, exploring her through layers of clothing with a crudeness that later shamed him. When he drew back, she was almost still, gazing up with stunned eyes and a sluttish open mouth that so clearly wanted more.

It was all down to her. He hadn't even tried to put her under his vampire spell.

Billy knew enough of the language to ask the girl her name.

'Selin,' she said, making the word sound like a gift.

By the time he'd got her to Nadir's courtyard, she'd sobered somewhat, and was a woman battling with the agonies of wanting it and not, outraged to have been kidnapped and yet thrilled to have been transported.

Urged on by Billy, she stumbled to stand before Nadir where he reclined on a divan spread with cushions, looking every inch the cynical old roué that he was. His black hair, freed from his turban, hung in a ponytail over one shoulders and his naked torso, spare and mahogany dark, was slashed with a silver scar, jagged like a flash of lightening.

Stone pillars edged the courtyard, and the walls gleamed with tiles of Iznik blue and turquoise, Koranic calligraphy forming a high elegant border. A plane tree dominated one corner and the air was heady with perfumes of night-scented flowers. A peacock wandered idly behind a row of pillars, its closed feathers trailing like an iridescent gown, and moths fluttered around copper lanterns. At the centre stood a marble fountain, burbling gently.

'Show her to me,' said Nadir. On the floor by Nadir's divan stood an empty goblet and Billy guessed he would want to fill it with blood.

Selin, standing before the divan, gave a pettish wriggle of protest as Billy began undressing her. He didn't touch her once, yet when her breasts were bared and she was in nothing but baggy shalwar and slippers, she was whimpering and breathless, her spine arching as she thrust herself forwards, greedy for a touch.

Nadir smiled and Billy, wanting to please his mentor, toyed with the girl's nipples, humiliating her by rousing a lust she'd rather hide. He traced his fingers over her skin, skimming beneath her breasts, and traced swirls on her back. Selin closed her eyes, flushing with shame, and her conflict turned Billy on all the more.

'She's a natural,' said Nadir. 'She'd do well at the harem. Or is that where you've come from pretty maid? A concubine cast out onto the street for being over fond of her role?'

'I'm no concubine,' breathed Selin, seemingly oblivious to the lusty sway of her hips.

'Show her your prick,' said Nadir. 'Let's see how she fares.'

But Billy was ahead of him. He had one of Selin's scarves in his hands and he tore it in two, leaving himself with a length of cloth perfect for binding limbs. He clasped her hands behind her back, and she made no complaint, only murmurs of delight, as he bound her. When Billy raised his brocade kaftan and freed his big cock, her mouth opened hungrily. She was falling under his influence.

Billy, fisting his erection, stepped back. 'Come on, then,' he breathed. 'Reach for it.'

It made Nadir laugh, and that pleased Billy. Selin fell to her knees and shuffled forwards, mouth gaping like a baby bird's, chasing his length.

'Please,' she begged. 'Please, *efendim*.'

Efendim. My master.

The word blew Billy's mind. He didn't deserve the epithet, not a bit of it, but it thrilled him she was horny enough to degrade herself by using it. And so he gave her what she wanted. She swallowed him, her head tipping back as he speared her throat, her neck arcing, muscles opening to encompass his cock.

'Hot little wench,' said Nadir. 'Send her this way when you're done.'

Selin was in Billy's power, rapt and stripped of inhibitions, and she didn't seem to care that another man watched. Centuries later, Billy could still summon up tactile memories of his cock sliding in the warm wet cave of her mouth, her lips slipping on him, her tongue dancing, and that undeserved word still echoing: *efendim*.

Cynics might call it a skilled blowjob, but Billy knew it was love. And he had a lot more love to give. He withdrew from her, and pulled her to her feet, clasping her around the waist and bending to suck on her small hard-tipped breasts. Her black hair streamed towards the floor and her pale torso arced deliciously, her groin thrusting at his muscled thigh.

'Be careful with her,' warned Nadir but Billy hardly heard.

He stripped off his upper garments and, from the scabbard belted at his waist, withdrew his kilij, a short sword with a nasty curved blade. Selin made little protest as he sliced at her shalwar, leaving her naked save for a jewel around her ankle and bangles around her wrist. Her nudity was creamy white and, as her religion dictated, the hair of her mons and armpits was shorn.

Metal clanked on stone as Billy let his knife fall. With easy strength, he carried the woman to the fountain where he draped her on the broad marble rim. She steadied herself, arms bound behind her back, and spread her legs wide, showing him the plump groove that glinted between her thighs. She really was a work of art, and the urge to defile her by reducing her to lewd, loose desire thrilled and repulsed. Thrilled, mainly. Billy was as hard as rock.

She tilted her hips to him, head rolling from side to side, splayed for him like some dissolute water nymph. Her black hair fanned out into the pool, undulating with the low bubbles, and sheets of water clung to the fountain's marble tiers, shimmering in the lantern-lit courtyard.

Billy dropped to his knees and fastened his mouth onto her pretty pink cunt. She tasted divine, as salty as the oceans, and he suckled and licked, hearing her bleats of pleasure surge and babble with the murmurings of the fountain.

The urge to feed was strong, and when she came, pushing tremors of ecstasy against his mouth, Billy was at his limit. He hurried out of his shalwar, watching the girl spread her legs like a harlot. Bending over her, he positioned himself, and her lipped entrance was a kiss melting on the dome of his cock. She cried out as he drove in deep, and she kept on crying as he plunged over and over, losing himself in her soft supple wetness.

He wanted to time his bite, fearing he might get carried away if he went in too soon. He recalled Nadir's words: *Feed wisely and we can have her again and again.* But the more she gasped, the more her beautiful little pussy seemed to liquefy around his cock, and the more impossible moderation began to seem. He wanted to sink his teeth into her neck and suck so hard the force would gash her skin. Nadir intervened, his motives far from altruistic, although in the end, it made no difference.

Nadir had Billy's dagger. He stood by them, levelling the curved blade at the side of the woman's neck. 'Do you want it?' Nadir asked Selin.

Selin didn't reply except to gasp and Billy gave her a series of slow juicy thrusts, each one jolting her lily-white body. 'Say it,' he snarled. 'Say you want me.'

'Don't be shy,' added Nadir. 'It's quite apparent you do and we haven't got all night.'

'Yes,' gasped Selin. 'Yes, I want you.'

Nadir chuckled. With a careful stroke, he whisked the blade across her neck. A thin line of blood seeped to the surface.

'Drink, don't bite,' he warned, and Billy fell on her neck, closing his mouth over the wound that was as fine and neat as a paper cut. Her blood trickled onto his tongue, sweet, warm and inadequate. Billy sucked harder, edging his tongue into the slit, widening it. He was rewarded by a thicker flow of blood. As he drank, he pounded into her, and when he used his fingers on her, he could taste the nearness of her orgasm.

And then she was coming, coming so hard that Billy was quite carried away. Her muscles quivered around his cock and her pleasure poured into his throat. Billy had never felt anything like it. There'd been other women, plenty of them, but Selin had a quality that touched some deeper part of him. He wanted more of her and he wormed his tongue further into her pulsing gash. Before he knew it, he'd bitten and her blood was spilling in hot coppery torrents.

She tasted good, unbearably good, meatier and richer than any blood he'd known. He drank deeply, telling himself he could stop any moment, could and would. In a couple of hours, her wound would heal and there'd be nothing to see except a dark-crimson bruise, a love bite. He gulped, feeling her orgasm course through him before it faded to a gentle throb. He continued to drink. The point at which he must stop kept eluding him. It was always a few seconds ahead.

'Stop it,' snapped Nadir. 'You're going to kill the bitch.'

Billy hardly heard. He was chasing a new pulse, the pulse of Selin's ebbing heartbeat. He was greedy for her death, and then a new thought struck him: no need! He would make her a vampire. He would drain her to near death then feed her with his own life. They'd be together forever and his quest for self-knowledge would be over.

Yes! She would be his for eternity. Her blood poured fast, spilling from the edges of his mouth, and then he started to come as he started to feel it: the slow thud of her heart as he took her closer to the edge. Some died in quick surrender. Others clung on and when they did, their death was all the sweeter.

Selin was a fighter. As Billy came inside her, her heartbeat drummed in his veins, a primitive beat that tugged at a dark need inside, feeding him with the bliss of stolen life as he lost himself to a mad, rapturous coming. And then the rhythm grew slower and the final pulses were fading as Billy gasped for breath, knocked by the force of his climax. He raised his head. Now was the moment. Now he would make her his.

He withdrew and Selin's head lolled back, her blood slicking on the fountain's rim, spilling into the water and tinting it pink. Reflected lantern light shattered on the surface and glistened on wet stone. Billy snatched up his kilij from the floor and slashed his wrist. His blood spurted then pumped and he cupped Selin's head, pressing his slit veins to her lips.

She didn't drink.

'Drink!' commanded Billy.

There was nothing. His blood tumbled over her lips.

She would find it soon. Any moment now.

Billy, though he'd never managed it himself, had seen

other vampires turn people. Their victims would seem comatose until something stirred them and they'd latch on.

But Selin had lost a lot of blood. The fountain was very pink, her blood and his. Rose-coloured water cascaded down the marble tiers. By Selin's head, threads of crimson spooled and wriggled in the bubbling depths.

'Drink!' he cried again, but still she didn't take. Her mouth was dead, and her flesh was cold and grey.

Panicking, he turned to Nadir. 'Help me,' he pleaded. 'I'm losing her.'

Nadir was composed and still, lounging on his cushioned divan. The scar across his torso glinted like a silvery line of fat in mutton. 'Too late,' he said. 'She's dead.'

'No,' breathed Billy, and he dunked Selin's head in the water, clutching her weedy hair, lifting and dunking in a bid to revive her.

The fountain turned a deeper pink, bubbling like a vat of borscht.

'Wake up!' yelled Billy.

From the tiered stem of the fountain, falling water formed curtains of delicate shimmering pink.

'She's dead,' repeated Nadir. 'I knew this would happen. You lack self-control.'

Billy hauled up Selin's sodden body and clutched her to his chest, blood and water running in rivulets over his skin. She was limp and heavy, and her pulse was gone.

From Billy's mouth came a noise that seemed not to belong to him. He tipped his head back, seeing a sky sprayed with stars, and howled like a dog in distress. He hadn't known he was capable of such a sound but then he'd never felt such wrenching, bottomless pain before. He'd killed her. She was dead. He'd destroyed the creature he loved.

Sobbing, he glared at Nadir. 'You could have stopped

me! Or helped me. You could have saved her. Made her a vampire.'

Selin's head lay against Billy's shoulder and he stroked her hair, tender and comforting as if she might feel the caress.

Nadir shrugged. 'I could have done, yes.'

'But you didn't,' accused Billy. 'You didn't.'

'No,' said Nadir smoothly. 'The best lessons are learnt the hard way. The fountain looks so pretty in pink, don't you find?'

4

A blizzard had blown in, worse than expected. Sleety snow darted across the beam of Esther's headtorch. Visibility was so low she might have been in her own personal snowstorm. They would never find Doug unless he spotted them and was able to respond. Or unless they stumbled across him. Or his body

'We need to do this more systematically,' shouted Bird. 'Get better equipped.' He approached Esther through the mauve-grey gloom, flakes slashing across the halogen ball encircling him.

'OK,' yelled Esther, knowing he was right. 'Just a couple more minutes.'

She felt guilty and afraid. Guilty because of the situation between her and Doug. She'd rejected him the day after they'd had sex, and he probably wasn't in a fit state to take such mixed messages. She hadn't realised how vulnerable he was, mentally and emotionally, and would have been more cautious if she'd spotted it.

Afraid because there was something out there, a green-eyed creature that moved faster than anything earthly. Whatever it was, it had left no prints to identify, just a few smudges in the snow by the window. Doug had dismissed them as nothing but evidence of a small mammal or a bird.

He didn't believe Esther had seen something, that much was obvious. How infuriating. If he thought she was a woman who'd use damsel in distress tactics to defend herself, he didn't know her at all. She generally preferred to make herself clear and if language failed,

Esther was perfectly capable of demonstrating her meaning with a knee in the groin. Unfortunately, Esther wasn't clear about what she needed to be clear about, hence the mess.

'Come on, Essie! Adrian!' hollered Bird. 'Back inside.'

In the quieter cabin, the white lanterns glowed softly. Johannes paced in the small space while Margret clutched her satellite phone, its thick antenna extended.

'Nothing,' announced Esther, stamping snow from her boots.

'I can't get through to anyone,' said Margret.

'We will try,' said Johannes. 'Margret and I.'

'Whoa, hang fire! Let's think this through,' said Bird. 'No point us walking over each other's paths. He can't have gone far. My guess is he's injured. We need to draw up a plan, grab some food and get a couple of skidoos out. We need to keep trying to get through to base, keep them informed. Schedule's off for the next few days. If we find him, he's going to be in no state to keep going. We can't get a 'copter out in this. Esther, stay here in case he comes back.'

'Bird,' said Esther. 'I don't think I'm the best person to be waiting for him.'

'Essie, you are,' said Bird. 'I'm not arguing. If it helps, I don't imagine he'll be coming back anyway. Not on his own, at least.'

Fifteen minutes later, the four of them were gone. Esther tried and failed to contact HQ, washed the pots from their breakfast of porridge and cranberries, and melted some ice on the stove for tea. Using fuel for one person seemed decadent and wasteful but if Doug came back, he'd need the heat. When Doug came back, *when*.

The slightest sound unnerved Esther: the whistle of wind through the log walls, the rattle of a door or the creak of wood from the cabin and outbuildings. Last night, she'd been convinced she'd seen a face at the window but now she wasn't so sure. Bird said it could have been someone else passing by. After all, they were on an old mushers' trail so it wasn't too far-fetched. But there were no marks in the snow.

A reflection, suggested Adrian. He had a point. A weak aurora borealis had been playing across the sky, a pale-green gossamer scarf, slow and balletic. Maybe that had cast a freaky light.

Esther began to think she'd imagined it. And she'd had such strange dreams in the night, a jumbled narrative that had left her with a head full of images: a peacock and a pink fountain; veiled women and turbaned men; a river bobbing with fishing boats; and a man with bright-green eyes who had such beauty and presence that she'd woken up wet, her lust spiked with loneliness and need, the intensity of which she'd never felt before. It had left her on the brink of tears.

She'd stayed in her sleeping bag, waiting for the others to wake up. To her shame, the discovery Doug was missing was close to relief. The panic snatched her right out of her pain.

She made tea and sat at the table, waiting. Bird was right: he couldn't have gone far. But, depending on his clothing, if he was injured he couldn't survive in sub-zero temperatures for long.

This was Esther's third major expedition. Once, two team members suffering from extreme frostbite had to be airlifted out but Esther hadn't experienced any major dramas. However, the threat was always there. If it weren't, there would be no challenge, no reason to do this, no glory in the final achievement.

Esther sometimes wondered what she would do if she didn't have the ice. She'd been on skis almost as soon as she could walk, her parents instilling her with a sense of adventure and wonder. The Arctic transformed her. She loved being here. It was both tranquil and savage, and, thanks to climate change, so momentary and fragile, a bubble about to burst. The sea ice was melting, coastal villages were under threat, livelihoods were at risk, polar bears could vanish.

Oh, where the hell was Doug?

Esther connected her palm-top to the satphone, thinking she might upload her blog, then realised she was being stupid. Comms were down. Last night's dream was muddling her brain. She was in half a mind to blog about the dream and was wondering who might read it when she heard a noise outside.

'Hello! He – ello?'

It was male and her first thought was Doug, even though it wasn't his voice. She hurried to the cabin door, thinking Bird or Adrian, although it didn't sound like them either. There was no German accent so that ruled out Johannes.

'Hello?' The voice was right at the door. Esther flung it open and a blizzard of snow whirled into the cabin. In the midst of the flurry, on skis, was a tall figure in a black ski suit, face concealed by a balaclava and visor, head haloed in almost a foot of grey fur.

'Hi!' he called, tipping up a ski pole in greeting. 'Mind if I come in.'

Esther was already ushering him in because in these conditions you don't ask for ID. The man stepped out of his skis and clomped in, his equipment clattering as he stood it in a corner. Esther slammed the door against the storm.

'Phew!' he said, and he quickly pulled off his headgear and visor. Sleek black hair spilt from his balaclava, and his dark eyebrows, as shapely and elegant as his finely-boned face, contrasted with his pasty complexion. When he raised his head to smile, Esther was startled to note he had one perfectly ordinary blue eye while the other was violet. It wasn't violet in the way Elizabeth Taylor's eyes were said to be violet. A better description might be bright purple.

'Are you OK?' asked Esther, alarmed. 'Where's your party? Or are you alone? A member of our team's missing. Have you –'

'Simeon,' said the man. He gestured with a gloved hand. 'I'm with a friend. We got separated. Silly fools. We're on a sponsored ski.'

Esther frowned, puzzled by too much. He was so pale he might not have seen the sun for months which was understandable if he'd been out here a while. But was that possible? He looked too delicate to be battling an Arctic winter.

'We're heading north,' continued the man. 'For the pole. We're raising money. For the, um, Haemophiliac Awareness Trust. And you are?'

'Esther,' said Esther, still staring at those eyes, one purple, one blue.

Simeon smiled broadly. His teeth were white and strong. 'What a pretty name,' he said. 'Esther.'

He removed his gloves and tossed them onto the table. 'How you doing, Esther?'

'I'm fine, thanks.'

'You're English, right?'

Esther felt slightly dazed. 'Yes,' she said. 'I am.'

'Listen, we found your friend. He's OK. My partner, my team-mate, he's bringing him.'

Esther snapped to attention. 'Where?' she demanded. 'We have to go to them. Where are they? How is he? Does he need medical attention? I can try to contact my team and they can –'

'Hey, don't panic,' said Simeon. 'He's cool, man. Just lost a bit of blood. Are you alone here?'

'Yes,' replied Esther, and she felt threatened by the question, remembering the face at the window and its luminous green eyes. 'Yes, I'm alone.'

That violet eye did something strange to her. When she looked at it, fragments of last night's dream swirled in her mind: the pink fountain, the veiled women, the man who'd left her wet with longing. She could vaguely recall giving him a blow job. The face at the window must have turned up in her sleep but his presence seemed more than a residue of the day's events. She felt connected to him and she guessed, from her layman's knowledge of dream analysis, he represented someone or something else, perhaps an ex-boyfriend or a yearning for home.

She turned away from Simeon's eye but it was a struggle because she wanted to stay in the emotions of the dirty dream. Maybe this was what Doug had been suffering from, a viral infection that induced mildly hallucinogenic states and an excess of desire.

'Where's your friend?' asked Esther, and the question seemed to carry more weight than she felt it ought. 'What happened to Doug. Are they far away? I've been struggling with sats and radio the last half hour. Maybe it's the blizzard. Do you –'

'Billy will be along shortly,' Simeon said confidently. He unzipped his ski suit and stripped down to thinner layers.

Esther began to worry. 'Aren't you cold?'

Simon pinched his black sweat-top. 'We're trialling new techno fabrics. Intelligent clothing. This is their thinnest yet. It's revolutionary. How many humans – people – in your team?'

'Six,' said Esther. 'Four are out there looking for Doug. I'm sure they'll be back any moment.' Esther didn't think it was true. They'd still be searching for Doug, not knowing he'd been found.

She felt she ought to be asking more questions and enquiring about Doug but all she wanted was to wallow in the soft trippy strangeness aroused by the coloured eye.

'My friend and I,' said Simeon. 'While we've been travelling, we've had this weird sense of something out there, something on the ice that's watching us.' He took a step closer. 'Do you guys ever get that?'

'Yes!' said Esther. 'Well, maybe me more than the others but I have had a sense of . . . of something.'

'Doesn't it bother you being alone here?' asked Simeon. 'In this little cabin?' He took another step closer, his rangy limbs slinky and reptilian.

Esther shrugged, standing her ground. 'I'm made of tougher stuff than that. Anyway, we have to find Doug. That's our priority right now.'

The man tilted his head and scrutinised Esther, lips twisting in a come-hither sneer. 'You're cute,' he said. 'Do you have a boyfriend?'

'Your eye,' said Esther. 'Why's it like that? Why is it purple?'

Simeon looked caught out. 'Ah,' he said. 'Contact lens. Must've lost one. 'Scuse me.'

He tipped his head down, and his thin white fingers fluttered briefly over the blue eye. When he lifted his head, both eyes were violet, shining with the translucency of gemstones. Esther didn't know if he'd added a lens or removed one. She was feeling somewhat detached, bizarrely attracted to this man whose skin wasn't pinched and raw, who didn't cough or wheeze, and whose haughty porcelain face was completely free of sores. He looked as if the cold had never touched him.

'Boyfriend?' asked the man again.

'No,' said Esther. 'I don't really have time.'

Simeon slunk closer still and stroked her jaw with long gentle fingers. Esther's groin flushed as if he'd touched her in a much sexier way.

'What are you doing?' she asked dazedly.

'Checking you out,' Simeon said in a new brisk voice.

With both hands, he tugged down the polo-neck of her sweater. For several seconds he examined her bared neck until Esther, worried, began backing away. Smirking, Simeon followed, a swagger in his lean hips, until she was pressed against the ridges of the log wall at the foot of the bunks.

'What is this?' asked Esther.

'Lust,' said Simeon and he unzipped her fleece with one swift pull. 'Dirty, greedy fuck lust. Blood lust. Lust for hot little whores called Esther.'

'No,' breathed Esther. Her heart thumped as the extent of her stupidity struck her. His talk of rescuing Doug was a con, of course it was. For miles, they were the only ones around, just her and him in a shed on the ice. Esther's sudden sense of solitude was so acute she wondered if this was how people felt when death was due.

'Yes,' Simeon said crisply. He groped her breasts through her layer of thermals and ground his big swollen crotch against her. 'And she's all alone on the icecap.'

'They'll come back,' said Esther. She pushed against him but she was weak in body and mind, all her training for the expedition disintegrating. He made her feeble and reckless. He was dangerous, she knew that, and though reason told her to resist, a stronger compulsion urged her to give it all up.

Simeon fiddled with the fastenings on her insulated trousers and, when he pushed his hand down the front of them, Esther was practically boneless with lust, with that dirty greedy fuck lust he'd suddenly inspired.

'Oh my God,' she breathed as his fingers drove right inside her, and her defences were gone.

He smiled at her, those violet eyes making her brain

dance as his fingers made her sex churn. 'Good?' he asked smugly. 'Want to suck my cock?'

Esther whimpered an affirmative. She was all his, and he was doing something magical to her – truly magical because, despite her clothes being awry, she didn't feel cold. In fact, she felt more comfortable than she had done since arriving. It didn't make sense, and yet it was all OK.

'My big hard cock?'

'Yes, oh yes.'

Esther wanted to fall to her knees, wrap her lips around him and feel his power in her mouth.

'Well, tough, you can't,' said the man. 'Maybe when Billy shows up he'll feed you a length. Would you like that? Huh, would you?'

Simeon's fingers were flying fast on her clit now.

'Yes,' she panted. 'Oh, yes.'

'Nice,' said Simeon. 'I can just picture you between me and Billy Boy, a cock at either end.'

Simeon's glossy black hair brushed against Esther's jaw as he leaned in to nibble by her ear. He nudged down her sweater, licked and sucked on her neck, his fingers still working her towards climax. The steady suck on Esther's neck made her feel like a schoolgirl smitten by some clumsy adolescent eager to mark her. But her thoughts weren't schoolgirlish, and she took the image Simeon had offered, conjuring up a picture of herself naked between two hard horny guys.

In reality, the stranger was kissing her neck, his hand deep inside her underwear, but, in her mind, she was on all fours, Simeon fucking her while she clutched the hips of another man, her mouth pulling on the bar of his cock. Oh, it was such a hot fantasy.

Billy. His name was Billy, Simeon's friend. And he was the man in the dream, the face at the window, an amalgam of fear, secrecy and desire. He had unearthly eyes and a powerful body, and he clutched her hair, taking control as he shunted into her mouth, echoing Simeon's words: want to suck my cock?

Esther, on the edge of climax, was tipped over by a dart of pain in her neck. She could almost feel the bruise forming under Simeon's lips, all the broken blood vessels blooming beneath her skin.

'I'm coming,' she gasped, slipping down the wall as the shivers gripped.

Simeon sucked harder on her neck, and her orgasm was spinning right out, holding her there on a plateau of bliss. She gazed past Simeon's shoulder, letting herself stream with the thrill, feeling dizzy and weak, the cabin blurring before her eyes.

And then a shadow passed one of the windows, the same window through which the eyes had stared at her.

'No,' she whimpered, trying to focus and get a grip as her orgasm ebbed away. 'No.' She tried to push at Simeon but her limbs were too heavy. She wanted to tell him they were in danger but all she could manage was 'no' and every time she said it, the pain intensified in her neck.

A shadow fell across the second window, darkening the room. For a brief moment, a pair of neon green eyes shone there in the lilac dusk of the snowstorm.

'No,' breathed Esther. A thousand tiny knives seemed to be stabbing into her neck. She was on the brink of collapse.

Then the door flew open with an almighty great crash. The blizzard whooshed in followed by a man from the military. He was a colossal figure in T-shirt and combats, staggering forwards with the bulk of Doug over one shoulder. A mohawk was shaved onto his head, and he was lightly tanned, big and beefy, his skin gleaming wetly. His white T-shirt, soaked from the snow, clung to the contours of his chest, his tight nipples pricking through the cotton. He shot Esther a look, and his eyes were as hauntingly green as the aurora borealis that sometimes lit the northern skies.

Esther screamed.

Simeon gave Esther a shove.

'Get off me, you slut,' he hissed. Blood dribbled from his mouth, and he drew his hand across his chin, smearing it with scarlet streaks. 'Billy,' he said. 'It's not what it seems, man. I swear.'

Billy unloaded Doug onto a chair where he sat, limp and stupefied, his brown beard glittering with lumps of ice. Doug frowned at Esther, looking confused. 'Hello, lady,' he mumbled.

Clearly enraged, Billy strode towards Simeon who stood motionless, lips glossed with blood, as if he realised he had no escape.

Esther's heart was going mad. She knew this man! He was the one in her dreams, and, dear God, he was even more beautiful. He had such a perfect face, strong and handsome, and his mohawk, dusted with snow, was the colour of mink. It lay in a stripe as exquisite as a pelt, and a vein on his temple was a thick blue knot. Esther wanted to run her hands over his head, caress the silky line of his hair, wipe the wet from his skin and soothe the tension that throbbed in that vein.

Billy cast her a cold glance then glowered at Simeon. He raised his fist, biceps taut, wet knuckles glinting, and landed Simeon a punch on the jaw. Simeon's head snapped back and he yelped, staggering from the impact, a hand to his face.

He might have fallen if Billy hadn't grabbed hold of his top and pulled him upright. The blizzard whirled into the cabin, riffling paper and blowing all the clothes and ropes that were hung about the place. The gas lanterns swayed, sending eerie shadows swinging across the room.

Simeon's lip was split, blood mingling with the blood already there. Billy kissed him fiercely, sparing no mercy for the pain he must have felt. Esther stared, stunned. They looked so hot together, a lanky injured man overpowered by a mean muscular soldier, cruelty and rage entwined. Shadows lurched and shrank as snow span around them, melting on their flesh and whipping Simeon's hair into a squall of black strands.

Then Billy pulled back, leaving Simeon dazed, his mouth now clean of blood.

'Oh, man,' mumbled Simeon.

Bending, Billy clasped Simeon's legs and heaved him onto his shoulders. He gave Esther another hard look, one that seemed to threaten, 'I'll be back.'

Then he turned and stalked out into the blizzard, Simeon draped over his shoulder.

T-shirt, thought Esther, he's only wearing a T-shirt. Then, for the first time in her life, she fainted.

'He's never punched me before,' said Simeon. 'Never!'

'Never?' asked Suzanne. 'I find that hard to believe.'

She sauntered naked into the white domed bedroom, blonde hair spilling over her shoulders and matching the clipped fluff of her pubes, a phial of Blud in each hand. *Hope's End*, sealed off from the outside world, had a permanent bluish-white light, and in it Suzanne seemed unreal, her hair glinting too brightly, her skin taking on a milky corpse-like cast. Simeon approved. She looked like an evil futuristic scientist bringing him test tubes of blood.

Billy he preferred in warmer tones and he put a lot of effort into keeping the main dome softly lit, candles flickering everywhere so the place resembled a gothic shrine in a massive igloo. Not that Billy appreciated it. 'Bela Lugosi's dead, don't you know,' he liked to mock. 'Get with the programme, Sim.'

But Simeon didn't want to get with the programme. He was old school – bourgeois and affected, if you listened to Billy – and would far rather be living in a mountainside castle, a coffin for his bed, a cape around his shoulders. He really wasn't cut out for modern life. It demanded so much of one.

'He hit me last week,' said Suzanne. She perched on the edge of the bed where Simeon languished in a sprawl of gawky self-pity. 'Here,' she said, handing him a Blud.

'Dude, that's different,' replied Simeon. 'I saw that. You said, slap me, daddy, you mean ol' brute.'

'Mmm, sexy,' said Suzanne, remembering.

'You enjoyed it,' Simon went on, speaking gingerly. 'What I mean is he's never hit me in anger before. We've been together since ... since 1726 and not once has he – What's this?'

Simeon looked at his phial of Blud, its glass casing clouded with cold.

'I put them outside a while,' she said. 'Blud Slush Puppies. Neat, yeah? I sugared mine. Didn't think you'd fancy it though. Sour's more your thing.'

Simeon pouted. 'Cheers, babe,' he said with camp offence.

Suzanne shook her phial, removed the top and tipped the icy red mush onto her tongue. Simeon followed suit. 'Yuck,' he said as he always did, before listlessly tossing the phial to the floor. His hair streamed like black silk against a stack of white pillows, his lip was a thick and pulpy strawberry, and he imagined he looked quite the consumptive, albeit a touch more debauched.

'Since 1726,' he went on. 'That's a long time, you know, Suze. Oh sure, we've had our ups and downs but I still love the guy. Man, he's been a cunt these last couple of decades though, a complete monster. I can't believe he hit me, can you?'

'It was only a little punch.'

'It was a big punch, Suze,' replied Simeon. 'He fucking hated me when he did that. He could've broken my jaw. And all because I was having a slurp on his piece of pussy. All because I beat him to it.'

'How could you beat him to it? Billy doesn't do humans.'

'Yeah, right,' scoffed Simeon. 'I bet you a penguin he'll do her. Do you think we make a good couple?'

'Sim, there are no penguins in the Arctic.'

'See? That's how much I care about this dump. I don't even know what's on the menu. *Do* you?'

'What?' asked Suzanne. 'Do I know about food?'

'No. Do you think Billy and I make a good couple?'

'Course you do. You're great together. Stop worrying.'

'Hmm.' Simeon sighed heavily. 'I sometimes wonder if we're only together out of habit. It happens in a lot of long-term relationships. I guess I always thought he was The One – in a non-exclusive, vampirey sort of way –'

'Companion in life, fellow traveller and main squeeze,' offered Suzanne.

'Yes,' said Simeon. 'And a great fuck. But hell, I'm not sure any more. Nineteenth-century England. That was our time, Suze. Everyone half in love with death. Ah man, Billy looked good in sideburns and a frock coat. So fucking hot. Berlin in the 1980s was kind of cool, too. You know how I am for those Teutonic types. But basically, it hasn't been the same since Queen Victoria died.'

'Here, put your head in my lap,' cooed Suzanne. 'I'll tell you a story. No, you tell me one. Tell me about Billy, tell me how you met.' She climbed further onto the bed and rearranged the cushions so she was propped against them.

'You know how we met,' said Simeon. He nuzzled up

to her, resting his head in her naked lap. He faced her feet and ran a hand down one slender leg before tracing idle circles around her knee. 'I'm always telling you.'

'Yeah, but I love it,' said Suzanne. Gently, she finger-combed Simeon's hair, drawing it back from his aristocratic face. 'It gets me so wet. Go on. It's seventeen twenty whatever, and you're in this Molly House in London . . .'

'Miss Tilly's Molly House,' said Simeon wearily.

'Yeah, cool,' said Suzanne. 'And Miss Tilly, she's like this prize whore who gets off on gay men.'

'Pretty much,' said Simeon. 'The tavern was full of peep-holes. She'd spend half the night with her eye fixed to a hole, gawping at mollies getting sucked off.'

'Even though she only had one eye.'

'Yes,' said Simeon. 'She wore a patch.'

'Because?' encouraged Suzanne. She wound a length of Simeon's hair tight around one finger and pulled steadily.

'Ouch. Because someone took offence one day and stuck a poker in the peep-hole.'

'Jeepers,' said Suzanne, unravelling the ringlet of hair. 'I love that story. And she still kept watching! What an amazing woman.'

'She was very, very dirty. A complete fag-hag.'

'Yeah,' said Suzanne, dreamy with admiration. 'I can relate to that though. Totally.'

'Man, those days were wild,' said Simeon. 'Billy was being Billy, you know how he is, a lone wolf prowling the streets, hunting for blood. He saw me lurking around St Paul's, thought I looked like trade, so he followed me and some other guy, can't remember his name. Followed us to Miss Tilly's. It was crazy in there, always crazy. Guys in drag, drinking and dancing. I remember sitting on Billy's knee, wearing some frilly dress in orange and blue silks, and wafting my face with a little Spanish fan.'

'Ha, you in a dress,' murmured Suzanne. 'It's hard to imagine.'

'Hmmm, well, *I* was hard,' Simeon drawled.

'Actually, scratch that,' said Suzanne. 'I just imagined it. It's very you. What was Billy doing?'

'Oh, Billy was God's gift that night,' said Simeon. 'He was acting like a real gent, stern and cool but, wow, so dirty. Man, he looked good, those bright-green eyes, that blond hair. It's such a lovely shade, like champagne. Not really blond at all. I wish he'd grow it again. And he had his hand up my petticoats and he was wanking me off, watching my face, really watching me. And all these other guys were whirling about the room, skirts spinning, squealing and laughing.'

'Oh, yum,' said Suzanne. 'And then you shot your load. Can we skip that part? Tell me how he made you a vampire.'

'You *know* how he made me a vampire,' sighed Simeon.

'Yeah, but I could hear it again and again, and I'd still be happy,' said Suzanne. 'You're like my favourite TV show, you know that? I love when it's repeated and the best episodes just get better each time.'

'My lip hurts, Suze. It's not easy to talk. Later, huh? Just keep stroking my hair, will you? I love it. It's so soothing.'

'Mmm, I like it too. Why's your lip taking so long to heal?'

'Blud,' said Simeon. 'It makes you weaker, reduces your vampire powers.'

'Ugh, I hate that shit. Tastes wrong, does you wrong. Nice Kitty. If we had a proper cat, I could stroke that.'

'Hey, don't diss my cat,' said Simeon. 'Renfield's just unusual, that's all. Do you want me to purr?'

'Oh, yes please.'

For a while, the two of them stayed like that, Simeon

with his head in Suzanne's lap, making rumbling noises in his throat as she raked his hair.

'Where *is* Renfield?' asked Simeon. 'I haven't seen him all day.'

'Dunno. Probably out mousing or whatever you'd call it up here. Can I put plaits in your hair?'

'Do what you want with me, babes,' murmured Simeon.

'Slut,' said Suzanne affectionately.

She drew strands of hair into thin threads and wove a slim plait which, because Simeon's hair was in such great condition, came half undone as soon as she released it.

'If you ask me,' said Simeon, 'the fact we've got a vampire cat should be our main worry. If anything's going to give the game away, it's Renfield, not you capturing a mortal and trying to keep him.'

'Totally agree. I think Billy was way over the top,' said Suzanne. 'One person wouldn't hurt, surely. And we're so well hidden here. They'll never find us.'

'I know,' sympathised Simeon. 'Oh, and Doug was such a bear. I really wanted to keep him. Our very own sex and blood slave.'

'Don't, it's not fair,' said Suzanne. 'He was hot. And such a yummy cock. It's been ages since I've tasted fresh meat.'

'You only got here the other week!' exclaimed Simeon. 'Ouch,' he added, touching his lip.

'Yeah, but I'm greedy,' replied Suzanne. 'And I'm not used to Blud. Hell, I wish Billy hadn't kicked off. Doug was lovely. Boy, he fucked me like a man possessed, like Billy does when he's on form.'

'I know. That was awesome. God, I so wanted it to be my turn next.'

'I'm getting hungry,' said Suzanne. 'Really hungry. Maybe we should think about leaving, Sim. It's the first sunrise soon. Isn't that usually your cue to start making a move?'

'Ha,' scoffed Simeon. 'Like we might leave while *she's* still around.'

Suzanne sighed and smoothed a hand across Simeon's forehead. 'Maybe we should bail and leave him to it. We could get to the coast under our own steam then head down to Kangerlussuaq. We could be on a flight to the States in a few days, maybe stay with Christophe and the guys in New York. I'm not really into all this returning to your roots shit. I mean, the temperature's nice here but that's as far as it goes.'

Simeon turned, squirming till he was comfortable and facing Suzanne's golden-haired groin. 'Tempting,' he said. He wriggled a finger into the slippery lips of her sex, trailing upwards to roll her clit. 'But the west coast's still some distance off, you know.'

'Mmm,' said Suzanne, half pleasure, half agreement. 'We could take my skidoo.'

'Sun's coming up any day now,' said Simeon. 'We'd need to be protected.'

'We could take one of the blackout tents,' said Suzanne.

Simeon gazed at Suzanne's clit as he fretted. 'It's quite a journey, babes,' he said. 'But, yeah. Maybe we could.'

Suzanne parted her thighs a fraction wider. 'Definitely we could,' she purred. 'All we'd need is a good meal inside us first.'

Billy was starting to realise that Blud had its limitations. If you wanted merely to exist, to operate in a state of vampiric numbness then Blud was your man, no problem. But if you wanted to thrive, to suffer and soar and to taste it all, then only human blood would do.

Since the birth of Esther, Billy had been living half a life. He'd been traipsing around the world's coldest, loneliest parts, resisting what he needed in a bid to resist her. It would've been better if she'd never been reborn. And yet all his vampire-life, ever since he'd killed her on the rim of the fountain, he'd been longing for her return.

She tormented him. It pained him that he'd killed her. It pained him that he'd once intended making her a vampire because, older and wiser, he could see that was an act of selfishness, not love. And this pain wouldn't leave him. He'd loved and fucked a lot of people after Selin, too many to count. Some he could remember well, others had faded or disappeared, but his one constant was Selin.

Every death he compared to hers; every fuck to their first and last; his every orgasm to the pure perfection of the one that had gripped him, surging through his veins as Selin's dying heartbeat had filled his body. But no matter how hard he tried, he couldn't fuck away the pain.

And now he'd seen Selin's eyes in Esther's. Without a doubt, it was her. Some externals were different, sure, but that was irrelevant. In essence, the two women were one and the same, separated by over three centuries. Billy, knowing how rare rebirth was, had never dared hope it would happen. Mortals didn't realise it, but only when a soul matched up with the right body was a person truly reincarnated. Most times, souls ended up in the wrong bodies, and that's why people suffered so. They were all in the wrong containers, searching for the right one which they sweetly described as looking for love.

Billy curled a barbell to his arm, straining up and down. He was sweating and tired but a long way from stopping. *Hope's End*, thankfully, was well equipped with facilities and various psychological comforts to ease the stay of whoever was meant to be there: researchers, soldiers, prisoners of war. Presumably, the US military once had big plans for it. Unlike the Arctic's Distant Early Warning stations, set up to detect Soviet bombers, the purpose of the dome was obscure. For all Billy knew, there might be dozens more buried under mounds of fake snow. There was even a sunroom for the dark winter months. Billy used it to top his tan. He didn't suit the coffin-cold vampire look.

In the gym, Billy would sometimes thank Gorbachev. Much as he loved the Arctic isolation, without the gym, he'd have cracked up. Exercise helped, really helped. It made him strong, physically and mentally. Lately, he could barely function for wanting Esther. The moment she'd arrived on the icecap he'd sensed her and the last couple of weeks had been agony. Now, idiot that he was, he'd done the thing he swore he'd never do: he'd tasted her blood.

He should have held back. He should have resisted. But when he'd burst into the cabin and seen Simeon there with her blood on his lips, her juices on his fingers, Billy had flipped. One swift left hook, and Simeon's lip was spilling with two bright-red bloods. Kissing him clean, the taste of Esther emerging fresh and strong, had been the best thing to happen to Billy since he'd quit killing.

He wanted more, so much more. He wanted more of her blood, her body, her heart, her cunt, her love. Nadir's voice came echoing down the centuries: 'You are a vampire, Wilhelm, don't fight it.'

If I could just ease off the slaying, thought Billy, maybe I could learn to manage it. He swapped hands and began curling the barbell to work on his other arm. He was aiming for three sets of ten but stopped when he heard a scream from the other room.

Hell, he'd forgotten to clear up. Stunned by what he'd done, Billy had headed straight for the gym.

He dropped his barbell and strode into the main dome.

There was no point trying to hide it. Simeon, hand pressed to his forehead was pacing back and forth, two paces left, two paces right. He glanced at the rug a couple of times, grimacing with revulsion.

Suzanne stood there, eyes sparkling with tears, a hand clamped to her mouth.

On the polar bear rug were the remnants of Renfield, a scrap of silver-blue fluff, his neck a gory wound edged with matted fur.

'Oh, man,' breathed Simeon, staring at Billy. 'You ate the cat. You ate the fucking cat.'

Billy, gleaming with sweat, glared back. He tipped his jaw defiantly, chest swelling.

'I was hungry,' he said.

Simeon rushed to embrace Suzanne. 'I told you,' he sobbed. 'He's a monster.' He turned to Billy. 'Dude, we are *so* over.'

5

Esther dreamt she was in a huge furnished igloo. No, not an igloo because it wasn't made of snow and the temperature was too warm. Dream logic. Dream igloo: an ice-white dome with a roaring fire, a polar bear hearth rug and candleflames like a pattern of amber petals. Nothing made sense.

She was kneeling on the rug, hands roped behind her back, her dark hair woven in a thick plait. She wore only a pair of undershorts. She had no idea how she'd ended up in this state of undress. Billy stood a few feet away, scowling down at her. Presumably it had something to do with him.

'You make me weaken,' he said in a steely whisper. 'Not your fault but you make me weaken.'

Esther had no reply. She was too scared to speak. This man ruled the room. This was his domain, and she appeared to be his captive. He stood stock-still, thumbs hooked in the belt loops of his camouflages, a tense stance masquerading as casual. Constrained anger. Green camouflage for jungles, not beige for sand. Snug white T-shirt over a broad muscular torso. The man who'd rescued Doug. Another crazy dream. Esther had had so many on the ice.

'I could hurt you,' he said. 'Really hurt you.'

Esther felt so exposed. Her breasts were bared and her bound wrists made them defenceless and tender. She wanted him to hurt her, to twist her nipples or kiss her like the man in recent dreams, remorseless, hard and greedy. And yet she didn't want that at all. She would die of shame. But something made her give a defiant toss of her head and say, 'Do it then. Hurt me.'

Billy laughed scornfully. 'You don't know what it means.'

'Try me,' said Esther, chin in a bold jut. Esther was tall, strong and fit, and had spent months in training. Her arms and thighs were honed for pulling, her mind was focused and she had the stamina of an ox. There were plenty of men she could wipe the floor with but Billy wasn't one of them. Bravado, however, was useful. 'Try me,' she repeated. 'Because I could probably hurt you just as much.'

How stupid that sounded when she was on her knees, hands tethered, and one garment away from naked.

Billy folded his arms and gave her a small condescending smile. He was brawny and fierce, a immense statue full of rippling potential. His hips looked stern, his biceps bulged and his combat boots were scruffy and worn.

Esther dipped her head, focusing on the boots. Shabby laces criss-crossed loosely over the leather tongues, and their toes were rounded as if capped with steel. She wondered how long she could keep staring at them. It was dangerous to meet the man's eyes and yet they pulled like magnetic north. Looking away was an effort. Looking up would cost her dearly. But, oh, how she wanted to.

Esther could feel herself unravelling. Those green eyes made her someone else, someone sumptuous, dirty and lavish. She liked being someone else, and she wanted the freedom to spread her legs wide and draw his mouth to her sex, to hook her thighs on his beefy shoulders and grind herself against his lips. She wanted to caress his bald head and stroke the band of his mohawk, moaning as his tongue twirled, making her hot, wet and orgasmic. The thought was enough to make her hips tilt with horniness.

She glanced up from the boots.

'That's better,' said Billy. 'Look at the boots again and I'll make you kiss them.'

It disturbed Esther that his threat made her groin loosen. She averted her eyes, gazing sidelong at the fire which danced with light gaseous flames.

'What do you want?' she asked.

'Really?' said Billy. 'You want to know?'

'Yes.'

'I want to destroy you.'

Esther's insides lurched, heart, stomach and head. 'Please,' she said, her voice catching on a sob. 'Please don't hurt me. Please.'

'But I love you,' he declared, his tone still coldly aggressive.

Esther shook her head. She was too confused. Billy was mad and terrifying, and his crotch was seriously swollen. He was hot, hung and powerful, and Esther fancied he'd twist her like a pretzel if they ended up in bed together. They seemed to be locked in a scary limbo of lust and resistance. Esther didn't know her future, didn't know what he had in store for her. She wondered if this wild talk of love was an attempt to reduce her by messing with her mind. Either that, or he was delusional.

'Then you shouldn't destroy me,' she replied, hoping to humour him. 'That's not love.'

'It is in my world,' said Billy. 'I'm a monster. I want what I love. I want all of it. I want to destroy the thing so I can have it.'

'Possessive,' said Esther. 'I've met your sort before.'

'No, monstrous,' said Billy. He began to circle Esther, stalking slowly. She kept her eyes fixed on the fire. 'If I don't destroy it, it torments me until I'm mad with wanting. I destroy it, and I'm mad with regret. Because I lose it, don't I? In having it, I lose it. So I'm still wanting.'

Esther began to feel sick. 'What are you going to do with me?' she asked.

'I don't know,' said Billy. 'I can't win. Either way, I can't win.'

Esther drew deep breaths and stared at the wall several feet away. It looked to be made of curved breeze block, and light glinted on a repair job of silver duct tape.

'I think that's desire,' she said. 'You can't top it, Billy. It's always going to win so maybe try accepting it. Give up trying to be the boss. You'll drive yourself insane. You have to want, Billy. Everyone does. It's inevitable. You have to want and resist and suffer, Billy. The day you stop wanting is the day you die.'

Billy, thought Esther. I have to keep using his name like cops do in movies when they're trying to talk down a madman.

Billy stood in front of her. The toes of his black boots were scratched and dulled. Esther looked up, wanting to see him. She caught a flash of green eyes as he pulled his T-shirt over his head, his body stretching to expose patches of underarm hair, paler flesh and the rack of his ribs. Esther turned to liquid.

Billy threw his T-shirt to the ground. He was beautifully broad, muscular but without the vanity of high definition. His abs were flat, his pecs taut, his lightly tanned skin flecked with golden hair. Around his neck, hanging from a leather thong, was a chunky pendant in dark oriental silver, a curved dagger like a weapon from *Sinbad the Sailor*. But what struck Esther most was the seam of a scar slashing his torso on the diagonal. She flinched to see it, and at the same time she felt certain she'd seen it before. It belonged in a memory or another dream.

Billy unzipped. 'You talk too much,' he said. 'Suck it.'

His cock sprang out, magnificent and thick, and

Esther sucked in great willing gulps. After all, she'd rather give head than try to fix a man's feelings. It was less debasing, easier to understand and the rewards were quicker. If Billy's soft grunts were anything to go by, he preferred it too. As Esther bobbed on his length, Billy said, 'You wanted me before. I saw it. You were hot for me, begging with your eyes like a greedy little whore.'

Esther recalled the look of dark promise he'd cast her before storming out of the cabin, Simeon over his shoulder. Had he seen it then? But that was a dream, wasn't it? Could he see into her dreams?

Billy grabbed clumps of hair either side of her head and withdrew from her mouth. He held her steady, his big red cock bobbing inches from her lips.

'Suck it,' he said.

Esther reached for him, mouth open, but he wouldn't let her near.

'Come on, girly, try harder,' he sneered.

Esther strained for him but he held her firm, his grip pinching her scalp. He teased her, rolling his hips so his tip skimmed her lips, its little slit seeming to leer and mock. Esther, now she couldn't have him, wanted him all the more.

'Please,' she said.

Billy released her hair and took a step back, clasping his cock. 'Come on, then.'

Esther cursed and shuffled after him, knees rubbing on the silky bearskin, mouth gaping. She felt weird, as if her dreams were overlapping.

'Come on,' breathed Billy, jacking his cock. 'Reach for it.'

Esther had a moment's *déjà vu*, a glimpse of a pink fountain, of ornate blue tiles. And then a word came from somewhere, one she didn't understand, and yet she heard herself speak it: '*Efendim.*'

Billy groaned and fell to his knees. 'Oh, God,' he whispered. 'I'm sorry.' His fingers fumbled over her face and he scanned her features as if he were seeing her anew, his gaze intense and pained.

'Don't look at me, turn away,' he said but it was impossible. Meeting his eyes, Esther felt she was falling into the Arctic, into phosphorescent nights and peppermint-green seas.

'I like looking,' she said, staring at him. 'It feels good. I like it.'

Billy's lips lifted in a quick smile, then he clasped her plait and kissed her so forcefully she could barely breathe. His hard torso squashed her breasts and her skin grew damp from his sweat. How could he sweat in sub-zero temperatures? Why weren't they freezing? Why did it feel so good when he made her feel small?

Esther was soft and wet, and when Billy eased up on his kisses, she began kissing him back, lusting after his force. He responded with a nip, taking her lower lip between his teeth and clamping on the tender flesh.

'Ouch,' said Esther as Billy pulled away.

Billy gazed at her, a smear of red on his lips, and Esther stared back, sucking blood into her mouth. His shoulders rose and fell, and Esther saw the tremor in his scarred chest as he fought to control his quickening breath. He liked this a lot. Esther thought she did as well but wasn't sure. Fear kept flickering, warning her to back off, play it cool. But she wasn't doing, was she? Didn't want to play it cool. Didn't want to be the responsible good girl. She wanted this man to toy with her. She wanted him like this, dangerous, cruel and as horny as a dozen men.

Esther gave him a steady look. 'Hurt me,' she said.

Billy smiled tenderly and stroked the line of her jaw. 'I am,' he whispered. He trailed his hand down her neck, drew swirls over her breasts and teased her nipples.

'What happened to you?' she asked, indicating his scar.

He ran his thumb beneath the swell of one breast, tracing around and up to her shoulder. 'I lived in another country,' he said. 'A long time ago. The people there, some of them, they thought you could kill a vampire by slitting him from his heart to his gut.'

Esther nodded, understanding. 'And you can't.'

Billy shook his head. 'No,' he breathed. 'Unfortunately not.'

Esther gazed at the silvery line. It slanted below one nipple, got jagged by his stomach and sliced across his belly. The skin was shiny, the tissue pinkish and puckered where the injury had obviously been messy.

'It was a deep wound,' said Billy. 'Usually they heal to nothing.'

'They nearly cut you in half,' said Esther.

'Nearly,' said Billy. 'But I deserved it.'

Esther didn't want to believe him but she knew it was true and she accepted it, just as she accepted he was a vampire. She wondered muzzily if being alone with him meant death, and she imagined it did. Yet she had a peculiar sense this man could threaten and protect her at one and the same time.

'Lick my scar,' ordered Billy.

Esther smiled. Her lip stung where he'd bitten her. 'Make me.'

Billy smiled back and fiddled with the pendant around his neck, watching her carefully. The miniature dagger was about two inches long and the blade looked sharp enough to cut, firelight winking on its razor-fine edge. Esther grew nervous again. She'd wanted him maybe to pull her hair, force her head to his chest and say something strict. His cool macho aggression excited her but knives were different.

Billy gave a tug on the pendant, releasing it from its

leather cord. Esther's heart bumped fast, faster still when Billy lunged for her. She screamed as she fell, slamming sideways onto her thighs. Billy grabbed her bound hands, tipping her forwards as he raised her arms behind her back.

'Please don't hurt me,' sobbed Esther. Her shoulders throbbed and her face was pressed into the fur rug, fibres sticking to her bloodied lip. 'Please!' Then she realised he was sawing at the ropes and seconds later she was free, woozy with relief.

'Sit up,' said Billy, kneeling opposite her again.

Esther did, giving her arms a little shake, glad of her freedom and less fearful of the knife. She dabbed her lip but the blood had stopped. Just a tiny nip. He wouldn't harm her, would he? Especially not now he'd just released her. She thought they were heading for safe ground but she had to rethink when he seized the waist of her undershorts. He nicked the elastic and ran a slit down the fabric, first one side then the other, before tossing the scraps aside.

Esther was naked.

'Put your hands behind your head,' ordered Billy.

He clipped the little knife back around his neck; a sign, thought Esther, that no, he didn't intend her harm. And so she obeyed, linking her fingers behind her head, shy and self-conscious, horribly aware of how the posture exhibited her. Billy flicked her nipples a few times with thumb and forefinger. 'Lick the scar,' he said. 'From top to bottom.'

His order made Esther flush with a dark sultry heat. Her sex was bloated and wet, and she felt empty inside, so hungry for cock. 'Make me,' she said again, starting to feel seductive and bold.

Billy arched his brows. 'If you don't,' he said, 'I'll stand up and I'll walk away.'

Esther bristled, cursing silently. His threat pulled

tighter than any bondage, the force of her lust outweighing the force of his muscle. She blushed for shame, knowing she couldn't refuse him.

'Fold your arms behind your back,' said Billy. 'And lick it.'

Trying not to resent his victory, Esther did as she was told, tipping forwards to touch the tip of her tongue to the tip of his scar. His fuzz of chest hair tickled lightly but beneath it the track of his scar was silky smooth. She traced it easily, moving from a flat dusky nipple to the confused patch of tissue below his sternum. Lingering there, she painted saliva swirls, unable to avoid thinking of the injury, of the viscera and bone right there under the skin she tongued.

She wondered how he felt about his mark. His body was beautiful and he clearly worked out to acheive that muscle but the mark was someone else's. To be licking it felt deeply intimate, especially since she didn't know how the scar had been acquired. Or, worse, how he'd come to deserve it. She felt she was tonguing his history.

She continued licking downwards, trailing wetly across his hard flat belly to his hip. He was trusting her with some fragility, asking her to accept and not judge. The scar ended and Esther's instinct was to suck his cock where it twitched from his open fly, but she resisted, not knowing whether that was allowed.

'Kneel up,' said Billy.

No, it clearly wasn't.

'Up!' corrected Billy when she sat back on her heels. 'Hands behind your head again.'

The severity of his voice turned Esther on and she knelt in the position he demanded. Kneeling inches away, his cock angled high, Billy grinned faintly and reached between her legs. Esther caught her breath, holding still as he massaged an inner thigh, his sure, steady fingers squeezing her flesh. He studied her face, his smile tilting higher when he ran a finger over her folds and made her moan.

'Nice?' he asked.

His touch was maddeningly light, teasing the wisps of her hair and making her crave firmness. Esther opened her legs wider. Billy obliged her by separating her lips and sawing along the wet groove of her sex, nudging her clit and teasing her hole.

'Please,' she whispered. 'Give me more. Inside me. This . . . it's not enough.'

Billy gave a harsh, knowing scoff. 'Not enough?' he said. 'Story of my life.' And he slipped a single finger inside her. He curled it forwards, making little taps there, and Esther was soon whimpering, her legs turning wobbly. 'Please,' she said again, struggling to keep her hands behind her head. She wanted to fall forwards, to lean on his big shoulders and suck his salty skin.

His eyes never left hers and he ignored her requests, smiling smugly at the way she pleaded. For too long, he teased with a tiny touch until he inserted two fingers and pressed his thumb to her clit, pinching her sex. He worked her like that, pulling and rubbing. Her juices clicked with his rhythm, running freely onto his fingers as her pleasure coiled tighter. And all the while he watched her, his lips parted, his eyes droopy. Esther was torn, wanting to escape his scrutiny as much as she wanted to bask in his attention.

'Good?' he murmured. Esther nodded, her mind too dumb for words, her throat too thick with breath.

Billy upped his tempo, his own breath rising, and soon Esther was gasping fast. 'I'm coming,' she panted, right on the edge. 'Coming!'

Billy snatched his fingers away.

'No!' cried Esther.

Billy caught her hands as she rushed to touch herself. 'I'm not ready,' he snarled, teeth clenched as she wriggled in his clutches.

'But I am!'

Billy glared, shoulders lifting, nostrils flaring. 'Turn around. Bend over,' he snapped, and he flung her around so she was on all fours.

'Please!' cried Esther. She tipped onto her elbows, pressing her buttocks back. 'Fuck me. Make me come!'

Billy grasped her hips, yanking her closer. His cock nudged at her hole, his end feeling stout and heavy, and Esther tightened for him. 'Oh please, please,' she said.

'Have it then,' hissed Billy and he crammed himself into her with a big savage jab. His fingers gripped her flesh and he began ramming her with wild angry energy.

Esther was lost, his impact shuddering through her body, his fuck thumping right at her core. She touched herself, just a few tiny nudges, and she was there again, her orgasm ready to break.

'Yes, now,' she cried. 'I'm coming.'

'Go on,' growled Billy. 'Come.' And he grabbed the rope of her plait, using it to pull her head higher. Esther arched her spine, fingers on her clit until she came, bleating and shuddering. As she peaked, Billy scooped her up backwards, a hand on her breast, another around her waist, and Esther howled as her neck exploded in dark brilliant pain.

Colours burst behind her eyeballs, flares of crimson, black and purple. And then the pain vanished and instead her neck began dissolving into Billy's mouth, his suck so beautiful that Esther was coming again, a second climax chasing her first, his cock still buried inside her.

The sensation was like nothing on earth. The wound on her neck was as soft and pulpy as her cunt, the tenderness of it sliding into Billy's violent, draining kiss. Esther was coming so hard she felt faint, the dark colours bursting in her mind until a new delirium took hold: snow and ice, a blur of tiny stars, a blast of wind, an enormous sky with the colours of a bruise seeping across it.

And then she woke with a sob, gulping for breath. 'Billy,' she gasped. 'Billy!'

She was in her sleeping bag in the dark cabin. There was no Billy. He was a dream.

Oh, God, Billy, come back.

A stab of longing made Esther's eyes prick with tears. Her thighs were slippery and wet. A dream. But how could he not exist? It had been so vivid, so sexy, so warm.

The cabin swam, its shadowy gloom quivering behind a watery veil. She ached for him, ached for a stupid dream vampire, for the man who'd saved Doug and now a phantom of her overwrought mind. It was too cruel.

Esther blinked and dashed away a couple of tears. Come on, Essie, she urged. Only a dream. Nothing to get upset about.

She wriggled up from the cocoon of her sleeping bag, her eyes adjusting to the dark. All the opposite bunks were empty, sleeping bags limp and twisted. She checked her watch. Mid-morning. Something was wrong. They wouldn't all leave like that. Why was she still in bed? Esther's heartbeat quickened.

'Hello?' she called, but she knew with a dread certainty no one would answer. It was too silent, the room too cold and empty. They'd left, and in a hurry by the looks of it. She peered over the edge of her bed to the bunk below, expecting to see Margret's abandoned sleeping bag.

Instead, she saw Margret, eyes bulging in shock, her skin a ghastly dough-grey, her neck ripped apart in a raw red gash. Her sleeping bag was soaked and on the floor was a neat puddle of blood.

Esther screamed, kicking her legs, running at nothing.

Then she drew breath and screamed again, over and over, her throat muscles pulling in pain. And, even while she was screaming, she knew there was no point. There was no one around for miles.

Billy was in agony, steel blades lacerating him inside. He was asleep, dreaming of a memory, of the Turks who'd tried to avenge Selin's death.

A servant had witnessed it from a window overlooking Nadir's yali. Billy was a marked man. It had happened so fast. Night time, wandering alone in the columned courtyard of the Suleyman mosque, insects chirruping. And then suddenly they were upon him, their approach as quiet as death. The cutlass flashed in the moonlight before it slashed Billy's body, and then they'd left him to die.

Billy was a vampire; his flesh mended fast. But that was one wound which had never fully healed. Like Nadir, he'd been left with a scar. Perhaps there was some truth in the rumour this was the way to despatch a vampire. Billy had lain on the ground, clutching his belly, trying to hold himself together in the shadows of an arched walkway. Blood poured through his fingers, and he squinted at a minaret spiking the starry night, willing himself not to lose consciousness. Perhaps this was the end, easier than he'd thought.

His thoughts swirled, and he wondered if he might join Selin in death. But no, it was impossible. She would be in heaven and he would be in hell. Maybe there was still time. 'Forgive me, Father, for I have sinned. I have . . . I have . . .'

Billy woke with a jolt.

'Selin!'

He was on the polar-bear hearth rug, the fire dancing with pale flames. His forehead was damp with sweat. Jeez, how many times had he had that dream lately?

He lay on his back and rubbed a hand over his face. Hell, he really was starting to crack. Esther was too close, much too close. Billy ran his tongue around his gums. He felt groggy, his mouth dry and sticky.

Damn, this was no good. He'd kept it together for years but this was testing him to the limits. All he ever thought about was her. Sometimes he woke barely able to breathe, the weight of her sodden body on his chest. And right now, she seemed so alive to him she might be there on the bearskin rug. He could almost taste her blood on his lips.

He needed to get the hell out of this place before he did something he might regret. Thousands and thousands of miles away. He would leave soon, very soon.

Any day now, the sun would rise for the first time that year. Suzanne and Simeon were up to something. Billy guessed they were planning to quit the ice, leaving him here to stew. That might have suited him a few days ago but not now. He was done. His time here was up. He would travel with them and then do his best to erase all memories of Esther.

She deserved a full life of love and happiness. If Billy stayed much longer, her second life would end the same way as her first, her dying heartbeat pumping down his throat.

Yes, she deserved better. She deserved to grow old and be withered by age, to feel her body decay and to treasure life because she feared death. God, how Billy envied her.

He would pack. He would leave. He would forget she even existed.

Suzanne had chosen a sky-blue dress with short cowboy boots for killing. The dress was printed with daisies, the flowers' yellow centres like little suns. It was pretty but it was even prettier now it was soaked in blood.

She sat cross-legged on the ice, making a snowcastle on her knee. 'Sim, I'm bored,' she said. 'Can't we leave now?'

Simeon lay propped on an elbow, his clothes and hair jet black against the whiteness of snow. Earlier, he'd been wearing his favourite black lipstick but that had long since rubbed off. 'Be patient,' he said. 'She'll be along any moment, I guarantee it.'

'You're so cruel, you know that?'

'Oh really?' said Simeon. 'Shit, and I was trying to be nice. I thought it might impress you.'

Suzanne laughed. 'Ah, you're right. This is going to be a riot. Me, you and Billy's bitch. Hey, look at me! I'm not bored any more. It's cool.' Suzanne began piling snow on her other knee, patting it into a pyramid. 'I vote we torment her for ages before the kill. You know what I love best? It's when they beg for their lives. It's so funny, especially when they can't even get the words out.'

'Oh, man,' said Simeon. 'I love that too. *Pluh ... pluh ...*'

'Pluh ... eese!' added Suzanne, laughing hard.

'Dude, I am so psyched for this,' said Simeon. 'That woman has dogged me for centuries.'

'Aw, dogging you how, babes? She's been mainly dead.'

'Oh, you know.' Simeon gave a dismissive flap of his hand. 'Billy's totally obsessed. I'm not kidding, Suze, it's no fun when your love rival's six foot under. They're always going to be perfect, aren't they? I never stood a fucking chance.'

'Hey, Billy loves you,' said Suzanne. 'Course he does.'

'Oh, sure. I know that. But I've always been second best. And now she's back on earth, I'm just some ... some piece of dirt on his boots.'

'Yeah, but high-quality dirt.'

Simeon shrugged and sniffed. 'Plus, he ate Renfield.'

'Don't get upset, babes.'

Simeon flicked his hair. 'I'm not upset.'

Suzanne pouted. 'I think you are.'

'Oh, OK then I am. But he made me a vampire, Suze. We'd spent weeks together in London, so hot for each other, fucking at Miss Tilly's, fucking in his lodging house. I was so happy then. And, even when he made me a vampire, I was still happy. It was like this whole new level of him I was getting to understand. And I've never resented him for it. Never.'

'I think I see her.' Suzanne indicated a dot of a figure in the south.

'Oh, cool,' said Simeon, glancing.

'Hungry?' asked Suzanne.

'Ravenous.' Simeon rolled onto his back, knees pointing upwards and flung out an arm. 'Give her a while longer, yeah? We'll lie low. She won't spot us for ages.'

Suzanne touched her fingertips to Simeon's. 'I'm thrilled we left her till last.'

'Yeah, me too.' Simeon smiled, slow and malevolent. 'The dessert course, and she's mine, all mine!'

'Hey, and mine.'

'Yeah, OK. What's mine is yours.'

Simeon sighed happily, looking up at the star-speckled, blue and purple sky. He closed his eyes. In a few days, they'd be in New York with a bunch of old friends. Simeon was so ready to kick back. Life got intense when it was just him and Billy. If Billy wanted to join them, fine, he could. But Simeon wasn't about to start begging for his commitment.

Nearly 300 years ago, with Simeon's blood spilling from his lips, Billy had said, 'You belong to me. I belong to you.' It was Covent Garden, a narrow rickety street. The place was full of brothels and taverns back then. Dark and seedy. Simeon's kind of place.

And though they'd since been apart for decades at a

time, Simeon had always felt the connection of that belonging. Probably always would, whatever happened.

Suzanne stood. 'Come on, I'm ready,' she said. She brushed snow off her skirt, and reached for Simeon's hand, pulling him up. They smiled broadly at each other, eyes glittering.

'Fast?' asked Suzanne. She looked radiant, her cheeks flushed from their earlier feed.

Simeon began to tremble with excitement. He'd been wanting to do this for longer than he could remember. He drew a deep breath. 'Fast,' he agreed. 'Faster than the fucking wind.'

Esther's snowmobile stuttered to a halt. She'd been expecting it.

She clambered out, removed her helmet, donned her fur cap and slung her pack over her shoulder. She'd brought her sleeping bag, the satphone, a flare gun, some survival essentials, plus passport, doorkeys, some Danish krone and her credit card. But, when you ran out of fuel on the ice, a credit card seemed like a sick joke.

She set herself south east and trudged toward the horizon's pre-dawn glow, leaving the skidoo sitting there like a hi-tech dodgem car. The blizzard had gone, thank God, and the morning was calm.

Margret's face kept jumping into Esther's mind. Each time it did, she had to stifle a sob. Crying cost energy. Esther would never make it if she cried. And yet she couldn't help it. She kept crying. She'd cried as soon as the skidoo had set off, weeping behind the visor as snow sprayed from the machine's runners, misting her vision. In the cabin, she hadn't shed a tear. She'd screamed and shook, gathering possessions in a whirl of terror while Margret lay on the bunk, waxy and bug-eyed. Before leaving, Esther had draped a jumper over the woman's face, wishing she could offer more dignity.

In the snowcat, Esther surged across the ice, praying she would find the others. Doug worried her the most. He'd been suffering ever since the skiers had found him wandering miles from the cabin, delirious and with no memory of how he'd got there. Bird had put him on a course of antibiotics and was threatening to do likewise to Esther. Like Doug, she had weird lesions on her neck, and was less than fit. She'd invented details about the two skiers because most of it was a blank. No way was she going to reveal she'd fainted or fess up about her strange dreams. She didn't want to be seen as a weak link in the team.

Five minutes into her skidoo journey and Esther began to fear she was the only link. The first body she found was Doug's. His great bulk lay crumpled on the ice, dressed in thermal long johns, bunny boots and parka. Esther had pulled over, not knowing what condition he was in. He was such a weight but she managed to heave him onto his back. His eyes were glassy, his beard lumped with ice, and blood gurgled briefly from the wound in his neck.

Esther had fled from him, urging the snowcat on and fighting her rising hysteria. She hadn't stopped for Adrian or Bird, recognising them only from the colours of their jackets. If Bird was dead, Johannes probably was too. And, if he weren't, he would surely want to be if he'd witnessed his beloved Margret's slaughter.

All Esther could do was get far, far away. God, what the hell was it? What was hunting them and what ground could it cover? And how come she'd slept through the attack?

But this was no time to dwell on what had happened. She needed to keep her wits about her and focus on the here and now. If she could make it to an Inuit village on the east coast, she'd be safe.

But the fuel gauge was low and, when the skidoo had

stopped with a whine and a cough, Esther began to doubt her chances. She walked on, knowing it was her only option. Staying still meant death. And she would not die here, alone in this sterile desert. She would not.

Having driven for miles, she clung to the hope she was out of immediate danger. The trek ahead might be her biggest threat. She had food, a stove, a sleeping bag. She could build a snow cave for shelter. If the weather and terrain were good, she could make it. Yes, she would make it.

'I will not die,' she panted, her breath puffing out. 'I will not die.'

All she needed to do was take one more step. And another. And another. Skis would have been easier but it didn't do to think that. She'd grabbed what she could. No use having regrets.

Again, the image of Margret loomed large. What monster had done that?

No. Stop thinking. One more step. Just one more step.

Before long, Esther had settled into a rhythm, the twilit blanket of snow numbing her senses. For almost twenty minutes, she was the only thing moving on the expanse of ice. And then, turning, she spotted a black speck to the north. Her heart pumped in fear. It could be good news, it could be bad, but she wouldn't know until it was too late. There were no snow banks to burrow in and her skidoo was less than a mile away, stuck there like a sign saying 'This way, please'.

The speck grew larger then separated into two specks, moving at quite a rate. Animals? People in skidoos? Esther extended the aerial of her satphone and tried for what felt like the hundredth time. Nothing. Dead. Her flare gun was clipped to her parka. Apart from a Swiss army knife, it was her only weapon.

The two blobs were getting bigger and bigger, their

speed disturbing, unnatural even. Esther began to run, as fat as an astronaut in her snow gear. Then she screamed, realising these were people and they were advancing with the speed of a cheetah. And then she screamed again because they couldn't possibly be people, couldn't be.

Hand in hand, the two things slowed and pranced towards her, a woman in a stained floral dress and a lanky man in black, the skier with the purple eyes. Simeon.

'Oh, shit,' gasped Esther, arms pumping, blood pounding in her ears.

Laughing and leaping, the creatures released each other's hand, frolicking this way and that as Esther stumbled on, boots sinking into the snow, heavy as lead.

'Hey, we meet again,' said Simeon. 'How's tricks? This is my friend, Suzanne.'

'Hi there!' said Suzanne, waving.

'Billy! Help!' cried Esther, hardly knowing what she was saying.

Simeon laughed. 'Billy, help,' he mimicked. His black hair flew behind him, his teeth flashed in a grin, and his eyes burnt like violet fire. Esther knew she mustn't look into them. Mustn't get caught.

A few feet ahead, Suzanne laughed, dancing in side steps, her blonde hair streaming, cowboy boots flicking up snow. Esther tugged off a glove and grabbed her flare gun. It was made of lurid-green plastic and she aimed it shakily at Simeon who gambolled alongside her like a tall jerky imp.

'Hey, Suze,' he called. 'She's got a water pistol!'

'Cool! Is it loaded?'

Esther turned to Suzanne, pointing the gun at her. The gun had only one shot and, while it wasn't deadly, at close range it could injure. When Suzanne skipped closer,

Esther pulled the trigger. A red light flashed, a bang followed and Suzanne yelped, doubling over and clutching her stomach.

Esther swung her pack from her shoulder and hurled it at Simeon with all her might. He caught it deftly and cast it to the ground with brisk contempt. Suzanne, still bent double, took a couple of steps backwards then raised her head. She glared at Esther through a tangle of hair, her eyes a dazzling sapphire blue.

'You bitch,' she snarled, spittle flying from her lips. 'Get her, Sim.'

Simeon launched himself, knocking Esther to the ground before she could even call out. He straddled her and tore at her parka, fibres spilling. Esther screamed, thrashing beneath him, snow flurries whipping up around them. Simeon grabbed her clothes and ripped the layers. One, two, three, and she was exposed, flesh bared to her bra. He grinned down at her.

'Please,' gasped Esther, skin scorched by the cold air. 'Please, no.'

Simeon fell on her, driving his teeth straight into her throat. Esther howled in pain. She tried to fight back, fists flailing but he was strong and solid on top of her.

'Stop! Let me go!'

The suction on her neck was furious, pulling on sinew and muscle, hoovering up blood. A hand slammed between her thighs and squeezed her hard, but it meant nothing to her. Her body seemed to be drifting into another realm. The pain subsided, and Esther felt her energy fading fast. Her struggles weakened and she stopped thumping him, fists too slack, arms too heavy.

'Stop,' she whimpered, dizzy and light-headed. 'Plea–'

The blood poured out of her veins, draining her mind and limbs. Her hands and feet grew numb and tingly. The world seemed muffled, time elongating.

I will not die, she thought. I will not die.

But she was slipping, losing the will to fight. Her vision grew dim. She saw snow through a filter of black hair then the snow receded, shrinking gently to nothing. A new blackness moved in her mind, wavering with peppered stars and with slow explosions of purple and blue, languid fireworks smudging her consciousness.

'Billy' she wanted to say but the word wouldn't form in her mouth and she didn't know what it meant anyway.

She tried to pull back, to reach the whiteness of snow again and understand the word. For a moment it was there, a brighter light, and a man who was both weak and powerful. Then she retreated, the blackness swarming and shimmering, and it might have been peaceful there, sinking into sleepy death, except her head was suddenly full of screaming, her teeth were chattering and the earth was splintering like shattered glass.

The weight lifted from her body.

Shrieks and voices stormed her mind.

'I'm on fire!'

'The sun!' screeched the woman. 'I'm blistering!'

'I can't see!'

'The sunrise!'

'Acid attack! I'm blind! My eyes are melting.'

'Run!'

'But I want her, Suze. I –'

'Sim, run! Here, take my hand.'

'But –'

'Sim, forget her! Come on. Run. The bitch is practically dead anyway.'

Billy was in the gym doing pull-ups, grunting through gritted teeth.

He was still in agony, his insides shredded with pain. Ever since waking, he'd felt as if he were being ripped internally from heart to gut. He guessed the dream in which he lay dying was somehow to blame. The pain was under his scar as if his old wound were opening up, threatening to burst him apart from within.

He pushed past it, heaving his chin above the bar then lowering himself to a dead hang. Normally, he'd do the exercise with weights on his legs but, Christ, not today. He'd kept his boots on and that was tough enough. The pain was worsening minute by minute and when a new shard sliced into his neck, Billy dropped from the bar, cursing. He tumbled to his knees on the mat, clutching his neck. Fuck, that hurt. Must've pulled a muscle.

He knelt for a while, filling his lungs with slow breath, squeezing his fists when the pain soared. Several minutes later, he heard the noise of a skidoo echoing within the dome. Someone was pulling on the starter cord.

Billy was on his feet in an instant.

Those two. Simeon and Suzanne. Of course. The evil fuckers, they were leaving, fleeing the scene of the crime, no doubt.

Because the pain wasn't just Billy's. It was Esther's as well. It shamed him that he hadn't recognised it. He was a fool, a useless fucking fool, so caught up with himself he could barely see beyond his own head. Esther was dying.

He strode for the exit, hearing the skidoo whinny and splutter. In a storage room off the tunnelled white corridor, Suzanne was pulling desperately on the starter rope while Simeon piled a sledge with possessions, his limbs angular and frantic.

'This fucking place,' he wailed. 'We're out of here! At least in New York you know when it's dawn!'

They were covered in blood, hair wild, faces scorched. Billy had no time for them. He grabbed his sunglasses then he was out on the icecap, nostrils twitching for the scent of Esther. The sun had just set, leaving a line of volcanic red bleeding into the dusk. It tinted the distance, the ice shimmering like a glacial poppy field, serene and unsettling. The first day of the year, and it was over almost as soon as it had begun.

Billy followed his senses, pain still gripping. He ignored it, running as fast as he could, fearing it might not be fast enough. Strength was leaking from him just as life was leaking from Esther. Minutes later, he saw her, a hump on the ice, and he ran harder still, muscles on fire.

When he reached her, he flung off his shades and fell on all fours, limbs quivering, gasping for breath. Esther lay on a stain of crystallized pink, her blood seeping down into the snow. Her dark hair was mussed and matted, and her neck was twisted at a grotesque, broken angle.

'Selin!'

Carefully, Billy tipped her to face him. She was as pale as a corpse, her eyes blank, her mouth slack.

'No!' roared Billy. 'No. Come back!'

There was no response. It couldn't happen again, it couldn't. To see a loved one die twice was beyond any hell.

'Stay with me. Selin! Esther! Stay!'

She gazed up at him with an expression he'd seen before, empty eyes looking right past him. Her dark lashes were tipped with frost and the snow was sludgy with the warmth of her spilt blood. Billy shuffled closer, rose-pink snow slushing around his knees. Oh, if he could be her, dying on the ice, and if she could have life, he'd swap in a heartbeat.

'Essie, please.'

It was hopeless. She was at her end now and so was he. He couldn't go on after this, no way. He would beg another vampire to stake his heart and bury it high in the Arctic where it would freeze for all eternity. If Simeon loved him, he would do it. He would put Billy out of his misery.

Esther's eyelids flickered. She seemed for a moment to focus on him then she was lost again.

'Oh, God.' Billy fell on her neck, putting his mouth to her gaping throat. He didn't drink but he felt the tremor of a faint pulse. She was alive, just.

Billy had no choice. He tugged the dagger pendant from his neck and sliced it across his wrist. Blood gushed. Cupping Esther's head, he pressed his wound to her lips.

'Drink!' he commanded.

His blood flowed over her face, dribbling into her ears and hair. Esther's lips didn't move. Billy might have been back in that courtyard, a dead woman in his arms, Nadir admiring the pink fountain.

'Drink!' cried Billy, and his voice cracked into a sob. 'Please! Please drink!'

Moments later, Billy felt her lips stir against his wrist. He hardly dared breathe. And then he felt what he'd so often dreamt of in re-imagining her death: the first blissful pull of her taking his blood.

'Selin,' he breathed.

His hopes began to rise as the pull strengthened, her lips fastening tighter on his wrist. Eternal life might be a curse but it had to beat eternal death. Her suck grew firmer, Billy's vampire blood pumping into hers, a poison to nourish her. Esther's eyes sharpened and she watched him with soft confusion before lowering her lids, drinking contentedly.

All Billy could hope was that she wouldn't hate him for this. He would help her through the transition, and if she loved him as he loved her, it would be a merry, hellish joy to tackle eternity together.

Billy dipped his mouth to her neck, taking a sip of her blood. He took a little more until he was slurping gently. He could feel what he wanted to feel: the weakening pulse of her human heart and the tinge of his own sweet poison. For several dying beats, it felt like he too had a pulse and a life. Then the moment was gone. Their hearts were still.

Billy raised his head, blood dripping from his smile, teeth stained pink. He wiped strands of sticky hair from her forehead.

'You belong to me, Esther,' he said. 'And I belong to you.'

Esther gazed up at him, eyes glowing with a new energy, bright and fierce. She smiled back, her teeth as pink as his.

'I know,' she breathed. 'And I always did.'

Buddies Don't Bite
Portia Da Costa

1

'Damn! Damn! Damn!'

Teresa Johnson trudged into the cosy, softly lit kitchen and flung her bag across the room, grimacing at the thought of her mobile and her PDA in a thousand bits, but in no mood to really care all that much.

'Idiot!' Avoiding a damage inspection, she headed for the fridge. First things first, she needed wine. Then a think.

Yanking open the big old refrigerator door, she stilled herself, closed her eyes, breathed deeply. Tantrums were pointless. And so was breaking things. Whether that be her wine or milk bottles, or the ones containing Zack's peculiar 'iron shake'.

'Chill out ... chill out ...' Reaching in for her Chardonnay, she wondered for the hundredth time what *was* in those dark-brown vacuum-sealed bottles lined up on the middle shelf. She'd opened one once, and it'd made her cringe. The heavy earthy raw-meat smell had been disturbing. Poor old Zack having to drink that mucky stuff for every meal. She didn't envy him his anaemia and food allergies.

Almost overfilling her wineglass, she teetered over to the refectory table and slumped down in a chair. Her anger was all but gone now and dim disappointment felt like a low pressure front.

'So what's it to be, Teresa?' She took a long slurp of wine. 'To wedding or not to wedding? Is it nobler in the mind to stay at home like a cowardly, boyfriendless reject? Or to take arms against a sea of smug marrieds and lovey-dovey couples and get laughed at because I'm a loser?'

'Talking to oneself is the first sign of madness, my dear, didn't you know that?'

Wine went everywhere, and Teresa's chair rocked on its back legs. She braced for impact with the hard kitchen floor and the thump of pain – then she found herself upright with her heart pounding fit to burst.

'Zack, for Christ's sake, don't sneak up on me like that! I hate it when you creep around and I don't hear you!'

She'd *definitely* felt her chair going over, but now it was four square again, and *she* was on her feet. And there was Zack, her tall, dark and handsome landlord, mopping efficiently at the spilt wine on the table with squares of kitchen roll.

Teresa glanced at the bottle, disorientated. Even allowing for spillage there was plenty left. She wasn't drunk and she wasn't imagining things.

Zack had put in one of his famous appearances right out of thin air.

And now – domesticated yet still manly – he was cleaning up her mess and making her ears burn with guilt. 'Oh, God, Zack, I'm sorry! I know I shouldn't yell ... it's your house and you're entitled to creep about if you want to.'

'No problem. I'm just sorry I startled you, love.' With his usual deftness and elegance, her landlord made short work of the clean up operation, and in what felt like a split-second, he'd poured her another glass of wine and was nodding for her to sit back down again.

Not for the first time, Teresa decided that it was a criminal waste to live every day with an unusual but desirable man like Zachary Trevelyan – and not be anything more than good house buddies. His narrow elegant face was alight with pleasure, even though he'd just been soundly bellowed at. What normal man would suck up such abuse and still smile?

'Better now?' Before the words were out, he was sitting down opposite her.

'Yes.' She was. It was always better to be looking at Zack than not looking at him. She loved his beautiful calming stillness that was such a contrast to the spookily swift way he sometimes moved. What would be even better was for him to move swiftly in her direction, take her in his arms and kiss her – instead of clearly observing the boundaries of their respective personal spaces.

In the interests of long-term house harmony and cordial landlord/tenant relations, Teresa always squished down hard on the temptation to think of Zack in 'that way'. But it was hellishly difficult when even after six months of friendship and platonic cohabitation he still did the maddest, hottest things to her hormones.

He was far from her usual type.

The accursed Steve and various assorted men who'd preceded him, had all been healthy, tanned, gym-buffed and metrosexual, and Zack was as far from that as it was possible to be.

The word 'Goth' always sprang to mind when she looked at him. Tall and lean and vaguely etiolated, he had all the characteristics of a typical night dweller, which wasn't at all surprising, considering he suffered from photophobia and sun sensitivity on top of his other problems. And yet his pallor captivated her. As did the stylish gauntness that seemed to suggest his bones were just a bit too big for his skin.

The lean sharp lines of his cheekbones and his jaw conferred on him a louche romantic glamour that reminded her of those sexy silent movie stars who dressed as sheikhs and wore eyeliner. Couple that with the kind of dark curly hair that could have looked like a yokel on anybody else, but suggested wild Byronic decadence on him and the most hypnotic blue eyes, the colour of a rare antique perfume bottle.

Teresa surreptitiously clenched her teeth. If exotic Zack had shown even the slightest hint of a whisker of a glimmer of interest in her, there would have been no need to go out with substandard men like Steve anyway.

'Come on, love ... what's the matter? You can tell your Uncle Zack.'

Slipping into 'therapist' mode, Zack crossed his long lean arms in front of him, and then settled into a perfect waiting tranquillity. Playing up to his own gothic image, he was wearing a loose frilled poet's shirt, half open down the front to show a tasty wedge of his smooth hairless chest.

Teresa stilled too. She'd whirled into the house in a maxi state about a micro drama, and now, after five minutes with Zack, she could barely remember what had been bugging her.

Looking into his clear blue eyes, she felt a low internal thud deep in her body.

This was the man she'd wanted to go to the wedding with, not Steve. It had never really been Steve. He was just a substitute and she almost felt sorry for him, despite the fact he was a rat. She'd only started dating him because Zack, her dearest friend, was off limits.

She'd fancied Zack, despite his peculiarities, ever since the first moment she'd set eyes on him, one night in a local coffee house. Then, as now, he'd offered sympathy – that time over her losing her flat when her previous housemates decided to sell up. They had been total strangers and yet he'd offered her the hospitality of his big rambling house and without thinking twice, or even once, she'd accepted.

Her fingers prickled with the desire to reach out, unwind those strong arms of his, and coax him to rewind them around her. She wanted to kiss his sweet red mouth, push her tongue between his lips, and find out if those large, white teeth of his were really as sharp as they sometimes looked. She wanted to rip his shirt all the way open and kiss his chest – and maybe his neck too. Perhaps she'd nibble him a bit? She often seemed to find herself imagining that. She wanted to peel off those tight black jeans that clung to his lean legs like liquorice – and see if the astonishing bulge she sometimes saw there was as magnificent as it was in her fantasies.

'Teresa?'

Zack's voice sounded shaken somehow, as if he had sensed her thoughts but wasn't sure he liked them.

'It's the wedding. I can't go!'

'But I thought you were looking forward to it?'

'I was ... I *love* weddings ...' Her mind filled with flowers, smiling faces and the sheer sentimental joy of romance. 'But I was looking forward to going *with* someone ... and not being part of the usual cattle market.' Zack's serious sculpted face bore a strangely wistful expression and she had a feeling he understood her perfectly. 'I was ... um ... expecting a hot, sexy, romantic weekend.'

'So what's happened?'

'Steve and I have split up ... well, technically he dumped me. I think I might have come over a tad soppy over the whole wedding thing and scared him off. So he bailed.' She shuddered, not because of the loss but at what she might have let happen. Encouraged. 'Unfortunately, though, because he's a friend of the groom, he's still going to the wedding ... with someone else.'

Zack's eyes were steady, thoughtful and heart-breakingly blue. 'Mmm. That's awkward.' He was as still as ever, but she could see him weighing up her options.

Suddenly, tears welled up, but they were nothing to do with Steve or the wedding. They were for something wistful and glorious that she'd never, ever have. A proper romance with pale and beautiful Zack.

'Hey! Hey! Hey!'

In another burst of freakish speed, he was in the chair *beside* her now, his powerful arms wrapped around her. And it felt so good that their unspoken boundaries were suddenly meaningless.

In Zack's cradling hold she was safe and cherished. He held her lightly but like a rock, like Superman to her Lois, he was so strong. In her mind, she flew back to a precious moment a few weeks ago. Another instance when he'd breached his personal space for her. She'd caught a virus that was going around and had nearly passed out. And sweet Zack had swept her up as if she weighed nothing and carried her all the way to bed.

Unfortunately, when he got her there, he'd left her with a hot water bottle, a selection of painkillers and decongestants and a steaming lemon drink – rather than climbing beneath the covers and giving her the sexual healing that she longed for.

But those moments of being swooped up off her feet and carried as if she weighed nothing at all had been exquisite, despite her congested sinuses and her head-ache. And being held now was equally sublime.

'You could still go, Teresa.' His hand was cool against her skin where he smoothed her hair away from her face. 'You're stronger than you think. Why not go any-way and show everyone how fabulous you are? Have fun and just be there for Lisa.'

You're so right, she thought. I will go. Why not?

Peering at him, blinking, she smiled a grateful smile, and then opened her mouth to speak – and brought forth insane words she'd never intended to utter.

'I don't suppose *you'd* come with me, would you? I mean ... not a "date" or anything? More a friend-type thing, really. You wouldn't have to be outside in daylight.

The wedding itself and the parties and whatnot are all either indoors or held in the evening.'

Nothing about the way Zack held her altered, but he was staring at the table, his pale profile intense, almost graven. A single jet-black curl dangled against his brow like an inverted question mark.

What have I done? Tessa thought. Now I've spoilt everything by opening my big mouth. But before she opened that big mouth again, knowing it was futile to even attempt to repair the damage, Zack spoke first.

With his customary measured grace, he unwound his arms from around her, pushed back his chair and stood up. Then he clasped his hands together, rubbing the fingers of one hand against the back of the other, studying them fixedly as if he'd never seen them before. Teresa couldn't have been more shocked if he'd run around the room, shouting and breaking things.

'OK ... why not? I'll go with you. I'll even be your "date", if you want me to.' His rather sultry red mouth curved into a smile.

What?

Teresa's jaw dropped, and the cosy familiar room suddenly seemed almost alien. This was studious Zack who worked from home writing scholarly historical treatises and never, ever went out during the day. This was Zack, who only ever ventured out at dusk, or at night, for long walks around the city streets. That was how she'd met him, in the coffee shop that night, and he'd been there for her then, just as he was now.

But this was different. *This* was amazing. Without thinking, Teresa leapt up, lunged forward – and kissed him.

And promptly forgot about weddings, and weekends, and perfidious weasel boyfriends.

Zack's lips were soft and cool and velvety. Twice as

luscious as she'd imagined and a hundred times more provocative. They were quiescent beneath hers at first, almost innocent, and deep in her groin pure lust kicked, and kicked again. There was something uniquely seductive about a man who was untouched, who was shy and pure. One of her deepest and most secret masturbation fantasies was to seduce a young sweet virgin man. It was an impossible dream when most men were sexually active well before they were even supposed to. But even so, the magical idea of it still burned in her imagination.

And Zack's beautiful motionlessness played right into those dreams. He simply accepted the kiss, but there was thrilling latency to the lush supple contact. The urge to hurl her weight forwards, wrestle him to the kitchen floor and accept the consequences raged through her.

But then, inside, something intangible tipped over.

Arms like steel bands closed tight around her, and his tongue gently pressed between her lips, demanding entrance. She let him in, loving the strange coolness of the moist and mobile pressure.

Her arms came up, hands roving over his hard back beneath his thin cotton shirt. And the touch of that was cool too, like woven cobwebs sliding over marble.

Although she'd lived with this man for months, she very, very rarely touched him. She'd almost forgotten the shock of his cold skin when they'd shaken hands to seal their house-sharing agreement, but now his hurried talk of poor circulation came back to mind.

But there was nothing wrong with his circulation today. Everything about him was active and hungry and full of life. Where before he'd been diffident, he was vibrant and eager now. Where before he seemed to be holding back, now he'd opened wide the gates.

Tugging at each other, they were suddenly on the kitchen floor just as she'd imagined, kissing like maniacs.

Zack threw one long lean leg across her, and acquainted Teresa with that star turn of all her erotic daydreams.

This is demented. I'm kissing my landlord and he's got a hard-on, she thought.

Unable to contain herself, Teresa surged against him, rocking shamelessly against Zack's sturdy erection. So much for keeping their distance and observing 'friends only' no-go areas. Her outburst had re-engineered the parameters. There wasn't anywhere that she couldn't venture now.

He had the most glorious backside. Tight and hard and round like a brace of ripe apples. And when she grasped it, he growled in his throat in a most astonishing way. Deep and fierce, like the call of a jungle animal, it bounced off the kitchen walls and filled her ears. If she hadn't had his tongue in her mouth, Teresa would have said, 'What the fuck is going on?'

But their tongues were dancing and she felt like growling too.

Deep in her belly, a famished hunger was gnawing at her. It was a long while since she'd had good sex. A real, hard, long wonderful fuck. She'd held back with Steve, and had been hoping this weekend would be their romantic first time. But now, she thanked every lucky star in heaven that she hadn't succumbed.

She'd never articulated it to herself, but she'd been waiting and saving herself for Zack, sure in the knowledge that her abstinence would be worth it.

Oh, I want you, she cried silently to him, massaging his sensational bottom, and squirreling herself against his cock.

Zack's answer was to growl again, a low feral sound. His lips crushed hers, his tongue thrusting, thrusting, just like the sex act. Where the kiss had been gentle and controlled at first, it was clear off the rails now. His mouth started to rove, moving roughly, messily, thrillingly over her face, along her jaw, as his hips rocked and jerked in that explicit rhythm that met and matched hers.

It was like being a horny teenager all over again, but magnified to the n'th degree. Every part of her was hot. They were rubbing against each other like crazy animals, and Teresa was the one making moaning noises now, unable to contain herself as Zack's hands went all over the place. Her breasts. Her thighs. The cleft of her bottom. He was surveying her physical geography, and he was impatient. His fingers wriggled between their bodies, tugging at her skirt and searching for access to her sex.

And all the while he was kissing, licking, tasting – and nibbling.

Nibbling? More than that – as his mouth reached her throat, she suddenly yelped and jerked beneath him.

Dear God, that is so hot! He's biting my neck!

It was pure sex. Shocking and primal. Painful but in a way that made her hips lurch against him of their own accord, seeking the touch of his fingertips where they pressed against her panties.

Am I flying? Teresa thought. This is weird.

She wriggled and parted her legs, not sure where the pleasure was, only knowing that it was like melting, dissolving, expiring – coming?

And then . . .

The rail-backed kitchen chair was hard beneath her thighs, and the glass cool in her hand. Her heart was thudding and there was a silvery hum ringing in her ears. But despite this strange physical phenomenon and an accompanying sense of dislocation, she felt calm, almost serene. Apart from a vague prickle of curiosity. She'd been panicking and fretting about something, but it was OK now. Zack had come up with a solution, hadn't he?

Looking up, she was surprised to see him standing by the sink. His mouth was uncharacteristically tense, his lips tightly pursed and his eyes looked huge and very dark. She felt a jolt of worry. Had her silly invitation distressed him?

'Are you OK, Zack? You're not sickening for something, are you? You don't *have* to come to the wedding, you know. It's wonderful of you to offer and God knows I appreciate it. But I'm a big girl. I think I'll be OK.'

There was a long pause. Zack's eyes seemed to skitter a bit, and he pressed his knuckle against his lips, as if pondering.

Teresa wondered what was the matter with Zach. He was not usually like this.

As she watched, Zack gave one long fluttering, almost slow-motion blink, squared his shoulders and lowered his hand to rest it on the forearm he had wrapped around him, reacquiring his stillness.

'I'd like to go. I need to get out more.' He gave her a cautious smile, his white teeth glinting. 'It'll be a change for me ... all this studying and researching. I need to kick over the traces and have some fun.'

'Um, yes, I suppose so.'

But later, when he'd returned to his books, his research and his computer, Teresa was left wondering about Zack's sudden decision. Wondering about that, and a few other things.

Like, why were her lips so tender, as if she'd been kissed to within an inch of her life?

And what the hell was that bright-red mark on her neck?

2

'Bloody fool! Bloody, bloody fool!'

Zachary Trevelyan fought the hysterical urge to laugh like a lunatic.

Of course, he was a bloody fool – he was a fool for *blood*. With an effort, he managed to control his mania but the irony still made him smile.

For decades he'd coped and adapted and made a semblance of a life for himself, without ever really fitting in. But ever since he'd seen a pretty brown-haired girl in a local street on a warm spring night, then followed her into a coffee house, it was no longer the placid existence he'd carefully nurtured.

And tonight he'd made it a hundred times more complicated. He might have gently tampered with Teresa's perceptions, but it was only a matter of time before she cottoned on to the anomalies. And he couldn't blank out his own memories of that kiss – or the natural and unnatural responses of his body.

In the sanctum of his workroom, he reached into the small beer fridge he kept there. It had never actually contained beer, although he did drink ale now and again. Instead the shelves were stacked with a row of small vacuum-sealed bottles. After flipping the top off one, he flung himself into his big leather wing-chair and took a long quenching drink.

His eyes fluttered closed as the rich familiar taste filled his mouth. The dangerous coppery flavour that defined him.

His roaring hunger calmed immediately. Heart, veins,

cells, they all glowed and returned to equilibrium again. The acute stiffness in his penis transformed from pain into a potential source of pleasure. Taking another long drink from his bottle, he laid the fingers of his free hand across his groin.

That had been a close, close call in the kitchen. Flicking his tongue over his lips, he captured a drop of the red fluid there, and then, still lightly cupping his genitals, he passed it slowly over the biting edges of his upper teeth.

They were altered again, just as they'd been ten minutes ago. Kissing Teresa, he'd felt his fangs descend as the crimson madness of desire, so long and so carefully avoided, had gripped him like a stranglehold.

What the hell had possessed him? He'd been at risk of revealing himself since the very day she'd moved in, and he still couldn't work out what had possessed him to ask her. But still he'd done it, wildly embracing the threat to his hard won peace of mind.

Oh, but the taste of her. The touch of her. She was everything he'd dreamt of, everything that had driven him time and again to red fits of frenzied masturbation. And all it had taken was the welling up of sympathy – his for her and hers for him – to tip him past the point of no return.

Zack remembered the first time he'd set eyes on Teresa.

Like any man, he'd first noticed her shiny teak-coloured hair, and her slender yet shapely figure as she'd strolled along, looking in shop windows. But then he'd watched, fascinated by an inner beauty, as she'd knelt down to talk to one of the homeless who sometimes bedded down for the night in the larger doorways. She'd stayed a while, actually talking to the man rather than just flinging the odd coin into his tin and scuttling away. Her face had been warm and animated and she'd stroked the mangy dog tied up to the man's pack. Then, eventually, she'd straightened up, and left, turning back to wave – but not before slipping what looked like a couple of banknotes into his hand, with an encouraging squeeze.

Later, in the coffee house, he'd been compelled to approach her, and expecting wariness and suspicion, he'd been greeted by a sweet open smile and an easy invitation to share her table. She'd welcomed him, a pale and probably rather odd looking total stranger, and generously engaged him in conversation.

Sympathy again. Sympathy, from beauty, for an outcast? Was that it? Was that what had made her the one to change his long cultivated habits?

You're a good woman, Teresa, and you're kind. But would you still have sympathy for me, if you knew what I am?

Would you give yourself as freely as you were about to if you knew that your hypochondriac housemate was really a bloodsucking fiend?

'It's a bit hot in here ... OK if I wind down the window?'

Not only was it warm in Zack's beautiful classic Mercedes, it was also getting difficult to sit still. Breathing in the scents of polished leather and Zack himself was making her crazy. She loved his old-fashioned floral cologne, but in a confined space it was acting like a drug. She kept drifting into a dreamy erotic fantasy.

Clenching her fingers on her bag with one hand, and a fold of her skirt with the other, she fought the pounding urge to slyly touch herself.

'Of course ... sorry. I always forget that other people are warmer-blooded than I am.' Zack's eyes were intent on the road. If she didn't know better, Teresa would have said that he was avoiding looking at her. Maybe he was having wayward urges of his own?

But that was nonsense. Zack was always the perfect, controlled gentleman. Alas.

Reaching for the window winder, Teresa frowned. There was *something* up with Zack tonight. He was different. Odd. Not his usual still calm self at all. And his beautiful rosy mouth was twisted as if he were smiling at a particularly bitter joke. Teresa eyed his perfect profile, and suddenly, as if he sensed her puzzlement, he turned briefly towards her with a warmer, less ambiguous, smile.

A second later, he was all attention to the road again and it was Teresa's turn to purse her lips, frustrated.

If you're not interested that way, Zack, why have you made yourself look so sexy?

She'd never seen Zack look all grown up and groomed this way before. Instead of his usual dark jeans, and floppy shirts that looked as if they'd come out of a dressing up bag, he was wearing a proper suit and smart shirt for a change. They were both dark midnight blue, and looked stunning with his pale skin and black hair. The look was restrained and semi-formal, and made a naturally dramatic man look even more dramatic. He'd slicked back his wild curly hair too, and that only added to the effect of sombre gothic elegance.

A quip about Count Dracula rose to her lips but, before it could get there, her head swam strangely. Pressing a knuckle to her mouth, she held in another gasp, all the time grappling with the impression that she was floating upwards in the car as if it were a space capsule.

Frames from a movie flashed before her eyes. And she was the star, seeing it from the inside.

Zack was kissing her, touching her, and holding her against his rampant body. His mouth was at her throat. Pain spiked there, but it was a sweet pain that induced pleasure between her legs. And as the stinging ebbed, that pleasure grew, and Zack lifted his face to look at her.

His eyes weren't periwinkle blue any more, but a wild and violent red — crimson to match the blood on his gleaming lips.

'Are you all right, love?'

No, I'm all wrong.

That hadn't been just a passing erotic fancy about Zack as a vampire. It had felt like a memory, not a fantasy. She could feel it in her sex.

She could feel it in her *neck*.

Her fingertips flew to the place where there had been a red mark. She'd dismissed it as a nervous blotch, but what if it'd been something else? And what if that slightly funny turn in the kitchen yesterday hadn't been due to her just being hungry?

Get a grip, Teresa, she reprimanded herself. Zack is your friend, and your house buddy, and you fancy him, that's all. There are no such things as vampires and you haven't even kissed him, so how could he have given you a love-bite?

'Teresa? Are you all right?'

His soft voice shocked her back into the real world of car journeys and impending weddings.

'I'm fine, thanks ... just wool-gathering. Car trips get me that way.'

She glanced sideways again, and their glances clashed. Zack's blue eyes looked cautious and wary in a way she'd never seen before.

'We can stop for a while, if you like? There's a service area coming up soon.'

He was trying to be kind, and the offer was tempting. The sudden change of atmosphere in the car — from dreamy sensuality to palpable tension — was uncomfortable. But they'd soon reach their destination anyway, and then they could both retreat to their separate rooms ... and their own space again.

'No. Thanks. Let's push on, shall we?'

'OK. Good idea.' With a smooth change of gear, he put his foot down.

Teresa sucked in her breath again, and stole another sideways look. Zack seemed calm and unruffled again, totally focused on the road. If he'd sensed her inner madness he wasn't showing it.

Turning to the window, and the darkness outside, Teresa squashed down her crazy notions – and thought of nothingness.

3

'You're kidding me . . . there's only one bedroom? When I rang, you said there'd be two.'

'I'm very sorry, Miss Johnson. I'm afraid there's been an error. The hotel's full for the wedding, and there's only one room in your name.'

Teresa hardly heard the rest of the spiel about folding beds and extra bedding *and* a refund. Her attention was locked on Zack and the stormy expression in his eyes. She'd never, ever seen him look this troubled, and it didn't surprise her when he took her by the arm and led her away from the reception desk.

'Look . . . I don't think it's such a good idea that we share a room. Why don't I leave you here and return again tomorrow night, in time for the wedding. It'll be dusk again then . . . and, if I leave the car in the garage, I needn't be out in daylight when I set off.'

For the first time ever since they'd met, Teresa felt annoyed with him. What on earth was the problem? They were friends. Surely even if they weren't a couple they could manage to rub along together somehow in the same room for a couple of nights? For such an intelligent and normally equable man, he was being ridiculous.

'Don't be silly. We can manage. It's not a problem.' Suddenly, though, it did seem like a problem. Zack was as still and unmoving as ever, yet he was surrounded by a strange aura of energy. Anger? Apprehension? Something else entirely? Totally unnerved, she said the first thing that came into her head. 'I won't leap all over you, if that's what you're worried about. It'll be strictly platonic.'

Fingers like the prongs of an iron trap tightened on her arm. 'It's not you I'm worried about, Teresa.' His voice was low, intense and unfamiliar. He released her arm, and automatically she rubbed it. 'This just isn't a good idea.'

'Why not? You're obviously not actually attracted to me or you'd love the idea of sharing a room!'

'You are wrong there, Teresa ... so very wrong.'

Zack pursed his lips, and looked as if he were about to elaborate, but from behind them the reception clerk asked, 'Shall I call housekeeping about the extra bedding, Miss Johnson?'

Well? Teresa didn't articulate the word, but Zack seemed to hear it. He closed his eyes for a moment, as if he were weighing up a thousand what-ifs in the space of a split second, then opened them again and nodded infinitesimally.

Her mind whirling, Teresa turned away from him and returned to the desk.

Up in the room, they stared at each other across their heap of luggage.

Teresa attempted a smile and, for a moment, Zack's face was inscrutable – a beautiful, blank, unwritten page.

Was he going to explain? Tell her what he'd meant, down there in the lobby?

'Zack, what did you mean downstairs ... about me being wrong?'

He looked away, towards the bed, and then his eyes flicked instantly away from it, as if it were the sun and the sight of it burnt him.

'You are wrong. I *am* attracted to you but it's just not a good idea for me to follow up on it.'

For a moment, Teresa wanted to cavort around the

room and shout, You do like me. I knew you did. I just knew.

'But *why* isn't it a good idea? You must have realised that I'm attracted to you too.' The urge to dance turned into a strong compulsion to shake him for his obtuseness.

'It's not something I can easily explain, Teresa.' There was wistfulness in his voice. She sensed some huge obstacle standing between them. It was hurting him, and it made her want to hug him, not for sex, just to comfort. 'Please trust me . . .' His shoulders lifted in a heavy, resigned shrug. 'But I still want to be friends . . . more than anything. If you can accept that?'

There was such yearning in his blue eyes that Teresa just melted.

'Yes, of course.' Still confused, but feeling better, she smiled. 'We're good, Zack, but don't ever try to tell me that it's us women who are the contrary ones. OK?'

Zack smiled back at her and the tension between them lifted.

'OK. And don't worry . . . I'm fine on the couch.' He shrugged in the general direction of a rather inadequate-looking settee. 'It looks perfectly comfortable.'

Teresa frowned. That was nonsense. The couch was a fussy, reproduction item, a triumph of style over practicality.

The bed, on the other hand, was deep, and well sprung and inviting – and it was more or less time to get into it. Zack's photophobia had meant that they'd had to wait until dusk to set off and now it was past eleven. There was nothing Teresa wanted more than to just crawl under that duvet and sleep. She didn't want to think about what amounted to their first ever argument. She just wanted to fall asleep, knowing that he really did care for her in his own weird way.

Then Zack shrugged out of his jacket and draped it over a chair back, and the sight of his lean body in that fine dark shirt woke her up again. All her good resolutions about boundaries and being 'just friends' melted like Scotch mist.

'But ... um ... what about your bad circulation? Won't you be cold just with blankets?' She glanced at the undesirable sofa. 'I could manage on the couch. I'm shorter. I'll fit better.'

Zack's whole demeanour seemed to lighten and he gave her an eloquently masculine look.

'No way.' He shook his dark head. 'I'm an old-fashioned man, Teresa. A lady's comfort must always come first.'

I'll bet it does. The thought was involuntary. As was the image of Zack, kneeling between her outstretched thighs as she sat on that very sofa, his long red tongue licking, licking, licking.

The entire surface of her skin seemed to tremble. She felt out of control, yet suddenly energised. On impulse, she strode across the room, squeezed his hard muscular arm and kissed his cool cheek. 'Thanks, Zack. You're a very sweet man. I don't deserve you.' Right in his personal space, she felt bold and crazy. She sensed danger, but she hungered for the taste of it.

When she pulled back, Zack was staring at her, his eyes wide and strange. He had his full sensual lower lip snagged in his upper teeth, and in the low light they seemed to glint like polished porcelain, sharp and deadly.

Almost dazzled, Teresa felt giddiness whirl her feet out from under her, and without knowing quite how, she found herself sitting on the edge of the bed.

'Wha–'

'Come on, Teresa, you need rest. It's late. Why don't you slip into bed and get some sleep?' Zack's voice was matter of fact. He was sitting a decorous distance away from her, inches and inches of clear space between their bodies.

'Er . . . um . . . yes, I suppose you're right.'

The soft thick duvet was tempting. These funny turns she kept having were worrying, and Zack was right, she'd be better off getting some rest.

She glanced from the bed to the bathroom. The prospect of getting ready for bed made her feel more tired than ever.

Zack seemed to read her mind. 'I think I'll go for a stroll in the grounds. Give you chance to get settled in.'

'But we've only just got here. And it's nearly midnight.'

'You know me and my nocturnal rambles. And I need to stretch my legs after the drive.'

Teresa's heart sank.

She should have let him go home and stay in his comfort zone. When this stupid wedding was over, it might be best if she looked for her own place again. This situation of liking each other but not being able to do anything about it was bound to become intolerable eventually.

Unexpectedly, a strong arm came around her shoulders.

'It's just a walk, Teresa. We're fine.' The arm squeezed, the pressure reassuring, but also unnerving. There was so much leashed power in that lean and elegant body, and he was still wound up like steel wire no matter what he said. 'I'm just giving you space to do your girl things.'

Emotion rolled over Teresa like a wave. This was all a mess but, even now, Zack was being wonderful.

'Thanks.' She flashed him a grateful smile as he released her and rose to his feet.

'I'll just put my bottles away, then I'll leave you to it.'

Ah, the mysterious 'iron shake'. Something picked at Teresa's tired mind as she watched Zack unpack several bottles from a cool-pack and stow them in the mini-bar fridge. One of these days she was going to have to ask him what was in that peculiar unappetising drink.

'I want you to be fast asleep when I get back,' said Zack firmly a few moments later. Teresa looked longingly at him, clutching a pair of eggshell-blue satin pyjamas from her case. He looked more relaxed now that he was about to escape the room, and his expression was almost brotherly. At least it seemed to be.

'OK, you're the boss of this dormitory.' She pinned on what she thought was a light-hearted, just-buddies smile.

But Zack was already out of the door and gone.

The night was beautiful, and the sky full of moon.

As Zack sped across the great park of Hindlesham Manor, he was aware that anyone watching him from the house would wonder if they were seeing things.

Things like a human-seeming figure devouring the yards at inhuman speed.

He was angry with himself. Not only had he muddied the situation between them by admitting his feelings, he'd given in to temptation and put Teresa at risk. And all he could think about now was her lovely body, clad in those blue pyjamas.

In bed.

Waiting for him.

Could he control himself around her for much longer? His cool heart soared at the thought of touching her, caressing her – entering her. Giving her pleasure while she was entirely conscious and her mind was unclouded by his psychic tricks. Making love to her, while she knew exactly what he was.

Would her natural sympathy allow her to see past his fangs and reddened eyes? Would the attraction he knew she felt towards him be enough?

Vampires had always had a bad press. Misinformation had extinguished the extended lives of many of his kind who didn't deserve their demise. As with humanity, there were a thousand different flavours of vampires. They were as different from each other as normal people were, each one's nature predicated by the life he or she had led before being turned, and the circumstances of how that process had occurred.

An evil murderous bastard was still an evil murderous bastard as a vampire – only more so. Likewise, a weak-willed person might also take the easy path and bite the neck out of man, woman or child in order to feed.

But a decent man would find a way to *avoid* harming others after his turning.

His own situation was unusual.

In 1932, as a novice in a Benedictine monastery, he'd fallen prey to a band of hungry vampires of questionable ethics who'd broken in and attacked the brothers. A beautiful female had sensed the diffidence of his faith, and zeroed in on him. Barely ten minutes later he'd lost that faith, and his human life forever, but unfortunately not his virginity. Swooping away, she'd laughed and taunted him, leaving him shattered, terrified, confused – and yet still aroused.

In the aftermath, he'd waited for the inevitable revulsion of his community, and received the surprise of his young, but altered, life. His brothers had been modern, forward-thinking twentieth-century monks and, far from casting him out or turning a Vatican vampire hunter on him, they'd helped him.

A new cynicism suggested that their kindness towards a bloodsucker in their midst wasn't entirely altruistic. His family was immensely wealthy, with old, old money, and the community wasn't about to pass up such patronage in times when other houses were closing. But, Christian charity or no, they'd made it possible for him to adjust and it seemed that the Church had been secretly handling cases like his for centuries.

And so here I am, Zack thought, a virgin vampire, who's in love for the first time in his long ridiculous life.

Hindlesham Manor was possessed of a large, traditional box hedge maze, and as Zack entered its perimeter, his enhanced senses savoured the delicious dewy air. Cool scents of wood sap, pine and moss were balsamic and intoxicating. They assaulted him like nocturnal elixirs, provoking and stirring.

But not as much as Teresa stirred him.

The journey had been agony, requiring a constant intense focus on the act of driving. Her perfume was delicate and floral, a beautiful expression of her natural sweetness and purity. Yes, he knew that she'd slept with men, but deep in her heart he detected a central innocence that no man had breached – an untouched and pristine state that mirrored his own.

But it was more than an artificial odour that had plagued him.

The fresh green smells of the night faded and were replaced with warmer richer human aromas. The lush musky scent of Teresa's body that had kept his penis stiff and his fangs right on the point of descent for mile after mile.

Haunting female sweat. Sex musk, from between her legs. And her blood, just beneath the surface of her smooth heated skin. It had called to him constantly, and it called to him still, demanding more self-control than he'd ever had to exert in all his years.

Plunging on between the tall hedges, he had no fear of losing his way. A natural sense of direction was one of his special gifts. The way was cool and dark, but it didn't chill his passions. He was erect again and he touched himself lightly as he walked, his mind flying back to the hotel room and the sight of Teresa in that huge tempting bed, her body twisting in sleep, her soft brown hair tousled endearingly.

Perhaps the jacket of her pyjamas might come unfastened as she tossed and turned, revealing her rounded breasts to his unholy gaze. With his psi abilities, it would be easy to touch her and pleasure her without her even waking. The remnants of his religious morality, never quite shaken off, abhorred such thievery, but when the blood fever in him was rampant, it would be hard to resist.

Teresa was exquisite, the crystallised embodiment of the perfect dream woman he'd wanted all these years. The woman he'd wanted even while he was an imperfect novice, struggling with his faith, before his change.

The only consolation was that she would *enjoy* the sensual dreams that he induced.

Connecting with his surroundings again, he found himself at the centre of the maze. He stepped into an open area, a spacious oval ringed by benches where explorers could sit and get their breath back, while they tried to work out how to get out again.

Zack didn't sit. Instead he walked across the central turf to the deep ornamental pond that shimmered like a dark eye reflecting the moon.

Staring into the water, he laughed softly, his lust muted by the perennial amusement of another shattered vampire myth.

In the black water, he saw his own face, and his chest and shoulders, clad in his dark shirt.

He was distinctly visible, although not quite as clearly as Teresa would have been if she had been standing beside him. His image was impressionistic, far less substantial than that of a normal person, expressing the remnants of his humanity. On the continuum of vampir-ism, he was at the 'light' end, complete with spirit, soul and conscience – and it was these that created his reflection in the water. A black-hearted villain probably wouldn't see a thing.

And yet dark passions surged inside him. His sleeping lust was red and violent, roused by Teresa, and whipped to boiling point by their enforced proximity. It had been insanity to come on this trip, but he'd done it all the same. He was still human in some senses, and subject to the wayward foibles of human nature. And a human need for love that compelled him to grasp at the fleeting chance for intimacy, both emotional and physical.

With Teresa safe in her bed, perhaps a quarter of a mile away, Zack surrendered to the chaos of his senses.

His fangs descended – a rush of sensation in itself. And as the truth of his condition was revealed he rhyth-mically cupped and caressed his genitals, fantasising that his own large hand was her smaller daintier one. His chilly skin seemed to burn with an icy fire and become painfully hyper-sensitive. His clothes irritated every nerve-end.

Ignoring the possibility of other insomniac explorers, he slid off his clothing, undressing far faster than any human could have.

Within seconds he was naked in the moonlight, but still his pale skin tingled. He moaned, knowing that only the gentle caressing touch of Teresa's hands could soothe him. Only her hands could both rouse and give ease to the fury of desire. His own hands, running over his limbs, his torso and his belly, only seemed to aggravate his need.

Yet he couldn't stop. He stroked his body, fingertips tracking over his dense musculature, imagining it was *her* fingers that were moving, sliding and tantalising. His cock was aching and heavy, standing out from his body now, a bar of darker flesh in the blue-white light of the moon, a strangely human phenomenon taking over the body of an other than human male.

At last, he took himself in hand, growling at the impact of his own touch, baring his fangs and tipping back his head, eyes closed.

'Teresa!' His voice was a low rumble of feeling as he began to stroke and pump his flesh. He knew it was not her hand, but in a state of passionate fugue, his own touch was the next best thing. His mind was able to trick him, and he seemed to see her beside him, and hear her breathing and smell her myriad delicious scents.

She was touching him, fondling him, loving him, making him moan with delight, his thighs flexing as he pushed and pushed into the delicious enclosure of warm, skilled fingers. He wrapped his free hand around his torso, but in his imagination, he was clasping her to him, even as she clasped and caressed his cock.

The sensations built and spiralled, the intensity mounting. His sharp fangs pricked at his own lips as he fought to contain his vampire roar of pleasure. He tasted his own blood, the flavour sweet but inert. It was no substitute for fresh warm, living blood, but the fact that it had once had life goaded and lifted him to the point of no return.

'Teresa,' he shouted again, no longer able to contain himself as his penis leapt and his spine felt as if it were melting in a white flame of climax.

Chilly semen jetted from between his fingers, creating a silvery arc that glittered momentarily in the light of the moon. And as it hit the dark surface of the pond, Zack groaned and swayed, his spent body crumpling as he collapsed and curled up on the damp turf, stunned and sobbing with release and renewed longing.

4

It was so hot. Longing for cool, and not sure whether she was awake or asleep, Teresa kicked off the covers.

Her eyelids felt heavy and it was an effort to open them. Blinking, she surveyed the unfamiliar room.

Yes, right. She was at Hindlesham Manor and she was sharing this room with Zack. Who was currently nowhere to be seen.

He likes me. I like him. But we can't do anything about it for some reason.

Groaning, she turned over again. Knowing what the deal was only made her want him more. When something was forbidden, it automatically became the most desirable thing in the entire world. Sod's Law.

Closing her eyes, she pictured his lean male body and wished that he hadn't shot away for a walk in the middle of the night. Even if they couldn't make love, it would have been comforting to sense his sleeping presence across the room.

She imagined his return. And that he'd changed his mind. She imagined him gazing at her, his beautiful blue eyes on fire with lust. He'd lick his lips and his sharp white teeth would glint.

Why on earth am I always thinking about his teeth? Teresa wondered.

Her hand flew to her neck. She seemed to feel the sharp prick of him nipping her there.

Squirming against the sheets, she touched the place where she imagined him biting her, and with her other hand she massaged between her legs through her pyjamas.

A low moan echoed through the room, and Teresa's eyes flew open again.

It wasn't her!

Across at the window, but looking into the room rather than out of it, stood Zack.

She opened her mouth to speak to him, but he made a shushing gesture with one forefinger across his lips. A fraction of a second later, he was beside her, and she felt too mesmerised to wonder how he could move so quickly and so soundlessly. The bed dipped as he sat down beside her.

Heavy inertia flooded her limbs. She couldn't move or speak, yet her senses were acute and the entire surface of her skin felt electrified, receptive, and tingling with an almost sentient longing to be touched. Her hand was still between her thighs, pressing against her sex, her clit. With her other hand she was still touching her own neck.

Zack just stared at her, as if the effort of speeding across the room had drained him and he was resting, restoring himself, feeding on the sight of her touching herself.

His hair was awry, his curls wild and beautiful. They appeared to float as he tipped his head on one side, even now hesitating. To Teresa's horror, he began to edge away.

No ... No, I shouldn't do this, she seemed to hear him say.

But, as he made to rise and leave, Teresa willed him to hear her silent command.

Stay!

Moving closer again, Zack smiled almost shyly, and the teeth she'd been so fixated upon glinted whitely in the moonlight filtering in through the fine gauze curtains. She wanted to sit up, reach out and run a fingertip over their sharp biting surfaces and test their keen edge.

In her imagination, blood welled from the pad of her forefinger – and, like fate, Zack lunged forwards, grasped her hands away from her body and pinned them in one of his, above her head.

Then he kissed her while his other hand searched and found her breast.

Oh yes ... Oh hell yes ...

There was an exquisite roughness about both the kiss and the caress. A fugitive lack of finesse that excited her senses even more. The way Zack's cool tongue probed, and his long fingers squeezed and fondled her only heightened her impression that these explorations were fresh and new to him. She mewled beneath his lips, her virgin lover fantasy surging up and taking flight.

Her response electrified him. Still kissing hard, and massaging her breast, he threw one long leg across her and angled his hips to rub his crotch against her thigh through her silky pyjama bottoms. He was hard as iron, cool and unyielding as he rocked his hips and circled his erection against her flesh.

Teresa began to wriggle in his hold, wanting to press more of herself against as much of Zack as she could reach. She could feel the chilly nature of his body through her pyjamas and the shirt and trousers he wore, but the near contact set flames of lust surging.

He was unusual. He was special. He was like no man she'd ever been with or wanted to be with before. Being kissed and touched and rubbed up against like this was driving her to madness.

'Zack, please ...' she finally managed to gasp when he allowed her mouth a moment of freedom and turned away, pressing his face into the pillow as if he were hiding it. 'Please let me free. I want to touch you.' She twisted towards him, trying to kiss him again, nuzzling his face. 'Let me look at you. I want to kiss you ... Please, Zack.'

'No!'

The word was extraordinarily loud and shocking. As if a lion had roared in her ear, Teresa shrank back, fearful yet more impossibly turned on than ever.

Zack released her hands, but with that strange, unnatural turn of speed of his, he was over her again, half lying on her before she could draw breath. With one long, cool hand he covered her eyes.

'Close your eyes.'

Teresa obeyed him instantly and without question. A part of herself – floating high above the proceedings – was outraged at such submissiveness, but the woman who lay beneath Zack accepted dreamily and complied.

Even when he took away his hand, her leaden eyelids didn't lift. She felt him move off her, but she couldn't follow. It was as if she were pinned to the bed by some force she didn't understand. Even her arms, free now, lay inert at her sides.

Moments seemed to stretch out like elastic as she lay there, and she could feel his cool gaze coasting over her satin-clad limbs. Obediently blind, she still seemed to see his dark head tilt again, in slow contemplation.

But then there was a sudden, sharp, tearing sound, totally unexpected. In the shock of it, the spell on her eyes was broken and they fluttered open. She saw a flash of movement, then all went dark again, and she felt smooth cotton being tied around her head in a makeshift blindfold. The cloth smelt deliciously of Zack's floral cologne.

What had he done, ripped a piece of a fine expensive shirt, just to cover her eyes?

He obviously had, and the action induced a rush of new excitement. There seemed to be no knowing what to expect next. One minute Zack was insisting they be just friends. The next, he was an innocent, tentative lover. And the next, he was dominant enough to play erotic blindfold games. Being with him was a switchback ride, like a sleigh on the Cresta run – her body was a well of pure adrenaline.

Now the effort of keeping her eyes closed was gone, another sensual gate opened wide. The tingling electric field across her skin ramped up sharply. The weight of her silky pyjamas against her breasts seemed to oppress her, and she inched herself restlessly about on the bed as if her body was reacting and fizzing like a volatile chemical.

Perfectly instinctive, Zack began to unfasten her pyjama top. He slipped each button from its hole, but didn't open the panels, moving all the way down to the hem with her body still covered. Then, and only then, did he pluck apart the leaves of satin and expose her. Warm night air sluiced deliciously across her skin.

'Touch your breasts. Show me what you do.'

The words were soft but they made Teresa shudder with desire. Swallowing hard, she drew in a great breath and tilted her head back against the pillow. Her face was hot beneath the blindfold. She'd never displayed herself this way, never performed for a man. She'd always wanted to, but somehow a fugitive spirit had stolen the desire away from her at the critical moment, whispering subversively that the man just wasn't worth the effort.

But now, in the face of strange, mysterious Zack, it was she who seemed to be the unworthy one.

Her face flamed brighter as she took her nipple between her thumb and forefinger and rolled it this way and that, enjoying the twist and tug of it, and the way she always managed to feel the sensation between her legs, as if a ghostly hand was shadowing hers, tweaking her clitoris in the same rhythm. Tonight, the phenomenon was more intense than it had ever been, and instinctively her free hand flew to her groin, so convinced was she that Zack had slid his fingers between her legs and begun to play with her.

But there was no hand down there but her own, and as she wriggled her bottom against the mattress, she clasped her sex and gripped it hard.

Zack uttered a low murmur of approval. She squeezed harder, making the breath catch in her throat.

The clock on the mantelpiece tick, tick, ticked as she handled herself and outside, in the park somewhere, an animal howled. Sticky juice began to trickle down into the cleft of her bottom, oozing from her as sensation gathered and massed.

'Stop a moment. I can't see . . .'

A cold hand prised her fingers away from her crotch, and then slid down her pyjama bottoms, leaving them bunched at her knees. Teresa groaned anew, imagining her exposure, and how rude and wanton she must look with her nightclothes opened and pushed apart to reveal her breasts and crotch to her cool eager watcher.

'Continue . . .'

His voice was still low, but there was a faint ragged edge to it. Teresa longed to see his face, and the desire and excitement painted on it. Again, she had that gut feeling that despite the odds against it, Zack wasn't all that experienced. And this situation was as new and exotic to him as it was to her.

Tentatively, she touched her belly. She didn't know what to do. Masturbation certainly wasn't new to her. She did it quite a bit. But in the dark, on this magic night, all her experience was stripped away from her. She felt new and innocent, just as she sensed Zack was. They were like two enchanted teenagers experimenting.

His hand took hers, guided it towards her cleft. Her heart turned over in her chest – he was trembling.

Oh, bless you, you beautiful man . . .

Then he withdrew his hand again, and let it rest on her thigh, cool and light.

Parting the lips of her sex, she slid in her fingertips, astonished by the swimming abundance of the slippery liquid there. She was wetter than she'd ever been. So ready for something. For anything. She sought out her clitoris, and gasped at the contact. She'd never felt so hyper-sensitive either.

Pinching the tip of her breast, and circling one finger-tip around her clit, she suddenly laughed, thinking of the old children's co-ordination game of rubbing your stomach and patting your head at the same time. It was quite an art, fondling herself this way, but she was excelling. The way her sex fluttered and leapt betrayed skill.

In a world of darkness she seemed to see Zack again, his face intense, almost intimidating. He looked nothing like the kind composed Zack who'd given her a home and his company and friendship. His expression was fierce, hungry, wildly feral. His eyes glittered with an unearthly light, and his mouth curved strangely.

His unfamiliarity frightened her, but there was no way to escape it. It was in her mind so closing her eyes, behind her mask, made no difference. There was only one thing to do – go on with her task.

She fingered her clit. She massaged her nipple. The sensation of gathering, deep in her belly, became an ever tightening knot. She couldn't keep her bottom still on the bed, and in her mind's eye, Zack devoured her lasciv-ious wriggling. His fingertips curved like talons into the tender skin of her thigh.

'Oh ... oh ... oh...' she burbled. And, between her legs, her sex rippled like a mirror, preparing to fling her over the edge into pleasure.

A hand joined hers in her cleft, one big male finger pushing inside her, sweetening the sensations, making them perfect.

Teresa shouted, her hips bucking, her core clenching and clenching on the cool unyielding intrusion that curved inside her.

Climaxing, climaxing furiously, she wrenched at the blindfold. She had to see him. See his face and his eyes.

But when she did – in the midst of orgasm – her consciousness slid sharply sideways and veered away from her.

Zack's eyes were red, and his beautiful mouth framed pointed fangs.

5

The rattle of crockery woke her.

'Hey, sleepy-head . . . Ready for breakfast?'

Her eyes fluttered open.

The heavy net curtains were still drawn but the room was light. It was daytime – with a dullish-looking sky, but perfectly normal.

And Zack, in a soft dark-blue casual shirt and jeans, looked perfectly normal too.

Teresa fought the urge to shrink back against the pillows. Her mind's eye overlaid Zack's pale but fresh-faced appearance with the terrifying modifications from her dream.

Surreptitiously, she fished around under the covers and found her pyjama jacket chastely buttoned and her trousers right where they should be. Even so, the sensations of the night were still vivid.

She'd been blindfolded, but somehow still able to see. And she'd blushed with furious embarrassment on exposing herself to Zack, and masturbating at his command.

But, oh, that hadn't been the most extreme thing.

Those last seconds; Zack's eyes red and burning – and his teeth.

Oh dear God, his teeth! Her vampire fantasies had invaded her dream now, and with bared fangs, Zack had been hell bent on biting her!

'Are you OK?'

Clear blue eyes regarded her with concern. White, even, but perfectly *un*-pointed teeth glinted in a smile.

He was holding a tray, set for breakfast for one, tempting and indulgent with eggs and bacon, toast and jam, and fragrant coffee.

Am I OK? Teresa wondered.

The juxtaposition between dream and reality still made her head feel vaguely woozy, and right at the edge of perception, she detected just the edge of a slight, peculiar hum. Tinnitus, possibly? She'd have to get that checked out when they got back.

'I'm fine ... thanks, Zack,' she lied, but, even as she spoke, the sumptuous aroma of a full English breakfast were setting the world and her thoughts straight again. 'It's just that I had a *really* weird dream ... I think it's sleeping in a strange bed though.' The silvery hum had disappeared, and she smiled back at him, and sat up straight. 'But I'm all right now. And this lot smells heavenly!' She patted her lap and Zack set the tray carefully in place on its folding legs.

'You're spoiling me! This is fab,' she mumbled a moment or two later through a mouthful of sublime savoury bacon. 'I haven't had breakfast in bed for years.'

'We'll have to rectify that when we get home. You need a decent breakfast at least once a week. A piece of toast and a mouthful of coffee as you run out of the door just isn't enough. You need more than that to see you through the day.'

Teresa's heart turned over. He was so thoughtful. But she suspected they both knew it wouldn't happen. There was no going back to their harmonious state of house buddies now. The thought of that cut like a knife, but there was no reason to spoil the next couple of days by dwelling on it. She returned her attention to mopping up egg yolk with fried bread.

And yet, as she munched and sighed with pleasure, she found herself watching Zack where he sat in an armchair, calmly sipping *his* breakfast while he read the paper.

What is that stuff?

When something looked like blood and smelt like blood, did that mean it actually was blood?

No, vampires are fiction. Dracula and Buffy aren't real. They're just stories.

He doesn't go out in sunlight, but he claims that because of his allergies.

Stop it.

He appeared to be in his mid- to late-twenties, but who was to say that was how old he really was. She hadn't known him long enough to tell.

Stop it.

But weren't vampires possessed of unnatural speed and strength?

Teresa's fork clattered on the plate, and Zack looked up from his paper. 'Something wrong with the bacon?'

'No, it's scrummy, thanks.' She applied herself to the plate again, even though her throat was suddenly too tight to eat.

Zack could move like lightning and lift her as if she weighed nothing.

No, don't be silly. You don't believe in ghosts, spoon-bending or Ouija boards ... why on earth should you suddenly start believing in vampires?

And yet still she pondered. Scoping him surreptitiously over the rim of her coffee cup as he turned another page of his paper, he looked just like a normal man to her. He was handsome as the devil and had rather pale skin, but there was nothing more sinister.

Mirrors! That was it! Had she ever actually seen Zack reflected in a mirror?

She sipped her coffee and wracked her brain.

No, she couldn't ever remember seeing Zack's reflection. But what did that mean? She'd never *looked* for it.

And she wasn't going to start looking now, she decided, carefully avoiding looking in the direction of the dressing table.

By eleven thirty, vampires were the last thing on Teresa's mind.

Ahead of them was a lunch, preceded by cocktails for guests who'd arrived early, as they had. And all her so-called friends would be there, the ones who'd been so solicitous – and slyly gloating – when Steve had dumped her. And everyone would have a significant other in tow.

It would have been a pure nightmare if it hadn't been for Zack.

When she emerged from the bathroom, fluffing at her hair and hoping her little silk two-piece wouldn't make her bottom look too big, she found him sitting on the bed, waiting for her.

If anything, he looked even more fabulous than ever.

She wasn't sure how many suits he had in his suit carrier, but this one was dark blue, lightweight and pure fluid elegance, just like him. His shirt was blue silk too, a couple of shades lighter, and he was frowning over a pair of toning ties.

Teresa's heart lurched. Why did life have to be so complicated? If Zack didn't have these mysterious issues of his, she could be straddling him on the bed right now, gorgeous outfit and vampire fantasies notwithstanding.

'You might not need a tie. I think it's quite informal.'

Zack whipped around, ties still fluttering from his fingers.

'Are you sure?' His head tipped to one side, light glinting on his dark curly hair, now immaculately groomed again. 'I don't want to stand out by being too casual.'

You'll always stand out because you're gorgeous, she couldn't stop herself thinking.

Teresa curved her fingers against her skirt to stop herself grabbing him. 'That's a beautiful suit . . . you look terrific.'

'And so do you.'

Suddenly, he was in front of her, looking down into her eyes. He lifted a hand, gently smoothing her hair where it flicked around her face. Teresa almost groaned at the effort of not turning and pressing her lips against his palm.

'Thanks . . .' She drew a quick breath, almost a gasp. His sweet cologne made her feel as if she was going to faint. 'Shall we get down there? I think it's probably started.'

She darted away for her bag and their key card, knowing that, if she stayed close to him, she'd do something stupid.

The perfect escort, Zack escorted her down the stairs, his hand lightly on her arm as they nodded and said 'hello' to fellow guests. In the busy reception area, a gilt-edged board, studded with plastic letters announced that the wedding cocktail party was in the Walcott Room. People shaking umbrellas indicated it was raining outside, which made things easier for Zack as the party would stay inside.

Vampire's luck? she thought, then gritted her teeth, squishing the idea.

The Walcott Room was large and airy, decorated in a sub rococo style with a lot more gilt, and ornate antique furniture lovingly polished. Brilliant light glittered from a magnificent chandelier. She was just about to gather up her nerves and lead the way in, when Zack's fingers tightened on her arm and he drew her quickly to one side.

'How do you want to play this?' he said, *sotto voce*. 'I'll do whatever you want –' his blue eyes twinkled '– but it'd be fun if we could give them something to speculate about, eh?'

I don't know what you are but you could just be an angel! Teresa thought.

The urge to hug and kiss him for real, never mind as an act, bubbled up again like one of the ornamental fountains outside, but she held it in check and just grinned. 'Yeah, why not?'

At least for a little while, she'd have a bona fide excuse to touch him and hang on to him.

The room's grand beauty faded into the background at the sight of the mass of assembled guests. They all seemed to swivel round to watch the arrival of Teresa, the recently dumped.

A strong arm slid around her waist, and she felt a soft kiss like thistledown settle on her hair. Obviously, Zack was going for the 'new lovers, can't keep their hands off one another' gambit. *My, how the gloaters would be taken aback at how quickly she appeared to be back in the saddle.*

'Look, there's the bride-to-be.' Teresa pointed to Lisa, between the clumps of chattering, drinking well-wishers. The bride's smile was already looking pretty set and strained as she kept glancing around to make sure everything was going all right. 'Let's go and say "hello".'

'Right ho.' Zack's voice dropped to a whisper. 'And don't worry . . . it'll all be fine. I'm right beside you.'

Doubt drained out of her like water through a sieve. Teresa smiled up into his face, her heart light and overflowing.

He might not actually *be* her boyfriend but, for the moment, he was the next best thing. He was a rock, and he looked utterly magnificent. And she could already see that most of the women in the room were openly ogling him.

Go on, drool, you lot, Teresa couldn't help thinking. *He's mine! Well . . . sort of . . .*

Even the bride seemed impressed. As they approached,

Lisa eyed Zack with a degree of interest that set her frazzled fiancé frowning.

'Hi, Teresa! I'm so glad you could make it. Isn't this place fab?'

It was obvious Lisa was fit to bursting with curiosity about Zack. The minute she released Teresa from their hug, her eyes skittered immediately to the tall dark presence at her side.

'Lisa ... Tom ... This is Zachary Trevelyan,' she announced proudly, 'Zack, this is Lisa and Tom, the bride and groom ... obviously.'

The greetings went smoothly, but both Lisa's and Tom's eyebrows shot up when they shook Zack's hand. Looking down at his fingers, he shrugged and smiled. 'It's a circulation thing.'

Lisa and Tom just smiled, but Teresa's brain whirled back into its former groove. That was another thing. Wasn't cold skin another vampire characteristic?

Leave it. Just stop thinking about it.

'So ... you and Teresa? Have you ... er ... are you ...'

Lisa's questions petered out, and Teresa's brain went blank again. That was the big problem with play-acting.

'Together?' Zack's voice was soft, almost sultry, and his arm slid back around her waist. Teresa stole a glance at his wickedly smiling face, and for a fraction of second, she half imagined that he winked. But just like so often with him, it was done so quickly that she couldn't be sure she'd seen it.

'Um ... yes ...' Lisa obviously hadn't been expecting such a straight answer. 'I know you're Teresa's landlord but I didn't realise you were a couple. Well, I thought ...' Teresa followed her friend's tracking scan of the busy room, bracing herself for the sight of Steve.

'What better way to get to know one another than by living together.' It was as if Zack was gently explaining the ways of the world to someone very young and naïve.

'I've been biding my time ... waiting until Teresa was free of commitments –' he paused delicately '– and for the moment when it would be honourable to ask her to be my lover.'

'Er ... yes ... right. That's great.'

Teresa hid a smile. Lisa couldn't seem to hide the fact she was desperately smitten despite the presence of her soon-to-be husband beside her.

I don't blame you, Lise, she thought.

Far more smitten, Teresa gasped inside when Zack pressed a light, but meaningful, kiss against her cheek.

'Shall we circulate, my dear? Other guests are waiting to meet the happy couple.'

They made way for members of Tom's family, and Teresa felt as if she was floating as they wove across the room, took a couple of drinks and found themselves a corner.

'Everything all right?'

Zack's eyes were twinkling. He was having fun.

Teresa twinkled back at him. It *was* fun being the envy of all her female friends. Especially the ones who'd expected a fine opportunity to pity her.

Here she was with the most handsome intriguing man in the room, whose presence beside her made her turn to jelly with longing. And on top of that there were all the exquisite little shows of affection – the kisses, the touches on the arm, the light guiding contact of his hand on her waist. They were part of a deception, of course, but that didn't diminish the pleasure.

Sipping her champagne, she watched Zack scanning the room, his keen eyes darting from person to person and from couple to couple as if he was an anthropologist studying a brand new tribe for a paper. Maybe it *was* something like that? She knew he wrote historical studies and treatises. Perhaps he was turning his hand to fiction, or pop psychology, and he was doing a little people watching?

Whatever it was, she had the oddest feeling that a gathering like this was entirely new to him.

'Have you been to many weddings?'

Zack swivelled round and smiled. 'No, this is my first wedding, would you believe?' He put his lips to his glass of mineral water and took the minutest sip. It was the only thing she'd ever seen him ingest so far, apart from his health shakes.

'Really?'

Unease crawled up and down Teresa's spine, and thoughts, conclusions and too many bizarre coincidences jostled and brayed at her. Focusing on the room, and its festive normality, she attempted to silence them.

'What do you think of it all then?'

'Fascinating. It's supposed to celebrate the welfare and happiness of the bride and groom, but, underneath, it's a hotbed of rivalry and envy and one-upmanship ... it's like a Roman arena full of designer lions.'

'I've never looked at it that way.'

And she hadn't. But Zack's beautiful blue eyes were clear and acute. He wasn't accusing anybody of anything, just enlightening her with his deadly accurate observations.

Until today, Teresa had seen weddings as sexy and positive and fun.

But now, seen through his sharp focus, the undercurrents were obvious. People were catching other people's eyes, people who weren't their own partner. Women were coveting other women's dresses, jewellery and men. Men were blatantly perving available girls and non-available girls with equal lustfulness.

'Actually it's more like Sodom and Gomorrah, isn't it?' she whispered as they dumped their glasses on a side table. Zack smiled like a conspirator as he snaked his strong arm around her waist again.

'But at least we're together –' he pulled her closer, the pressure of his fingertips like electricity through the thin stuff of her top '– and we can guard each other against the prowling hyenas.'

But who's going to guard me from you? Teresa couldn't help thinking.

At that moment, she turned around and saw Steve across the room, apparently devouring his new girlfriend whole in front of an audience.

'Is that him?'

Zack's hold tightened, and strength poured through the contact between their bodies. Her vague doubts about Zack forgotten, Teresa leant in, and the effect increased. Steve and his trollop looked ridiculous and she was invulnerable.

'Yes, I'm afraid so ... although I'm hard pressed to know what I saw in him now.'

Beside Zack's lean grace and refined Gothic style, Steve was a clod. And fat too! With new clear eyes, Teresa noted that he had a rather angry shaving rash.

'Shall we say hello?' Zack's fingertips caressed her waist, the gentle pressure both sensual and confidence building. With him at her side, she could do anything.

'Why not? I'm bound to run into him at this gig sometime, so let's get it over with sooner rather than later.'

'That's my girl!' Zack's mouth brushed her hair in another fleeting kiss and just like before her feet felt as if they were lifting off the carpet. This was only a charade they were playing for an audience, but the perquisites were blissful.

Steve and his rather voluptuously enhanced lady friend were still playing tonsil hockey, so it required a discreet but pointed cough from Zack to get their attention.

'Hi, Steve, how are you?' Teresa smiled brightly as the two disentangled themselves. 'Smashing do this, isn't it?'

The girl – Suzy, Teresa remembered – looked astonished, as if she couldn't believe her eyes. A dumped woman confronting her 'ex'? How could that happen?

Steve, on the other hand, seemed about to collapse or have apoplexy or both at once. His eyes widened, not just with surprise, but with astonishingly unfeigned lust as his eyes cruised up and down Teresa's figure.

Take a good look, buster. It's all for him now, not you.

With Zack's hand on her waist, she could understand what the proverbial million dollars felt like.

Steve's mouth dropped open, but no words emerged. His eyes continued to skitter from her breasts to her legs to her face and round and round again until he suddenly seemed to notice that she wasn't unaccompanied. And as he tilted his head up to meet the eyes of a very tall man, the expression on his face made Teresa want to giggle.

I never noticed you were so short, Stevie-boy.

'Pleased to meet you ... I'm Zachary Trevelyan.' Zack's voice was firm and no nonsense, while Steve still couldn't seem to locate his own tongue.

Teresa had a hard time containing herself as she watched the handshakes.

Like the rest of the female guests, Suzy seemed bewitched by Zack, but also distinctly annoyed now that her own specimen of manhood was clearly substandard. She shook off Steve's grip and favoured Zack with a pouting smile as she proffered her hand.

'Ooh, cold hands, warm heart.' She batted her mascara-clad lashes at him.

'Something like that.' Zack's response was a finessed

combination of exquisite politeness and a complete lack of reaction.

Steve winced. There was no other word for it. Zack didn't appear to be exerting very much pressure as he gripped the other man's hand, and his smile was amiable. But Steve's face went bright pink and, as Zack released him, he visibly fought the urge not to wiggle his squished fingers.

'You're the landlord, aren't you?' Steve's tone was belligerent and Teresa hid her smile. Her ex was faced with a taller, fitter, altogether far superior male, and she sensed he was seriously regretting his decision to dump her.

'Yes, he's that as well.' Beaming, she slid her arm around Zack's waist just as his arm went around her shoulder.

Steve's eyebrows lowered in a scowl when Zack's cool lips momentarily caressed the side of her face.

'Shall we get another drink, love?' Zack's words against her skin sounded exactly like a sinfully obscene suggestion that Steve and his babe weren't supposed to have heard.

Teresa turned to look up at him, loving the wicked glint in his glorious blue eyes. He was clearly enjoying baiting her ex just as much as she was.

'Or would you prefer to get out of here?' He licked his lips ever so slightly, his black lashes lowering lasciviously.

Oh, hell, yes!

It was just a game, but suddenly it felt real. Zack's dark head tilted, as if he was monitoring her every thought and for a moment, he frowned infinitesimally. Then he winked like a demon, his pale beautiful face all aglow.

'Better circulate just a bit more, for politeness sake –' she paused, giving him a devouring look that was worthy of Suzy '– and then I'm all yours ... would you like that?'

Zack laughed, his eyes on hers, and then swivelled towards the nonplussed couple beside them. 'We'll probably see you later. Nice meeting you both.'

Then his strong arm deftly turned Teresa and he began to guide her away through the throng.

They found a corner, and some more drinks, said 'hello' to more people. But, as the moments passed, Teresa found it impossible to focus on the party.

Would you prefer to get out of here? The words tolled in her head.

It was all an act, but she *did* want to sneak away to do what Steve and Suzy gloweringly suspected. And what various other couples, drifting away, were clearly planning on.

Plenty of time for a long lazy session in bed before the wedding at nine p.m.

In the heady miasma of high-end women's perfumes and expensive aftershaves, Zack's delicious cologne sang like a clear clean note. It was playing havoc with her. Her body tingled in the places he'd touched so decorously, and down between her legs a needy pulse was steadily throbbing.

Wedding lust. Mating rituals. The whole atmosphere was ripe with pheromones and sex.

She turned to Zack and found him staring at her, his eyes dark and strange-looking. His expression was an irrational blend of intense desire – the mirror of hers – and what could only be described as apprehension.

What have you got to be afraid of?

What have I got to be afraid of?

'Look ... I mean ... do you *really* want to get out of here?'

The words floated in the air as if they suddenly had a life of their own. It wasn't at all what she'd meant to say, but it was too late to call it back. She swallowed, feeling hot blood rush into her face and neck. 'Damn it, I've embarrassed you, haven't I? Forget I said it.'

She couldn't look him in the eye, but Zack lifted her face to his with one finger under her chin. His expression was more troubled than ever, complex and sexy, and slightly wild.

'No! I want it too –' his voice was odd too. Gruff and deep, yet it seemed to ring. Several people looked around, frowning curiously in their direction '– but as they say in those soaps ... it's complicated. More complicated than you can possibly believe.'

Staring down at her, his eyes were hot and confused. He pursed his lips and then seemed to run his tongue over his teeth, again and again, as if examining them somehow.

Checking for fangs, Zack?

Her unspoken words seemed to electrify him. He took her firmly by the arm and hustled her from the room and into a small adjacent lounge that was conveniently deserted.

Pushing the door shut behind him, he backed up against it and hauled her into his arms.

His mouth came down on hers, hard and sweet and demanding, just as it had been in her fantasies. The sharp contrast between her warm lips and his cooler ones made her tremble with an excitement that was beyond sex. It was a strange stimulus she was at a loss to understand.

Zack's tongue was cool too. Cool and bold and greedy and undisciplined. There was a rough unpractised quality about the kiss that made her blood sing and her knees go weak as jelly.

Throwing her arms around him, she pitched herself into the embrace, sucking on his sweet chilly tongue and pressing her belly against his, blatantly enticing him.

The pressure was intense, and raw, and she couldn't get enough of him. It was as if her body was trying to climb inside his and be closer than his skin.

A moment ago, Zack had expressed doubts, but now they were forgotten. He pressed his pelvis back at her, circling the hard knot of his erection against her softness, growling in his throat as she reciprocated, rocking and pushing against his cock.

I knew you wanted me. I just knew it.

Her exultation was silent, but she could tell Zack had read it. He dug a hand into her hair, angling her head as his lips left hers and began to travel across her cheek, and down the line of her jaw and neck.

The touch of him and the taste of him were exquisite. His breath was almost scented, and it lingered on her lips where she ran her tongue over them. Her mouth felt bruised even though the kiss had only lasted a few moments.

Zack's lips were like thistledown on her skin, the contact magically light and circumspect as he explored her. She sensed that elusive reticence in him again, an impression of caution and lack of experience. Moments ago he'd been a wild man, but now he was holding back.

Sliding her hands under his jacket, she slid them down his back until they reached his firm male buttocks. Then, cupping the delicious muscular rounds she gripped him and pulled him against her belly.

He growled again. Deeper this time. The sound seemed to bounce around the small room as if it were a cathedral, like a feral utterance coming from another dimension. It was the weirdest thing, but it only made her surge against him. And then utter a groan herself as his mouth opened against her throat.

She felt the questing touch of his tongue, licking, searching – and then the contact of his teeth, sharp and hard, against her skin. The sensation made her sex clench involuntarily. Though his mouth was cold, it was the hottest, most exciting moment of lust.

'Please ... please ...' she heard herself implore, tilting back her head to give him better access to her neck.

She pressed her groin against him, to ease the ache and reinforce her invitation.

And then she felt it.

Tiny, sharp and keen, his teeth broke the skin of her neck in a little bite. It was pain, but it made her hips lurch, rocking harder and seeking closer contact. Her entire body was burning and silently screaming to be naked against him.

'No!'

Zack's cry was deafening. Teresa swayed, with her back against the door as she clutched and scrabbled at it in order to stay on her feet.

Across the room – impossibly – Zack was standing as if staring at a tall glass-fronted bookshelf full of leather-bound volumes. His dark-clad back was a wall of raw tension and, at his sides, his pale hands were two clenched fists.

He was here. And now he's there. What happened?

He was kissing me. Now he can't look at me. What have I done?

'What's the matter, Zack? What is it? Did I come on too strong?' She started towards him, but he stilled her with a chopping gesture, as if he'd seen her. The air between them seemed to hum. Like an external expression of that strange interior phenomenon she'd attributed to some inner ear problem. 'I'm sorry ... I don't usually behave like a trollop ... I thought you wanted me.'

'I do,' he said, his voice low, tormented, 'I want you more than you can possibly understand and in ways ... ways that you won't understand.'

There was pain in his words, agony in his taut body.

Teresa felt a great surge of compassion that somehow melded with her desire.

'Try me, Zack. I'm here for you in any way you need me. I'm crazy about you. Surely you realise that?'

He let out a noise like a sob, as if the news were exactly what he wanted to hear, but painful too.

'I – I'm crazy about you too, Teresa. Really. But this can't possibly work. I thought it might, but I was wrong. So wrong –' his tense shoulders lifted, and then subsided '– I couldn't have *been* more wrong.'

'But why?'

Watching him closely, achingly, Teresa suddenly braced herself – half dreading, but now almost *knowing* what she'd see when Zack turned to face her. Every breath of air whooshed out of her body, and she began to sway.

Then, as if time itself were mutable and malfunctioning, Zack spun slowly towards her.

His eyes were red, and his canine teeth were sharp white fangs.

6

Someone was gently tapping her cheek, and a dear familiar voice was speaking softly but persuasively in her ear.

'Teresa, my love, are you all right? Come on ... snap out of it. Please talk to me.'

Teresa's eyes fluttered open, and the first thing she saw was Zack's face, pale, handsome and worried. He was kneeling in front of her, and she was slumped in one of the large damask-covered armchairs that were arrayed around the small room.

She had absolutely no idea how she'd got there.

Zack took a glass of water from the low table beside her chair, and offered it to her.

Teresa sipped, feeing numb and weird but with her hackles on the rise, aware of something, she knew not what, barrelling towards her.

'Oh, God! Oh, God! Oh, God!'

It all returned to her.

The glass started to tip, but Zack caught it faster than the eye could see and set it back on the table.

Unable to look him in the face, Teresa stared at the glass, then at his hand, long and smooth, still holding it.

'You *are* one, aren't you?' Her heart thudded, fast and hard. Her mind felt like a wild pony, cantering about, trying desperately to avoid the truth. 'A vampire? They're real, aren't they? And I've been living with one for six months!'

An overload circuit tripped somehow and, without thinking, she whipped out her hand and fetched Zack a ringing slap across the face. He could have deflected it without effort, but he stayed still.

There was no red mark on his cheek where the blow had struck.

'I'm sorry.'

His apology came before hers. She hadn't really intended to hit him, it'd just happened. A reflex.

'I wanted to tell you, Teresa. Time and time again. But I didn't think you'd believe me. And if you did believe me, I was afraid it'd make you run for the hills – and leave me.'

His whole face was full of remorse. Full of humanity. No hint of pointy teeth or ruddy eyes.

Teresa dragged in a shuddering breath, totally at a loss. This was the most momentous discovery of her life. A critical turning point. She needed advice. She needed someone to turn to. Someone to tell about this completely unbelievable thing.

But the only person she longed to tell was the man staring worriedly into her face.

Laughter bubbled up in her throat. How could anyone, ever, manage to get themselves into a situation as ridiculous as this? She'd finally found the perfect man – a decent man, who she wanted as a friend as well as a lover, and who was spine-meltingly gorgeous into the bargain – and he was a vampire!

Hysterical laughter broke free, took a hold of her, and got out of control. Her body shook and tears of manic merriment trickled down her face. Zack's strong arms slid around her and she could feel his chest heaving with laughter too.

Several chaotic moments followed. They rocked together, bonded in a bizarre glee, until the door to the little sitting room opened and someone popped their head in.

'Whoops, sorry!' They were gone again before either

Teresa or Zack could stop, but the spell of their mad fit was finally broken.

She stood up, forcing Zack to rise gracefully to his feet too.

'Well, as they say in every romantic film or drama I've ever seen, we need to talk, don't we?' He smiled down at her, his beautiful mouth quirking.

'That's putting it mildly, dark prince.' She reached for his cool hand. 'Shall we retire to our chamber?'

Zack shrugged eloquently. 'I think we'd better.'

In the lift, Teresa noticed something she hadn't seen the last time they'd ridden up.

'Hey! I can see you ... sort of ... I thought you weren't supposed to have a reflection?' She pointed to a small courtesy mirror at the back of the lift. In it was Zack's image, faint and shadowy, but definitely visible.

'Don't believe everything you see in movies or read in books.' In the glass, Zack's beautifully curved mouth was hazily reflected. 'There are degrees of vampirism, and as many different kinds of us as there are normal people.'

'I didn't know that.'

'Yes. And I suppose you'd say I'm at the more human end of the spectrum.'

She thought of his kindness towards her, and the way she always felt cared for and protected by him. His attitude had been help, not harm, from day one.

Or at least it had seemed that way.

'So you're not planning to ... to drain me dry and either kill me or make me into a vampire too, then?' She tried to speak lightly, but her voice wavered.

Emotion played across Zack's face, complex and haunting, and she felt guilty for betraying her lack of trust.

But – but he was a vampire. A *vampire*. Human end of the spectrum or otherwise.

'I would never intentionally do any of those things ...'

He bit his lip, and Teresa thought of all the times she'd naively noted how white and shiny and sharp his teeth looked. No wonder they were sharp, didn't he bite necks with them?

She put her hand on his arm. He felt so strong, so normal – and so human. But still she trembled.

'What do you mean by "intentionally", Zack?'

The lift door sprang open, to reveal a couple who Teresa vaguely recognised, waiting outside. She smiled briefly at them and then led the way towards the room. It would be easier to talk there, but her heart still thudded. How foolhardy was it to lock herself behind closed doors with a vampire?

'So, "intentionally", Zack,' she repeated once they were alone.

Instead of answering, he walked towards the mini fridge. He took out a whisky miniature for her and poured it into a glass, then a flask of his 'iron shake'.

'I'm so stupid ... I didn't even work out that was blood!' She grimaced as she took a sip of her own drink and she sat down on the bed. She'd never been a whisky drinker, but these were desperate times. Clutching her glass, she stared long and hard at Zack's throat as he took a swallow of his own 'drink'. Dark, terrifying thoughts began to circle.

'Please, for God's sake, tell me that's *animal* blood!' The whole universe seemed to hinge on his answer. Was she just feet away from a mass murderer?

Zack frowned. 'It is ... and you did, actually ...' He put aside his flask, as if he'd lost his appetite. 'Work out that it was blood, that is.'

Layers of shock piled on one another. Teresa drank more whisky, not tasting it.

Slowly, he shook his head, lingering across the room from her as if daren't approach.

'What do you mean, Zack?'

'This is so complicated ... so hard to put into words. What's happened to me, the way I am – and the stupid, selfish things I've done.' He studied his long narrow hands for a moment, running the pad of his thumb across a nail, then suddenly made a strange elegant gesture, a kind of pass.

Accompanied by that elusive, silvery humming in her ears, images, impressions, sensations all flooded in. Blanked out memories and exquisite, unearthly pleasure.

'You bastard!'

Teresa flew across the room as if she was the one with vampire powers. Fired by confusion and fury, she thumped and beat at Zack's chest and shoulders. It was like belabouring a statue made of granite. He didn't lift his arms to protect himself. He just took it.

'I'm sorry,' he whispered when the energy had gone out of her, and she stomped back across the room, retrieved her glass and sloshed down more whisky.

'How could you?'

Deflated, Teresa slumped, and let her jumbled emotions settle.

She felt bemused, still angry, slightly betrayed, and bizarrely, as before, she suddenly wanted to laugh.

She'd just beat up a supernatural being who could probably snap her neck in a heartbeat – and she'd got away with it. Eat your heart out, Buffy.

'So why the mind-games?' Across the room, Zack was standing just as she'd left him, but he winced visibly at her words.

'Because, if I'd let you see the truth, you wouldn't have stayed in my house.' He seemed to have regained his beautiful stillness. Something Teresa realised now stemmed in part from the fact he didn't breathe and his chest never moved. 'And if I'd let you remember me touching you, you'd have remembered the biting too.'

His gaunt face was tormented and whiter than usual,

if that were possible. Self-recrimination made his eyes darkly haunted.

Teresa put down her glass again, and held out her hand to him as her muddled feelings dropped into place like the tumblers of a lock. She was afraid of his strangeness, and the fact that he was fiction and magic made real. But he was still Zack, and she still wanted him – and loved him.

Despite everything he'd just admitted, he was a troubled soul and she wanted to hold him and comfort him and soothe him. For all his supernatural potency and his sly mind-warping powers, he was still that lost innocent boy she'd always dreamed of. Still the beautiful virgin she'd longed to initiate.

How she knew this, she hadn't the faintest idea. Maybe it was vampire telepathy, working in reverse?

'Come here.' She slid her free hand across the bedspread. 'You're obviously able to control yourself.'

Zack's eyes were troubled, but unexpectedly he complied, striding across the room and sitting down beside her.

'I'm not so sure of that,' he said, as she reached for his cool hand.

He looked away for a moment, then squared his shoulders and turned to face her again. He took her hand, turned it over and then folded it into his. The process was almost a transformation, the drawing upon an inner strength and dignity to face a crisis. Something he must have done before, many times, to survive.

'The thing is –' his fingers traced her palm '– for my kind, lust and bloodlust are two sides of the same coin. One triggers the other. I don't want to harm anybody. I don't want to damage anybody. So to avoid one, I have to avoid both.'

'But you've been experimenting, haven't you? With me.'

For a being that didn't need to breathe, Zack sighed heavily and looked towards the ceiling.

'I'm not sorry.' When he looked at her again, his smile was a chiaroscuro of emotion. She saw remorse, and genuine penitence, but also the slow impish beginnings of seduction, like a naughty but very grown-up boy beginning to flex his sexual powers, 'You're beautiful . . . and I adore you. I wanted to give you pleasure.' He paused and heaved another faux vampire sigh. 'But it's not safe. I might not be able to hold back another time.'

'How do you know unless you try?'

Teresa's heart was thudding fit to burst. This was the most dangerous thing she'd ever done – but she'd never wanted anything more intensely in her life.

Zack's eyes glittered, brilliant with those conflicting emotions. But Teresa knew she was winning. The fine line of red around his blue irises told her so. 'Teresa, this isn't a game. I could easily kill you.' He ran his tongue around his lips, then over the edges of his teeth – checking. 'And I'm . . . well . . . not experienced. It'll be like handing a learner driver the keys of a Lamborghini.'

'But you're not going to learn anything – least of all how to master your darker urges – if you don't try, are you?'

Are you sure? he seemed to ask silently. His eyes were changing, changing, even as she watched him, and his white fangs were already sharp points of danger.

'Don't worry . . . if you get out of hand, I'll just knee you in the groin,' Teresa answered, 'that's usually guaranteed to stop *any* man . . . alive *or* dead, hopefully.'

Tired of bargaining and coaxing, she released Zack's hand and slid her own up his arm and around the back of his head, drawing him to her. As their lips met, his suppressed growl rang in her brain.

With his tongue in her mouth, he tipped her

backwards onto the bed, pushing her effortlessly across its width and moving over her.

The taste of his mouth was astonishing – both exotic and familiar – and the brush of his extended canines set her nerves shivering with a delicious sense of peril. She felt it tingling in every part of her body, not only against the tender inner skin of her lip. She pressed her tongue back against his, daring to flick swiftly at the sharp points.

As she tasted the tiniest drop of blood, her sex clenched and Zack growled, his hips rocking.

Still kissing, they tugged at their clothes, the tangling and fumbling only adding to the thrill of struggle. Shoes clomped onto the floor, and cotton, silk and high-quality suiting all went flying into heaps, willy-nilly. As the pieces came off, they paused to press skin to skin, and it wasn't only Zack who made unearthly sounds of hunger.

Naked on the bed, he was an object of pure beauty. His skin was milky pale but had an exquisitely dense sheen like polished marble. Muscles in fine long slabs adorned his arms, his torso and his thighs.

His cock was astonishing. Large, jutting, fiercely hard, it reared up from his body, silky and seeping and rosy pink.

'I thought your sort didn't have circulation ... how does this come about?' She ran her fingertips along it, making him hiss and clench his jaw. A tiny trickle of his own blood stained his lip as he bit down.

'It's not circulation – just hydraulics.' His voice was low and ragged. 'I don't know how it works but right now I'm just glad it does!'

Tipping her back on the bed, he started to explore, his cool fingertips travelling over her body in sweeps that were both hungry and tentative. Again, she got a strong impression that he was in brand new territory, that he was a novice – but one whose powers of instinct and empathy were phenomenal. Maybe it was something to do with what he was? And he could read her feelings and her thoughts? Whatever it was, his touch was perfect without any need for coaching.

Teresa trembled as his mouth began to move on her. Studiously avoiding her neck, he kissed first the line of her jaw, and then darted straight to the curve of her breast, his cool tongue flicking out and tasting her skin. The short, scurrying licks flickered around her nipple, but didn't settle on it. Round and round he went, skirting the sensitive areola but not closing on it.

You teasing devil. Teresa slithered against the quilt, unable to keep her hips still. Every part of her wanted him. She groaned out loud, gripping his strong shoulders, her nails digging into his astonishingly hard muscles.

And then he sucked, hard, on the tip of her breast, his lips pulling, his tongue circling like a rude little serpent.

'Oh God!' she gasped, her molten core rippling as his mouth moved instinctively. She pushed her hips against him, her sex blindly seeking his. Her hands roved over his magnificent back, his flanks and his bottom.

Her body seemed to shout with hunger as his lips parted and she felt the prickle of his fang-tips against the crown of her breast.

Bite me. Please bite me, her mind screamed.

It was madness, sex and yet not sex. Grabbing at him, Teresa's mind grabbed at something indefinable, other, far greater than the fleeing confluence of their bodies. A sense of yearning flooded through her, the longing for a communion that was immense and monumental, beyond time itself.

Zack jerked back.

'No!' he gasped. 'I can't . . . I shouldn't . . .' He shook his head, his dark curls tossing. 'I don't care if I live a thousand years and *never* have a woman!'

The concept she'd been reaching for, dissolved like mist, and despite her desire, Teresa reached up to touch Zack's dear face, frowning as she processed his words.

'Zack, love, what do you mean? What do you mean "never have a woman"?'

How could that be? He was beautiful, exotic, and virile – with hypnotic powers into the bargain – how could he not have had scores of lovers in an unnaturally long life? She'd relished her 'virgin male' fantasies. But surely that was all they were – fantasies.

Sitting up, he turned away from her, his white back a wall of tension.

'It means just what you think it means.' He lifted his hands, smoothed them over his hair, gripping the thick, shiny curls at the back of his neck. Letting his hands fall again, he turned back towards her. 'I've never been with a woman. I've never dared.'

Teresa sat up too, reaching for him. Despite the high sharp thrill of his admission, it was sympathy she felt most strongly. What kind of torment must his long life as a vampire be? He had a soul. He was a good man. And his principles had prevented him from ever putting a woman at risk. Even if the woman *wanted* that risk.

I love you. The thought popped into her head.

So impossible, but she felt it, and knew that the emotion had been with her a long time – probably as long as she'd known him. And all the time her heart had secretly recognised his sacrifice.

But she was still curious.

'What about *before*? Wasn't there anybody then?' But when *was* before? 'How long have you been a vampire?'

Zack seemed to relax. He flashed her a wry, boyish smile.

'I was turned back in the 1930s, so that would mean that I've been what I've been for seventy years, although I've tried not to keep count.'

'But they had girls in the 1930s, didn't they?' Teresa smiled back at him, 'I mean ... well, you look about twenty-five. Surely at that age you had girlfriends? What the hell happened to you?'

The thought of Zack with other women gave her a bit of a stab, even though they were most likely dead by now.

'I was a novice in a Benedictine monastery, Teresa. Pure as the driven snow, you might say.' He laughed, a shrug lifting his finely formed shoulders.

'Crikey!'

'Crikey indeed,' he intoned, still smiling, 'although after I became a vampire my religious faith took quite a knock.'

Teresa made a decision. It was perilous and foolhardy, but there was no way she was going to let this glorious man deny himself any longer.

And she wanted him more than ever. A thousand-fold.

'You've got to trust yourself, Zack. You're a good man, despite the fangs.' She inclined herself towards him and kissed the corner of his mouth. His fangs had retracted a little but she could still feel their points as she pressed her lips against his. 'And I believe you can control yourself.' She kissed the other corner of his mouth, flicking her tongue between his lips, seeking out the sharp badge of his condition. 'I'll help ...'

His arms came around her, cool-skinned, yet warm in intent. He was shaking, and she imagined tears like jewels trickling down his beautiful face. A moment later she felt the moisture against her cheek.

They kissed again. Slowly at first, yet growing wilder and wilder with every second. Teresa felt free and confident and full of desire, stirred to elation by this miracle of a man, who was her dearest fantasy, and yet so very, very, very much more.

And Zack relaxed at last. She could feel him smiling as he kissed her, his lips curving against her skin, even as his fangs slid against it.

'If I start to bite, don't forget that knee in the groin.' He was laughing as she slid her sex up and down the muscular length of his thigh, loving the friction as she curled her fingers around his chilly but magnificent cock.

'I've thought of that.'

And she had. It was perfect. Rising up over him, she pushed him down onto his back against the covers. He looked like some kind of crooked angel with his dark curls against the crisp white cotton pillowcase.

'I just want you to lie back and think of Transylvania!' She swirled the tip of her finger around the head of his penis, and watched him snarl silently, his upper lip curling to reveal the strange beauty of his fully extended fangs. They were awesome, but she wasn't going to allow him to make a mistake with them.

How long would a man who'd been waiting seventy years for sex be able to last, she wondered. Especially one who had vampire fire burning in his blood?

Still touching his penis, she lowered her lips towards it. Forming an 'O' she guided him safely in.

So cool. So hard. So sweet and clean, not at all like any man she'd ever sucked.

'Oh, God, Teresa!'

Zack's voice was plaintive. Full of wonder. She imagined him masturbating, perhaps frequently, but if he'd never been with a woman this would be a revelation. She let her tongue dance, exploring his sumptuously flared shape, while out of the corner of her eye, she watched him writhe and tear at the bedclothes, his face contorted and his eyes crimson red.

She tasted him slowly, carefully, her exploration circumspect. No harsh suction. No bobbing up and down.

Just delicate strokes of her tongue, while her fingers gently played his shaft and balls.

His enraptured cries became more feral. He growled. He snarled. He ripped the sheets, his hips bucking wildly as he thrust himself into her mouth, making a mockery of her carefully measured pleasuring.

'I want you! I must have you!' His voice was ferocious now. He was all primal magic and otherness. Teresa felt fear, the kind that exhilarates and hurls the spirits skywards. She was a mountain climber challenged by Everest, a hang-glider about to freebase off a sheer precipice. Wracked with savage terror, her blood surged with a wild anticipation and sheer joy in the embrace of no going back.

Hauling herself upright, she looked down on Zack's magnificent cock, pale and shining with his own juice and her saliva. Deep inside her, she felt her womb leap and cry to him. Could he make her pregnant? She doubted it. And as a virgin, he was free from disease, surely?

It was his fangs that were the danger to her. But with them, she'd take her chances. She had no choice.

Throwing a leg over Zack's lean hips, she positioned herself over him, his tip at her entrance. Then as he bucked up again, she bore down, taking him in.

7

It was heaven. Paradise. Perfection. More than he'd ever imagined, and he'd had a long time to imagine it.

First her sweet mouth, now her beautiful warm body. The sensation of being enclosed and caressed was exquisite and chaotic. As intense pleasure surged, the call for blood raged in his mind and his veins. He looked up at Teresa, drinking in every glorious facet of her gentle curves and her gleaming rosy skin, seeing her sweet face all haloed in shimmering red.

I must resist, I must resist, Zack repeated to himself.

The battle of his senses was titanic. The knowledge of what his fangs could do to her clashed again and again with raw ravening hunger. A lust for blood such as he'd never experienced before, even in his earliest and most untutored struggles.

And yet the conflict prolonged the pleasure. The primal skirmish between man and vampire kept him from simply thrusting like a maniac, coming and ejaculating almost immediately. Fighting his own urges gave him an edge, just enough so that he could think of Teresa's pleasure.

Reaching out, he clasped her hips, holding her tight and rocking her on the fulcrum of his penis. He knew he was big and hard, and he filled her and caressed her with that hardness. Her eyes and her mouth were wild with sensation and her throat was flushed. As she moaned, and rocked in time to his movements, he felt her channel ripple and embrace him with its heat.

'Oh, God! Oh, God!' he roared, naming the deity he was no longer sure he believed in, 'I can't ... I ...'

And yet still she pleasured him, flexing and clenching the very quick of her sumptuous body around him. His head was spinning, a red vortex of raving desire. Wanting her to share something, some human essence of this sublime sensation, he slid his fingers between her legs, finding the apex of her sex, almost where their bodies were melded. He knew his touch was clumsy and untutored, but her response was a sweet whimper of pleasure, and she pressed her hand over his as if to affirm his efforts.

Then he felt it. Her body reaching the pinnacle. Fast, hard contractions around his flesh. Her fingers gouging into the back of his hand, and his thigh where she was supporting herself.

'Zack! Oh, God, Zack!' she shouted, her triumphant shout as unnaturally loud as his own blood cry.

Beyond control, he reared up, grasping her to him as the red fire of bloodlust boiled in his loins and in his soul. At the last moment, he tried to turn away his head, but she wouldn't let him. Still climaxing, she buried her hands in his curls and brought his face to the curve of her neck, pressing his mouth against the soft damp skin of her neck.

'Do it, Zack!' she commanded him, her voice ringing like a queen's, compelling him to do her will, 'Do it, Zack ... take my blood. It's what I want.'

Unable to defy her, he bit down softly, and drank her sweetness.

Her human blood was warm with life as his cock jerked inside her and his cold seed spilt and spilt and spilt.

'I now pronounce you man and wife. You may kiss the bride.'

Don't look at him. Don't look at him.

It was useless. Teresa could no sooner not look at Zack than she could stop breathing.

I'm going crazy, she thought.

Zack's idea of formalwear was a gorgeous black Edwardian evening suit, complete with high collar and elaborately tied cravat. She knew now that he could never have worn such a suit when it was actually in fashion, but she loved his quirky fondness for vintage style.

Everybody cheered and clapped as Lisa and Tom kissed enthusiastically, but like herself, Zack appeared vaguely distracted. When he met her eyes, his expression was complex. Part triumph, part confusion, part guilt, part lust – all mixed up with a sweet warmth and tenderness.

She wished he would listen to her when she told him he had no reason to feel guilty.

She'd been the one who'd pushed him into biting her.

His eyes widened as if he'd read her thoughts, and unable to stop herself, Teresa flicked back to those breathtaking moments.

It'd been like falling and flying both at once. There had been pleasure in her belly like a boiling, swirling whirlpool that she also felt in every cell and atom of her body.

She'd never come like that in her life before, and she knew it was because Zack had been feeding at the same time.

The little pinpricks itched suddenly, and Zack's eyes narrowed as she adjusted the silk scarf she'd slung around her neck to hide the evidence. He'd taken barely a few mouthfuls, but it was the act, not the volume that was significant.

The ceremony over, murmuring and jostling guests began to move away from the rows of seats set out in front of the little rose bower where Lisa and Peter had taken their vows. Next on the agenda was the reception, and the groaning tables of delicious buffet food and inordinate amounts of booze behind the open bar were calling.

Dusk had fallen, and there was a tiny bit of descending sun on the horizon, but the weak rays didn't seem to bother Zack too much.

'It'd have to be full daytime sunlight for me to crisp,' he'd told her as they'd made their way to the outdoor ceremony, 'Other than that, I'm fine.'

Teresa circulated through the noisy hectic reception in a dream. Everyone was having a fine old time, ribald jokes were being told, and people were drinking, eating, laughing and flirting. But to her it all seemed at a great distance. Her only reality was the tall elegant man at her side.

From time to time, she caught other women eyeing him, their blatant envy of her written on their faces.

Oh, yes, he is a stud, she silently taunted them. And he's gorgeous. But you don't know the half of it, and if I tried to tell you, you'd think I've lost my marbles.

Sipping from a glass of wine, she wrinkled her nose because it had no flavour. She supposed that normal human pleasures lost their impact when you were in love with a supernatural being, and you'd just been to bed with him.

Dancing began on the specially laid floor. Teresa watched people jigging and gyrating, and women doing various kinds of sexy wiggle in order to snare themselves a man for the night. At one time she would have enjoyed strutting her stuff too, regardless of whether she was hoping to find a nice man or not. But tonight she felt weary and detached from reality. It was if someone had photoshopped the wedding party into a blur.

'Are you all right?'

Turning from the dancing throng to Zack felt like leaving the shadows behind to embrace the sweet light of the moon.

'You look tired.' His fine broad brow was puckered with concern, but all Teresa wanted to do was reach out and touch the single loose curl that dangled across it, having escaped from his scrupulously groomed coiffeur.

Trying to think straight, and not get sidetracked by kiss curls and eyes that turned red, Teresa gave him an encouraging smile.

'I'm fine, Zack, really.'

Liar.

'I'm perfectly OK.' She dropped her voice. 'You haven't harmed me. In fact, I feel wonderful.' She touched his arm, thrilled all over again by the feel of hard muscle and unnatural strength beneath her fingers. 'It's just that I'd far rather be alone with you than amongst this crowd.'

Zack frowned again.

'Don't do that.' She reached up and smoothed her fingers across his brow as if to erase the frown. His skin was cool, but the contact prickled like electricity. 'What we shared was wonderful. And I want to do it again. As soon as possible.'

Biting his lip, Zack looked heavenwards, a picture of confusion. There was the slightest bit of extra pointing on his canines, and she could feel desire pouring off him like discreet magnetic waves.

He took her by the shoulders, and looked deep into her eyes, his own already ringed with red.

'And do you think I don't want that too?' His voice was raw. 'I waited for three-quarters of a century for what happened between us, Teresa, and it exceeded even my wildest imaginings.' His long fingers tightened around her shoulders, and the little pain of it was scary yet delicious. 'And next time . . . next time I know will be even better.' His crystal-blue eyes had a red halo. 'But I'm not sure I'll be able to control myself.'

'Right on, mate! I know what you mean! She's a cracker!' slurred a drunken wedding guest as he passed them, swaying and bleary-eyed.

Zack's eyes flared crimson and he glared at the man ferociously. The very air seemed to vibrate with a silent roar of fury.

'Sorry. I'm really sorry,' apologised the chastened guest in a tiny voice, before scuttling away, white as a sheet and terrified.

'See what I mean?' Zack's eyes were normal again even though his voice was still softly fierce. 'Around you, I can't contain myself – I thought I could, but it's a thousand times more difficult than I expected.' He closed his eyes for a moment, thick black eyelashes like two silken fans sweeping down. 'I ... I love you, Teresa ... and I don't want to hurt you. I can't bear the thought of what I might do.'

Teresa swayed, and almost before she could register what had happened, Zack's arm was around her waist, holding her up.

'You're *not* all right at all, are you?'

'I'm fine, I tell you,' she shot back, her voice sharper than she'd intended. She couldn't think straight. Her head was spinning and her heart was flying up, like a bird.

He loves me.

She stared around. The wedding seemed to recede away from them – become unreal. New dreams flooded in, swirling and blending with her wild erotic fantasies of vampire sex. She saw herself and Zack, walking hand in hand through a beautiful night, silent in contentment and companionship. For all eternity.

'Come on, let's get away. It's great ... but we need time to ourselves,' she gasped.

Zack looked doubtful, alarmed, almost angry. And Teresa knew it wasn't anything to do with breaches of social or wedding etiquette. 'Don't worry ... nobody will miss us. We're not the bride and groom.'

I wish we were. I'd give anything to be the Bride of Dracula.

'What's so funny?' Zack asked as they sped away from the wedding party. Teresa realised she must have laughed aloud. As they left the marquee, shadows were falling like a cloak across the garden.

'Nothing. Just silly thoughts.'

They were silly – but also deadly serious.

To *be* Zack's bride, she'd have no choice but to die.

Driven by some vague, dark compulsion, Zack headed for the maze again, drawing Teresa along at his side.

This is madness, he thought. We should have stayed with the wedding ... You'd be safe there, my love. I couldn't feed on you with an audience of hundreds.

And yet a part of him knew that he had it in him to do just that.

Now that he'd tasted the bliss of lovemaking and the beautiful alchemical blend of blood and sublime sexual pleasure, he knew that the comfortable arrangement that he and Teresa had shared until now would never be the same again. He couldn't go back now, but perhaps *she* could, if he could persuade her to leave his house and the danger he presented.

And in the meantime, somehow, he had to maintain control. He had to think. Reason. Explain to Teresa what had to be.

The tall fragrant hedges of the maze loomed around them as they entered. The night scents were cool and fresh, intoxicatingly sweet. But nowhere near as dizzying as the delicious odour of Teresa's perfume, and the delicate but piercing aroma of her sex.

'I hope we don't get lost.' She looked up at him as they walked, her face glowing in the light of the newly emerged moon. 'Or can you fly and see above the hedges and find a way out again?'

Zack shook his head, amused despite everything.

'Yet another myth from stories and movies.' He squeezed her fingers, almost wanting to moan aloud at how much the simple contact roused him. His fangs were already dangerously lengthened, just from holding hands. 'I can't fly and I can't turn into things. You'd be surprised how very normal most vampires are.'

'No bats? Wolves? Green mist?'

'Fortunately, no.'

She shrugged, and the slight, subtle lift of her breasts made a jolt like liquid silver speed through his veins. Everything she did, everything she said, and everything about the way she looked only made him more aroused. He was just about to draw her to a halt, and insist they return to the marquee when they turned a corner and found the centre of the maze. The stone benches sat in a silent, accusing circle around the dark pool where he'd spent his passion last night.

Teresa gasped.

'This is so beautiful! What a magical place!'

She drew him forwards, and then looked down into the near black water.

'I love it that I can see you,' she breathed, and then turned to smile at him.

Zack stared down too, looking not at his own faint reflection, but at the clear image of Teresa, her bare shoulders gleaming in the moonlight, beautifully revealed by her elegant dress with its narrow straps. As he watched, she pulled off the silk scarf that had been wound around her neck. Her throat was white and smooth, apart from the twin crimson punctures of his bite.

Lust, both for blood, and in the form of simple human desire, raged through him like a tidal wave. His penis stiffened like iron, and his fangs descended fully.

He had to get out of here. He couldn't resist. He had to be in her – and he had to feed.

Teresa watched the magical change. Crimson gleamed in Zack's eyes and the points of his sharp white teeth glinted in the moonlight. A frightening yet delicious feeling of weakness and yearning enveloped her. It was coming from him she knew, but she guessed it was a subconscious rather than conscious emanation.

It didn't matter which though, her body still sang with need and longing. Her skin tingled, especially around her bite marks, and between her legs her sex melted and grew liquid with raw desire. Moving without effort or conscious volition, she pressed herself against the length of Zack's body, tugging at his collar and then laying her lips against his cool throat as if that might compel him to reciprocate.

She could feel his great strength, and how he was using it to fight her and put her from him, but her own surge of strength and power was almost equal to him. Sighing, she wound her arms around him, opening her mouth on his neck, licking and tasting the delicious flavour of his skin.

'Teresa, no!' he groaned, but there was resignation in his low voice, and a pleasure that was impossible to hide. All these months with her he'd held back, and all the decades before, when he'd kept himself apart and out of temptation's way. They were like a great mass of dammed up emotion bursting forth, a force of nature that could no longer be turned or diverted.

His arms tightened around her, and as she threw her own arms around his neck, he cupped her buttocks, lifting her and moving her against the knot of his erection. She felt her feet leave the grass beneath her as he held her effortlessly, crushed against the length of his body.

'We mustn't, Teresa, we mustn't –'

It was a last-ditch attempt.

'Oh yes, we must,' she purred, wriggling and rocking sinuously against him.

For a moment, all around was a blur of motion, and then Teresa found herself lying on her back, on the grass. Zack was lying half over her, a hand moving seductively over her breast while he supported himself on the elbow of his other arm. Somewhere in the transition his jacket and his elaborate tie had disappeared, and his white silk shirt was hanging open, baring his chest.

Teresa laughed. She was naked on the turf.

'So ... you've changed your mind,' she murmured, lifting her knee, sliding it against him, her hips twisting, coaxing.

'Yes,' he said roughly, his hand sliding from her breast to her belly, fingers flexing, the middle one tracking down towards her cleft. 'But no biting ... absolutely no biting! I swear it!'

But his eyes were red and his fangs were long. Teresa shuddered, revelling against all reason in the power of her lover's most basic instincts.

And then he touched her, and as she moaned with longing, he howled, primal exultation ringing and rebounding in the intimate space enclosed by the high hedges.

Only his caress existed, only his long cool body, only his scent. All rhyme and reason and the world of the normal and the sane, cautious and prudent was forgotten. She groaned for the vampire's kiss, and the possession of his body. Somehow he was already naked and moving over her, his heavy penis searching, searching, and searching for its perfect sheath.

Teresa tilted her hips, inviting him and facilitating his thrust. Her hands grabbed at him, clawing at his back and cupping his backside, encouraging him, goading him on, her nails digging in, breaking his skin.

When he pushed inside her, her head went light and she wailed and sighed and thrashed as if she too were in thrall to the lust for blood. Her hips lifted, pushed, thrusting back at him. She wanted him to be inside her, really inside her – inside every nerve and cell and blood vessel. She wanted to be with him, and *be* him, right down to the tiniest denominator of what made them, and she wanted to be inside of him too.

They slid and rocked together, limbs working, bodies pressing and slapping against each other in a natural instinctive dance of the flesh. Great waves of delicious sensation swept through Teresa's belly, her legs, her arms, her fingers and toes. Even her hair seemed to be tingling with delight and almost standing on end.

But she knew there was more, and even in the midst of such a cyclone of pleasure, she recognised again the greater and more life-changing lure. Embracing its ultimate call, she arched her neck and offered her throat, her fingers digging deep into Zack's black curls to draw him to her.

He roared again, a huge sound resonant with joy and triumph, but also a fatalistic 'no' of horror and resistance. But it was too late, those basic instincts were in control.

The pain, when it came was immense. This was no little nip, and the drawing of a few mouthfuls of blood. This was the real thing.

Hard unforgiving teeth plunged through her skin, probing for and then finding the rich pulsing vessels they sought. Hot blood began to flow, sweet and abundant. Teresa moaned again as her pleasure spiralled and became unrecognisable. Perhaps the pain was pleasure? Or the pleasure was pain? She couldn't tell. She only knew the exquisite joy of feeding and being fed on by her love.

On and on it went, her sex rippling and clenching and contracting around Zack in time to the steady pulsing surge of blood from her throat. The sensations were sublime, and she was aware, somewhere in the centre of them, that Zack was ejaculating inside her, and yet he stayed hard, his cock unflagging, solid and cool.

She began to float, as if weightless, insubstantial. She was drifting on a sea of warm primitive feelings, cosseted and buoyed up by love, suspended in a drifting crimson cloud. The pleasure seemed to melt and change, become ever more languorous, drowsier and less substantial. There was no effort in the union now, just ease, and gliding, flowing sweetness . . .

From a great distance, she seemed to hear an agonised voice, crying, 'No! Oh no!' but it could have been merely her imagination.

Is this a dream? How strange it is. Am I awake or asleep?

Still drifting, Teresa became vaguely aware of motion, things happening around her and to her. It was disorientating, but she wasn't scared. Zack was with her. Zack was taking care of her.

With very little help from her, he was helping her back into her clothes, while she just stared around, dimly registering her surroundings and even her own body. She could smell blood, rich and tantalising. Staring at her own fingers, she found traces of red on the tips and around the nails, and it being the most natural thing to do, while Zack was searching for her shoes, she popped each finger into her mouth, one by one, and licked off the life giving fluid. It tasted just as appetising as it smelt.

And then she was being carried along, her arms around his strong neck, her face buried against his scented skin, against his unbuttoned collar.

'I'm so tired,' she murmured, nuzzling, 'I could sleep for a month ...'

'It's OK,' her beloved whispered, 'you'll soon be back in bed.'

Teresa wanted to say how nice that sounded, but before she could frame the words, she was already fast asleep.

8

It seemed to Teresa that it was many, many weeks before she finally woke up from that dream.

She recalled the carrying to bed, the putting to bed, and then the next morning and conversations with Zack as the two of them packed up their belongings and then drove back to town.

How easy and tranquil it had seemed, chatting to her friend – her buddy – about this and that, and making plans, some vague, some definite, for the weeks and months to come. The only thing that bothered her was the return of her tinnitus now and again. She'd resolved to see a doctor sooner or later.

What an excellent idea it seemed to begin to look for a new flat of her own while Zack was away, visiting his old friends at the Priory of St Benedict in North Yorkshire on retreat. Yes, it really was time she stopped presuming on the generosity of this kind man. She had some savings – in fact her bank account was unexpectedly healthy – and it would be fun to decorate a place exactly to her own taste. And with her out of his hair, Zack could get on with his research and his writing, and they could always pop around and see each other when she was settled, couldn't they?

She was sad to see Zack leave for Yorkshire, and she'd shed a few secret tears. But ever the thoughtful one, he'd arranged for his cleaning lady come housekeeper to put in a few extra hours in his absence, so Teresa would have some company around the place while she was looking for that flat.

Everything was planned, organised and trundling along smoothly. At least it seemed that way at first.

But then the changes began. Or perhaps it was just that she started to notice changes that had already occurred – and her memory began to sharpen.

And that wasn't the only thing that got sharp.

She began to wake in the night from hot red dreams about Zack. Wild erotic flights that left her aroused and yearning and voraciously hungry. But when she opened the fridge, there was nothing in it she fancied.

One night, she dove into the freezer and found some icy packages of Zack's iron shake – the ones he kept for emergency when fresh supplies were delayed for one reason or another. Inexplicably, her mouth began to water, and the shape of it felt strange and unfamiliar.

Defrosting the hard frozen red pillows, Teresa absently ran her tongue over the edges of her upper teeth – then squeaked out loud when she got the shock of her life.

Then suddenly she saw an image of his hand, fingers crooked, moving strangely.

But there was no need for a magician's pass now. The delicious odour of blood brought everything back. Everything he'd blanked out in his misguided attempt to 'save' her.

She smiled.

In the small hours of the morning, Zack let himself into the still, dark house. His housekeeper never stayed overnight, so it should be empty – but the back of his neck prickled when he sensed a vague presence.

Teresa!

She shouldn't be here. He'd deliberately stayed out of contact for the six weeks he'd been away, hoping it would be easier for both of them that way. It was difficult trying to blur the mind of someone as sharply intelligent as his beloved, and if they were separated, the dangerous memories would fade to nothingness.

But she was here. He could tell, but even if he hadn't been a vampire he would have been able to detect her. That was what a never-dying love could do for you.

Jumbled feelings roiled in his heart.

He felt pure joy that Teresa had stayed in his house – and red anger with her for resisting his influence and putting herself in danger.

Racing up the stairs, he felt almost alive. He could swear his heart was pounding in anticipation, and the blood was surging through his veins. It was an illusion, but despite his confusion, it was exhilarating.

The door to Teresa's room almost broke on its hinges, but the emptiness of her room made him want to howl. Had he been wrong? Was it just the memory of her presence he'd been sensing?

He smelt the air.

The essence of her was strong in the room. Maybe that was it? Her glorious perfume and the lingering sensual odour of her body made him catch the breath he no longer needed. He felt both unmanned and also wildly, insanely aroused at the same time.

Stomping away down the corridor, he sought his own room, still absorbing the scents of Teresa as he went.

In his own bedroom the lights were out, but he could still clearly see that there was a hump beneath his quilt, and tousled teak-brown hair poking out onto his pillow. In the blink of an eye, he was ripping back the covers.

Teresa peered up at him, rubbing her face sleepily. He knew it was feigned – he could sense her sharp mind rising to meet his.

'What the hell are you doing here?'

'I thought you'd be pleased to see me, Zack.'

Her delicate nightgown slipped from her shoulder as she sat up, baring her neck and shoulders, now perfectly smooth and unblemished again. Zack suppressed a groan as his cock went rigid and his fangs instantly lengthened.

He shook his head, more confused than ever.

He wanted her. He felt pure joy because she was still here and in his bed – but the danger, the danger. Last time, they'd gone so close to the edge that he'd feared they'd crossed the line.

'I am ... but I thought we'd agreed that you were getting a place of your own?' The words came out muffled. He had his knuckle pressed to his face, hoping to mask the state of his canines. There was still a chance to get out of this gracefully, without hurting her. There was still a chance to set her free, so she could live and not be cursed by the condition that defined him.

Teresa laughed – a pure twinkle of sound.

'You don't have to hide. I know what you are. I woke up from the spell you put on me.'

Zack dropped his hand from his mouth and glared at her.

'All the more reason for you not to be here. You know how dangerous I am to you.'

'I don't care.'

Her head came up, her chin lifting. She looked different somehow, he realised, more beautiful than ever if that were possible. Her skin was pale and creamy and her lips were rosy. There was a gleam in her eyes, dark and knowledgeable.

'Well, you should! You can't stay around me. You're not safe.' His fingers tingled with the need to touch her, especially when she came up on her knees in the bed, reaching for him, her face sultry and challenging. Unable to stop himself, he grabbed her by the shoulders, gently shaking her. 'You have to leave, Teresa. Please, for my sake! I couldn't bear it if I harmed you ... if I changed you.'

'Too late, my love.'

The words were quiet, but they seemed to land in the centre of the room like a great stone.

'No!'

Zack's words weren't quiet. His great shout seemed to bounce off the furniture.

Teresa was smiling at him, the beautiful colour of her eyes ringed with crimson. Her neat white teeth were made uneven by delicately pointed canines.

'But you didn't feed from me.'

He cradled her jaw, running his thumb lightly over the points of her fangs. They were rudimentary, only slightly pointed, not true vampire teeth.

Yet.

'I tasted a little of your blood on my fingertips. From where I scratched your back.'

Zack quickly wracked his memory, sifting through all the lore he'd studied when he'd first been changed himself. If she'd only taken a few drops, she could still revert. She could still be normal and live a human life. If she got away from him now, and took no more blood.

'Please, Teresa, you've got to go. If you stay around me the compulsion will only grow . . . and I won't be able to resist you.'

'Whose compulsion? Mine or yours?'

'Does it matter? Please, my love, just go!'

But her eyes were clear, despite the crimson. He sensed her intelligence. Her will. Her full knowledge of what lay ahead. And her desire for it.

Most of all, he read love in her expression.

'I can't go, Zack.' Her arms slid around him. 'I love you. I need to be with you.'

A sudden last urge to free her welled up.

'What if I don't love you?' he demanded, trying without success to shake her off him. But she was already far stronger than she'd been before, and she laughed softly, pressing her face, and her body, against him.

'You might be a vampire, Zack, but you're a poor liar.' She pulled open his shirt, kissing his skin. 'And I've already got ... well ... powers.'

She kissed him again, her tongue stroking against his collar bone.

'It's no use telling me you don't love me because I know you *do*!'

Oh, but you feel so good!

Teresa smiled against Zack's cool skin as she waited for him to admit what she knew was true. He didn't speak, but his arms closed around her. The sense of being enclosed, and of being cherished made her feel like swooning. It was an old-fashioned word, one she'd never have used before she met him, but it was the only one that fitted.

'I do love you.' His voice was low and clear, but she could tell that the confession cost him. 'I love you ... and I want to be with you forever.' His arms tightened, and he tilted his head back, as if looking to heaven for knowledge.

'So what's the problem, Zack?' She rubbed her face against his cold-as-marble skin, loving it smooth silky texture, loving the fact that it would never go slack, or sag, or grow sallow with age. Loving the simple joy of the contact.

His hand settled over her hair, gently stroking.

'But forever means just that, my love. Forever. And ever.' A deep shudder passed through him. 'And if you choose it, you'll never walk in the sunshine again. And in a few years, your friends, your family ... well, even if they wonder why they never see you much in the daytime again, they'll certainly start to notice that you're not ageing.'

He put her from him, looking into her eyes. Teresa saw that his eyes were reddened, and with her already-sharpened senses, she could taste his desire. Despite the stress of the moment, he couldn't stop himself wanting her.

'*You* are my friend, Zack. I love you and I want you, but you're my buddy too. You *always* will be.' She reached out, took his face in hers, made him look at her. 'My parents are dead ... my sister and I aren't close. And I'll deal with everything else when the time comes.'

'Are you sure?' His eyes were crimson now, burning – happy.

'Completely! Now come on, finish the job. I want to be like you, not just half and half.'

'With pleasure ... with pleasure, my love,' murmured Zack, his voice gruff with emotion as his arm swept around her again and with his free hand he cradled her face.

Tenderly, he kissed her, his soft lips sweeping over her mouth, then her jaw and on down her neck to the tenderest, most vulnerable spot. She felt his tongue caressing her skin, over the vein, as if soothing the place in readiness.

And then – ah, the pain of the bite! Sharp, blade-like fangs plunged in and immediately the blood began to flow and with it the pleasure. He was supporting her in his arms, his hold on her almost chaste, but it felt to her as if he were caressing and stimulating every nerve-end in her body, most of all her sex.

The sensation was sweet, mind-bending and exquisite, like tumbling and soaring at the same time. She felt both weak and strong, and the very quick of her body was shimmering and rippling with an intense sublime glow. As he drew on her powerfully, she spiralled to a peak, crying out and coming.

As she floated, still in that impossible state of ecstasy, he lifted his mouth from her neck and kissed her on the lips. She tasted her own blood like a sacrament –

and hunger surged in her to drink from a different source.

Still supporting her, Zack leant back, ripped open his shirt and, in the classic romantic vampire's gesture, he drew a nail across his chest, over his heart.

Dark-red blood oozed from the little wound, the ultimate temptation.

And the final step.

After this there would be no going back, no further chance to retain her humanity.

But as she looked up into her lover's red eyes, she embraced her choice.

Inclining forwards, she began to drink – and to change as Zack cried out in his own ecstasy.

Afterwards, they made long, slow, simple human love. Sliding and rocking against each other they kissed gently and stroked each other in leisurely exploration. There was no biting or exchange of blood, just pure sensual pleasure, sublimely heightened by supernatural senses.

Eventually, Zack lifted himself free of her, lay back against the pillows, and pulled her to him again. Teresa smiled. He no longer felt cold to her. Their body temperatures had equalized.

'So we don't bite each other any more then?' she observed, touching her fingertip to his chest where the little cut that she'd fed on was already as good as healed. 'Presumably I can't feed on you and you can't feed on me.'

'Oh we can, but only for mutual pleasure.' Zack's fingers slid down her back teasingly, and to her delight, Teresa felt lust begin to stir again. Before tonight, she would have been too exhausted to go again so soon after such a prolonged dance of love. But now she had strength and energy to spare and she could feel that Zack was ready again just as soon as she was.

'Ooh, I like the sound of that.' Her sex rippled spontaneously at the thought of Zack at her neck again.

'But for nutrition purposes, I'm afraid we're confined to animal blood from now on. Not quite as tasty, but still perfectly acceptable.'

'Don't worry, I've tried it. It's not bad.' She kissed his chest.

'I'm glad of that,' observed Zack wryly, his voice teasing, then immediately, she sensed him become more serious. She no longer had to look at his face to perceive his emotions, she simply *knew* them. 'It's a huge transition, my love. Your life has changed utterly now. Everything's different.' He paused, his strong arms tightening around her. 'But I'm here – I'll always be here. And I'll do everything I can to make things easier for you.'

And he would. She knew that. She had no doubts.

There was an adventure ahead, a different life and an unimaginably long one.

But as they began to make love again, her still heart glowed with perfect happiness.

Zack was her best friend as well as her lover – and everything was possible with him at her side.

Forever.

Under her Skin
Mathilde Madden

Day 1

She's running down the corridor. She hasn't stopped running since the letter came this morning. Running, running, running, running on adrenaline.

She tried to go to the library. The one here and the one at her parents' house, but she was so damn jumpy that the words wouldn't lie still on the pages of each book she tried to read.

But that doesn't matter. She doesn't need to read up on vampires now. She's known about such monsters since before she could talk.

She has to be at the castle by six. Time is getting short. She practically crashes though the door of the private hospital room at Cobalt.

Her mother looks up blearily, as though she might have been asleep in her chair – uncharacteristically crumpled. Her usually tight precise up-do is all skew-whiff and shedding tendrils of grey-brown hair around her face. Her eyes are red. She's been crying. Did she cry herself to sleep?

'Merle!' her mother says as she gets to her feet, the upper-crust bark of her voice shadowed with fatigue.

'How is he?'

'He's ... He's ...' Her mother trails away a couple of heartbreaking times and in the end she has to steady herself to stop the falter in her voice. 'He's the same. Comfortable. Critical.'

This is it. Merle just wishes she felt numb right now –

blank. She doesn't. She feels like she's going to be sick. She looks at her father in the bed which – along with the machinery that surrounds it – takes up much of the room. He seems to be nothing more than a mass of pipes and tubes and skin and sheet. Not really a person. Just a body. The beeping, flashing machines that are doing the work of his traumatised internal organs seem more alive than he does.

She crosses the room until she is close enough to touch the pale skin on the back of her father's limp hand. Her fingertips look so pink next to his. Thrumming with life. With blood. But she doesn't want to start thinking about things like that. About blood. Her blood. Her blood and who might want it. 'There's no chance of us finding an antidote ourselves?' she says, knowing there isn't, not knowing what else to say.

Her mother shakes her head. 'I'm not even sure what's in the poison. A cocktail of magic and science. Classic vampire work. Black Emerald Clan written all over it. He must have got it from their vaults. I've managed to identify some of the components but I'm nowhere near.' She indicates the bottles of failed potions on the window still. Each one contains a sparkling liquid. Some are rusty or red in colour. Most are golden – glittering with their broken promises.

Merle looks back at her father. 'Right.'

Merle's mother has this face. This this-is-my-final-word face. That's the face that is looking at Merle right now. 'I'm still not going to let you take up Cole's offer. This isn't your fight.' Merle has never defied that 'final' face before. She's also never got such a strong sense her mother *wanted* her to defy it before. She's telling Merle not to take up Cole's offer – of course she is, she's her mother. What else can she say?

Doesn't mean that's what she wants.

'But it is my fight,' Merle says. 'It is now.'

Merle's mother turns away and picks up Darius Cole's letter which is lying on the table by the bed. It's so typical vamp. Thick vellum, sealing wax and words designed to devastate. Merle's mother peers at it like she's looking for a loophole.

Merle knows she isn't finding one. 'It's the only way,' she says, coming up close behind her mother and touching her shoulder.

'Look, Merle.' Merle's mother turns and she's really close. Merle can smell her expensive old-fashioned heavy perfume lying over the scent of her grief. 'Your father and I . . . We never meant to involve you in anything like this. In our work. And the thing about Darius Cole, well, the thing about vampires in general, is they play games. They can out think humans. They find it fun to trick them. What it says in this letter, well, it just won't be as simple as that.'

'What it says in that letter is that if I don't go and spend 25 days with Cole dad will die.'

Merle's mother just looks at her. And Merle sees it sudden and sickening. Her mother is being asked to choose. Being made to choose between her daughter and her husband, and of course her mother knows she should choose Merle, but it hurts. While Merle is thinking this, her mother shakes her head and turns away.

'You want me to go, don't you?' Merle says to her back. 'Part of you does. Deep down.'

In a very quiet voice Merle's mother says. 'He's dying. We have to do something.' But when she turns back to Merle her face is severe and familiar. 'But not that. Charles would never forgive me if I let you anywhere near that vicious undead creature.'

Almost before her mother finishes speaking, Merle's father bucks up and begins to convulse in the bed. He screams loudly in real agony and starts to thrash around. The sheet slips and Merle sees his half-naked body, pale-grey and sheened with sweat. It hits her so hard it's like being winded. My father. My dad. *Daddy*. Broken and suffering. Dying. Merle takes a shocked step backwards.

Merle's mother has already grabbed a syringe of something from a trolley of medical ephemera. She dashes around the bed, shouting at Merle to get back and sticks the needle into the IV line. Merle's father stills quickly.

Merle's mother turns away from the bed. She's out of breath, her shoulders heaving. 'He's already so full of morphine I keep thinking the next dose'll kill him. And maybe that'd be kinder.' She looks like she's going to cry.

'Well, then,' Merle says. 'Look at him. You can't tell me not to go. How can I not?'

Merle's mother doesn't say anything.

'I have to be at the castle by six,' she says, knowing for sure now she has to do it. If she ever had any doubts they're gone now. If part of her hoped her mother was going to expressly forbid it.

Merle stiffens and takes a step towards the door. Then stops and look back at her mother who seems to be frozen by the bed. What is there for her to say?

Merle holds her eye. 'And when I get that antidote I'll do what you should have done years ago and put a stake through that bastard's silent heart.'

It takes a tube, a train, a taxi and a little more than an hour to get to Cole's castle. Merle takes the time to give herself a pep talk. Now this is really happening. After the distinct lack of any kind of eleventh-hour reprieve.

As the daughter of two of the most famous vampire hunters in the world – as the daughter of the founders of Cobalt – Merle knows more about the undead than most. She knows that they exist, for a start. She also knows that they are disgusting, rotting things and that the only good thing they ever did was decide to keep themselves completely separate from human society centuries ago. Darius Cole was a vampire who didn't agree with the Clan Council's ideas about segregation. He wanted to overthrow humanity. Enslave them for food. Taking down Cole was the reason Cobalt was set up in the first place. It represented human and vampire working together for the first time in hundreds of years – probably for the first time ever – all because of Darius Cole. And they'd succeeded. Thirty years ago Cole had been captured and Cobalt had handed him over to the Black Emerald Clan to be dealt with under their laws.

Merle grew up with Darius Cole as her personal bogeyman. She has always hated him more than anything. And that was before he escaped, killed or enslaved the Black Emeralds and started poisoning Merle's family.

One of the most dangerous things about Cole is that he has super highly developed psych-powers, even for a vamp. Cole can control minds like no other vamp recorded: telepathy, suggestion, persuasion, hypnosis. Merle knew that in 25 days he could potentially do anything to her. Twist her mind.

But she also knows that vamp psych-powers aren't irresistible. It's just a matter of keeping her emotions in check.

A lot of what is said about vampires isn't really true according to Merle's mother. But one of the legends definitely is. You have to invite them in.

Like all vamp places, the Black Emerald Clan's castle is heavily warded. Invisible and undetectable. Merle has the taxi driver drop her off in what looks like the middle of nowhere and throws the little iron ball that came with the letter into the trees. Reality fractures like broken glass, and suddenly the huge stately castle in front of her is so real it is impossible to imagine how this view looked without it a moment ago.

She crunches up the drive and pauses outside the

castle door, waiting for the exact dot of six. When her watch says 5.59 she reaches up, poised to grasp the enormous door knocker, but before her hand touches it the door creaks open.

The woman who peers around the doorframe, taking care to keep out of the last shards of sunlight, is clearly a vampire – she is also an image of pure decadence. She has a bird's nest tangle of blonde hair wound lopsidedly on top of her head. Her breasts, hips and lips are all lusciously plump. She is wearing a white froth of a dress that seems to reveal more of her luscious body than complete nudity would. She looks like Marilyn Monroe cast in some pornographic version of the life of Marie Antoinette. Except she looks like she'd been the one eating all the cake.

There are fangs in her mouth and some dried blood on her bottom lip.

She makes Merle feel totally sexless with her short straightish hair, and short straightish body. She's wearing plain blue jeans and dark-blue T-shirt with a muddy brown cord jacket. She hadn't wanted to look like she'd got dressed up. But the woman at the door makes her wish she'd found something a little more exhilarating to wear.

The woman not only exudes sex, she makes Merle feel like exuding sex is the only acceptable way to be. She feels herself starting to hunch her shoulders in the hope that the woman won't notice her comparative lack of breasts or hips. She takes a deep breath. 'I'm Merle Cobalt.'

'I know who you are, dear,' says the woman, before turning away and stalking into the castle. She looks like a ship at sail, rolling, swirling and billowing with every silky step.

Merle trots after her. The space beyond the imposing front door is an enormous entrance hall, five times the size of the reception at Cobalt. It's magnificent, totally old school vamp – circular and cold with echoey flagstones.

'Leave your case here,' the woman says, not looking round. 'You will follow me to the dungeon.'

'The dungeon?' The hairs on the back of her neck are tingling. Her stomach is flipping over and over. She's been feeling so sick with nerves for so long it's almost become normal.

The woman is already approaching a small wooden door that is secured with heavy bars. She draws them back and heaves the door open to reveal a flight of dank steps leading down into the realms beneath the castle. Then the woman glances back at Merle once – her gaze like steel – before starting to descend.

Swallowing hard, Merle follows her.

The steps go on for ever. Down and down, getting darker and colder and damper. The real world recedes. The only light is from some pathetic candles guttering in little recesses set into the walls. If this whole descent into the dungeon is meant to intimidate the wretched prisoner, it really works.

At the bottom of the stairs is a narrow corridor and leading off it at regular intervals are four small wooden doors with barred windows set into them. Cells.

Merle digs her fingernails into her palms as she follows the woman all the way along the corridor to the fourth and final door.

The woman turns and gives Merle a cold smile. 'You might know this story,' she says darkly. 'After your parents captured Darius Cole they turned him over to the Vampire Clan Council. He was found guilty of treachery and sentenced to live. To live here. In the custody of the Black Emerald Clan.' She yanks open the door which squeals on its hinges like it hasn't been used in centuries.

Merle gets a glimpse of a tiny dark space. A slickly wet floor. Black stone walls. A wooden bench along the farthest wall. 'In this very dungeon cell. He rotted for twenty-five years. Let's see how well you endure twenty-five days.'

Merle takes a deep breath, lifts her chin and stalks inside.

It isn't until she hears the bolts being drawn that she feels her throat start to ache with the effort of not letting herself cry.

Day 2

She really didn't think she would be able to sleep in the cell. But sometime later – must have been the next morning – she wakes up on the wooden bench. Her whole body aches.

She's hungry and thirsty and cold. And yet, despite how awful she feels, weirdly, she can't help thinking about Darius Cole. About the fact that she's facing 25 days like this, when he endured 25 years.

Did vampires feel the cold? Did they feel hungry and thirsty like this?

She's still thinking about this when the door to the cell squeals open. She must have become accustomed to the dark, because she has to screw up her eyes at the sudden invasion of light. A man is standing in the doorway.

'Darius Cole?' Merle says, her voice sounding scratchy thanks to her bone-dry mouth.

Despite growing up in a house of vampire hunters. Despite learning to fear Cole above all vamps. Merle had never seen a picture of him. She has no idea what he looks like. Vamps don't photograph and all the drawings that were done of him were handed over to the Black Emerald Clan by Cobalt along with Cole himself.

The man doesn't reply. Instead he takes another step

into the cell and Merle can see him properly. He's smiling and he's so damn vampirey it hurts. He has a swirl of silver hair, a refined jawline and a stance that is almost too erect. There is a strange sour smell in the room that seems to have come in with him. But is he Cole? Merle feels pretty sure he isn't going to tell her straight out.

He is carrying a small wooden tray that holds a plate of toast and a glass of water. Merle bites at her dry bottom lip and finds herself staring at the water.

The man sets the tray down on the floor and takes a few more steps towards Merle until he's standing right in the middle of the cell. She finds herself shrinking back against the wall.

'Hello, Miss Cobalt,' he says. 'Are you hungry? We don't really have much food, I'm afraid. I sent Kristina out last night to buy something for you – but she didn't really do very well.' He looks down at the tray with an expression of disdain.

'That's OK, really. Could I have the water now?' Merle stands up and takes a step forwards.

'Sit down!'

Merle sits right back down at once. The wisp of intimidation that she had felt from the moment the cell door opened suddenly explodes inside her chest. God, he can be scary when he wants to be.

'No manners, really,' the man mutters to himself then he meets Merle's eye. 'You should be chained.'

'What? Why?'

The man doesn't bother to answer. He just walks over and in a simple and business like way begins to unfurl a set of manacles mounted into a bracket above the wooden bench. The chains are rusty. They clatter and clank as he picks up one wrist cuff. This close up, the sour smell coming from him is almost overwhelming and undercut with a taint like rotting meat.

'I'm here of my own free will,' Merle says, trying to talk and hold her breath against the stench at the same time. Not easy. 'You don't need to chain me up.'

'Yes I do. For –' he pauses and looks thoughtful for a moment '– for authenticity.' And then he snaps a sudden cold metal bracelet around Merle's right wrist.

Merle stares at it in disbelief. Feeling the weight of the metal along with the weight of what he is saying. 'Authenticity! You mean they kept you chained for 25 years?'

'*He* was chained. You should be chained so you know how it was for him. That is the point of this, I believe. That you should know what they did to him. How he suffered for you.' He starts on the second cuff.

'"For me"? "How *he* suffered for me"? So you're *not* Darius Cole? And why was it for me?'

The man doesn't answer. Answering Merle's questions is clearly not his thing. He snaps shut the second bracelet and takes a step back. The cuffs around her wrists are attached to long chains, so long that the manacles would really only be a mild inconvenience rather than a restriction. The man smiles. 'Very nice. They suit you.'

Merle shakes her head with exasperation. She just wants to know now. She doesn't even care about the manacles or his creepy comments. '*Are* you Darius Cole? Was it you who was chained up down here for 25 years?'

The man laughs. 'Maybe.'

Merle frowns. She looks past him at the tray on the floor. Suddenly she stops caring about who this man is as the glass of water starts calling to her dry throat. She looks up at her captor. 'Are you going to let me have something to eat now?'

'Maybe. If you earn it?'

'If I earn it. How do I earn it?'

'Kiss me. Kiss me nicely and I'll bring the tray over.'

'Kiss you. I'm not kissing you, Cole, you murdering traitor.'

'Ah, so I am Cole?'

'They said Cole would play stupid games, so, yeah.'

'But all vampires love to play games with humans. Perhaps I'm just a friend of Cole's. Perhaps I just wanted to play with his new toy while he was busy. Perhaps I actually find you just as repulsive as you do me, blood sack.'

'So, you're not Cole?'

'Kiss me and I'll tell you.' The man bends down, his lips inching closer.

'Get away from me!' Merle lashes out at him, not really thinking about anything except how really, really grossed out she is. But she hits the man right in the face. Not so very hard, but it is enough of a shock that he staggers backwards. Away from her, taking his death-smell with him.

When he recovers himself – backing up even further – his face is livid.

Merle is shaking.

'Oh, now that wasn't nice,' he says. He turns and makes to leave. As he passes the tray on the floor he kicks out with his foot. The water spills, the glass breaks and the toast scatters on the dirty floor. 'Oh dear,' he says. 'That's a shame.' As he reaches the cell door and opens it he turns. 'See you tomorrow, Miss Cobalt.'

Day 3

'Hungry enough to kiss me now?'

He's back, holding a tray just like the one from yesterday.

Merle stares at him at him. She still doesn't know for sure if he's Cole or not. Which is weird because if some-one is your own personal bogeyman they might at least be kind enough to introduce that fact properly.

'Or thirsty? Let's see.' He sets the tray down on the floor like before, but this time walks over to Merle holding the glass of water.

Merle looks at it longingly. She'd actually managed to scrape up some of the water from the floor after he'd left yesterday, but it hadn't been enough and she's still horribly thirsty.

He's very close to her now, but holding the glass carefully out of easy reach. 'Just a kiss.'

She has to drink. She doesn't have a choice. She has to kiss him. But now he's this close the fact he might be Darius Cole isn't half so appalling as the smell of him. Like blocked drains on a summer's day. Merle holds her breath, screws up her face and pecks him on the cheek.

When she opens her eyes he hands her the glass and she drains it.

'Oh,' the man says, 'you *were* thirsty. I'll bring a bigger glass tomorrow. I am sorry. We really have no idea how much humans need to drink.'

'Eight glasses a day,' Merle says tautly. Like he didn't know that.

'As much as that.' He pauses and looks as if he is making some kind of mental calculation. 'I'll have Kristina bring a pitcher down.' He turns and walks back across the cell to collect the toast. As he picks it up he says, 'We gave him no blood for a month. Nothing. We didn't know what it would do. He started to hallucinate. We kept him naked and he knew we were watching him lose his mind. Do you see those marks there on the bench?'

Merle looks down next to where she's sitting. There are a number of deep gouges in the wood. 'Yes.'

'He bit right into it.'

Merle's brain seems a little clearer now she's had some water. 'You said "we", "*we* gave him no blood for a month". You're one of the Black Emerald Clan.'

The man nods at her as he carries over the plate of toast.

'I thought Cole had killed you all.'

'Not quite all,' says the man. Now Merle isn't so thirsty she can feel her hunger gnawing and burrowing inside her. The toast isn't particularly nice. Limp plasticky white bread, barely browned, but the sight of it is making her feel light-headed. The man reaches out and runs a finger down the front of her T-shirt. 'I won't bite you,' he says, clearly amused by this not-very-hilarious statement, 'then he'd kill me for sure. But now, your food, I'm afraid the price is another kiss for the old man. On the lips this time. Your food for my food.'

The man is gross, but, Merle knows, she can't go 25 days without food. So she just sits quite still and lets him move in and kiss her on her firmly closed mouth. His lips are inhumanly cold and the smell is nauseating.

'Ah, the warmth of it after so long on plasma packs. Too rich for an old man,' he says as he pulls back. Then he sets down the plate of toast before turning away, almost sulkily, and stalking out of the cell.

Day 4

No longer close to delirium from hunger and thirst, Merle starts to actually get bored.

So bored that she's almost pleased when the repulsive male vampire arrives. He's carrying a tray that holds a jug of water, a bowl of soup, an apple and a bar of chocolate. Merle's heart twists. Food that isn't toast! Instantly she feels almost desperate for the food on that tray, but at the same time slightly sick with the idea of what she might have to do to get it.

The vampire smiles. 'Cole has been a little more specific about what you are to receive for nutrition.'

Merle nods. Darius Cole. Here she is in Darius Cole's castle and after four days she still doesn't even know what he looks like. 'So he isn't ever going to come and see me himself? Not at all.'

'Darius Cole saw no one for months at a time. He didn't need food or water. When they did give him blood they just pushed it through that hatch there.' He points to the door where a much smaller hatch is set into the bottom. Merle had thoroughly examined it a couple of days ago while searching for any weaknesses her prison might have. She'd found none. 'They were scared of him. His powers to manipulate were legendary.'

'Is that how he finally escaped? How he took over this castle?'

'You ask such strange questions. What you should be doing is asking me what you have to do to earn this food.'

Merle swallows, looking back at the food. Her salvia glands tingle. 'What do I have to do?'

'You have to answer *my* questions.' The vampire smiles unpleasantly and comes and sits down on the bench next to her. Merle moves away from him a little, her chains clanking and clattering. They're making her wrists sore and achy. The vampire leans still closer – making her attempts to move away from him futile. He whispers, 'Does the idea of Darius Cole keeping you a prisoner here excite you?'

Merle swallows hard. She's been thinking about Darius Cole all her life. Thinking about scenarios exactly like this. Thinking about him. Obsessing. Wondering if he ever, even once, thought about her. But this imprisonment, the reality of this, well she can safely say this isn't exciting at all. 'I can't imagine anything less exciting. Being here on my own, hungry, thirsty, in the dark . . .'

The vampire smiles and everything horrible about him seems to increase several times over. 'Not the reality of it, the *idea* of it. Why do you think he wanted *you*?'

'To hurt my parents.'

'He could have imprisoned them?'

'This is worse for them, much worse.'

The vampire cocks his head at her. 'OK, let me put things another way, Miss Cobalt, did the idea of Darius Cole, a notorious dangerous vampire, your parent's nemesis, wanting you to come and spend time with him in his castle excite you? Did it *arouse* you?' He raises his eyebrows like he's her co-conspirator. 'Did you think he planned to desecrate you?'

And, oh, God, that's the question. The one she's been torturing herself with since they got the letter. Was part of her thrilled by the idea of this? Not the reality. The idea. Her nightmare wanting her. She knew she couldn't hide feelings this strong. Not from a vampire. The blood rises to her face. She tries again to move away but there's nowhere to go except off the bench onto the floor. There's only one escape route.

Merle turns to look the vampire right in the eye, holds his gaze while the blood rushes in her ears and her cheeks grow hotter and hotter and she swallows hard and says, 'Yes.'

The vampire stands up. 'And now you are disappointed that he hasn't.'

Merle gets up too. 'No, I . . .'

'That wasn't a question.'

Day 5

When the vampire appears the next day he seems rather more vigorous. He carries a similar tray to yesterday's and sets it down before he approaches.

'Yesterday, the questioning, that was Cole's orders. He wanted to know about that stuff. And he was watching me with his telepathy so you got an easy ride. Today is different. If you want *this* food remove your clothes.'

'What?'

'You heard me.'

'But when you kissed me, you said it was too much.'

'Yes, well, perhaps I was wrong about that. Perhaps it was too little.'

Merle shakes her head, mostly in disbelief – some horror, but she's not actually that scared because she knows she'd rather starve. 'I'm not going to take my clothes off. There's no way.'

'Fine, I'll do it for you.' The vampire rushes across the cell at her, his dark coat billowing out behind him. Merle is sitting on the bench and he knocks her back, hard against the wall. Before she even realises it, he yanks at her T-shirt so hard that the fabric starts to tear. She's screaming.

With a grunt of effort, he pulls her down onto the floor. She's kicking and scratching at him. He's so strong.

Then a familiar breathy voice above them says, 'Oh for goodness sake, use your weapon. Hit him like this.' Merle looks over the vampire's shoulder and sees Kristina standing over them, looking almost bored. She bends down and picks up some of the slack from Merle's chains and uses the doubled length to strike the vampire's skull. He collapses onto Merle's chest.

'See. Easy,' says Kristina. 'You know that might be why Darius wanted you to wear the chains. He used them as weapons every chance he got.'

Merle's pushes the unconscious vampire onto the floor and gets up shakily. 'Well, I guess I'm not an expert in these things. Dungeon self-defence.'

Kristina gives a snorting laugh. She picks up the tray of food and brings it over. 'God,' she says, putting it down on the bench, 'is that all he brought you? I made much more. He was probably trying to make sure you were always hungry, the dirty sod.' She pauses a moment then looks at Merle with one hand on a curving hip. 'He was only doing it for the kick of playing with you, you know. He wasn't actually attracted to you.'

'Oh,' Merle says, not really sure what to think about that. 'Right.'

'I'm just saying that because I hate the stereotype that vampires are always trying to get it on with humans. It's the biggest lie out there. We're not interested in you like that.'

'Right,' Merle says again.

Kristina claps her hands together. 'Now eat up and I'll try and find the rest of your food. That old corpse Oberon will probably try and claim that he doesn't remember how much humans eat. But I do.'

As she leaves, Kristina takes hold of Oberon's body by the legs and drags him out of the cell.

Day 6

The next day Kristina brings the food.

As Merle is eating she says, 'OK, Darius has dealt with Oberon and he says he'll come and see you himself later. How about that?'

'Um, OK.' And suddenly Merle doesn't know what to think. Maybe she'd resigned herself to the idea that she wasn't ever going to meet Cole face to face. That maybe that was part of the game he was playing. But maybe this is still part of the game. He's making the rules after all.

'He says he is sorry, too,' Kristina says, pouring out a cup of coffee. 'He made it pretty clear I was to tell you that.' Kristina gives Merle the coffee and takes her empty plate away. 'You're getting another meal later, by the way.'

'Wow, it's getting like a five star hotel around here.'

Kristina gives Merle a sour look. 'Well, as you mention it Darius did also say I should ask if there was anything you wanted.'

'The antidote to what Cole gave my father.'

'Yeah, yeah, let's take it as read that you asked for that and I told you no, shall we? Anything else. Something within reason perhaps?'

'Something to read?'

'Now that I can do,' Kristina says, her ever-changing mood flipping over back into perky. She picks up the tray of empty dishes and starts for the door.

'And some light to read by,' Merle shouts as the cell door slams shut.

Kristina doesn't return that day. But the promised second meal is slid through the hatch at the bottom of the door.

And later, as she's drifting off to sleep, Merle thinks of Darius Cole. Of how it must have been for him locked up here all alone.

Did you think he meant to desecrate you?

'And you said "yes".'

Merle sits up, startled. There's someone standing in the darkness of the furthest corner. A tall lean figure – achingly still.

'Darius Cole?'

'You know who I am, Merle,' he says. His voice has a soft mesmeric quality. It almost sounds like it's coming from somewhere else.

'You can read my mind.'

'I'm in your mind, Merle. You're dreaming.' And he steps out of the shadows. Darius Cole. Her nightmare. Her forbidden. Her taboo. He's standing right in front of her. And it's so strange to think that she never knew what he looked like until now. Stranger still that somehow she sort of recognises him.

As he emerges into the dim light, a long forgotten memory flares. He's so familiar.

He has thick dark hair that hangs just lower than his collar. He's wearing dark colours, black and grey, soft fabrics. His style is informal, like an off-duty vampire. Sort of vampy-lite. He's tall and lean. Hard. Holding himself in a way that makes her sure that he is muscular and taut under his clothes with more strength than his tight physique would suggest. He has a long thin nose and a mouth that has a mean little suggestion of a top lip paired with a bottom lip that is almost obscenely sensual and full.

He moves towards her and there's nowhere to go but harder against the wall 'What are you doing here, Cole? In my head. What do you want?'

'Didn't Kristina tell you I'd come. Here I am.'

'She didn't say you'd come in a dream.'

'She didn't know. She's a dreadful eavesdropper. But she can't listen to us this way, can she?'

'She can't listen to us? Listen to us doing what?'

'Oh, Merle, is your mind still on your desecration?' Cole says, laughing a little, 'You are so very endearing. You don't know whether to be scared of me or excited by me, do you?' He takes another few steps forward and drops into a crouch in front of her. She can see his face very clearly now. Dark eyes, stubbled skin, shaded brows – the sharp, bright flash of his teeth: his fangs.

'That's not true. I'm not scared of you, and I'm not turned on either, all I am feeling right now is how much I want to go home to my family.'

'Don't tell me lies, Merle. You know I can read these things in you as easily as you can read a newspaper.

'Well, your reading's off. Go and read something else.'

'Oh, I'll go. Very shortly. I will leave you alone, I promise. And you will ache with disappointment when I do. But first I want to tell you something. I want you to be assured that nothing bad is going to happen to you while you're here under my charge. At the end of your twenty-five days you will be free to walk out of here with an antidote that will restore your father to exactly as he was. Neither I nor any member of my household will touch you or violate you in any way. Unless you request it.'

'Unless I request it? I'm not going to request . . .' She trails off and screws up her face. 'And anyway, it's a bit late for that, isn't it?'

'I know.' Cole glances down. 'I know I shouldn't have left you with Oberon. I just wanted you to know how it felt. To be scared and alone. Abandoned. I'm sorry. I should be the last person to wish that on anyone.'

'They really kept you down here, alone in the dark like this, for twenty-five years?'

There's no reply . . .

Merle opens her eyes. She's alone in the cell.

She gets up from the bench and checks every corner as far as the limits of her chains will allow. But nothing. Not even a rat.

When she finally lies back down it takes her forever to get back to sleep. She half hopes that Cole will still be there in her dreams.

He isn't.

Day 7

'Who ordered books?' Kristina cries as she flings open the cell door.

Merle sits up, rubbing her eyes. 'What?'

Kristina is pushing a small trolley. 'Books. I've brought your books. Oh, and some muesli and some orange juice. And a newspaper. It's today's paper. God knows where it came from. Someone must have gone out this morning before it got light.'

I can read these things in you as easily as you can read a newspaper.

Merle gets up and walks over to the trolley. She picks up the paper. That day's copy of *The Times*. She turns the pages, forgetting the chains on her wrists for a moment. One hits the orange juice and sends it flying.

'Oh yeah,' says Kristina, 'that reminds me.' She produces a large iron key and grabs Merle's left wrist.

Merle watches in a daze as the manacles fall away one after another, leaving red raw skin behind.

She rubs it, feeling a kind of conflicted gratitude. She wants to thank Kristina, but at the same time, she knows she's one of them. Part of the problem. She rubs the damaged skin on her wrists harder, to remind her of what's happening. 'You can tell Darius, I mean, you can tell Cole, that orange juice and newspapers don't make this comfortable. I'm still locked in a cell.'

After Kristina has gone, Merle finishes her breakfast and looks through the books. They clearly all come from the castle library. They're history books – a complete vampiric history series. A history she knows well. The stuff she was raised on. Her bedtime stories.

It begins with the twelve Vampire Clans and the forming of the Clan Council. Detailing the peace pact to stop killing humans 250 years ago. The law about not converting humans into vampires without unanimous Council approval. The eventual withdrawal of the vampires entirely from any contact with human society. The self-imposed seclusion in their hidden castles that lasted more than a century.

Had lasted until the rise of Darius Cole.

But even reading these familiar stories is better than staring at four dark walls. She ends up reading all day.

When she finishes the book that ends with the beginning of Cole's rise to power, she notices she still has two more volumes of the series to go. Strange. This is where most history series ended. Cole is usually thought of as too recent to be included in vampire history yet. Too unresolved. She picks up the last two volumes one at a time and skims through the pages. They're all about Darius Cole. The rise and fall of Cole and his Righteous Power movement. Neither of these books had been in her parents' library. She'd never read anything about Cole. She only ever knew what her parents had told her about him. Evil. Tried to turn vamps against humans again. Too strong for vamps to control themselves.

The books follow that same story. Cole came from nowhere. A vampire with extraordinarily strong psych-powers and an agenda. Righteous Power – the notion that vampires were a superior race, that they should use their psychic abilities to enslave and control humans. RP wasn't a new idea, but Cole brought this dangerous rhetoric back. Seductive and smooth and with those damned psych-powers, the fact that he had no clan and no lineage hadn't seemed to matter. Cole had quickly converted three of the vampire Clans to his dangerous way of thinking.

That was when the Clan Council had decided they needed help to contain him. Vampires, it seemed, were helpless against Cole powers and so the Council turned to humans.

Merle turns the page. The next chapter in the book is titled 'Cobalt'. On the facing page is a black and white picture of her parents. Her mother. The same tall elegant creature, but much younger, without a single grey hair. In the monochrome of the picture her shiny dark brown locks look jet black. Next to her stands Merle's father. A shade taller, with the slightly flared nose that Merle inherited, too much pale hair and a crooked grin that looks slightly untrustworthy.

Merle stares at the picture for a long time thinking of her father in his hospital bed and her mother crying herself to sleep in the armchair beside him.

After Kristina has been and gone with more juice, another newspaper, eggs and a mug of coffee, Merle picks up the book again. It's still open at the picture of her parents. She fell asleep staring at it the night before.

But now she turns over and reads on.

Cole was massing an army to storm the castle of the Black Emerald Clan. This castle. The army marched by night and were incredibly vulnerable to human attack during daylight hours if their whereabouts was known.

Somehow Cole was captured when he left the march to travel alone to London. After sometime in captivity, Cole revealed the whereabouts of his army. Betrayed them. They were all killed by a Cobalt team and Cole publicly denounced his previously held beliefs in Righteous Power.

No one knew why Cole had done it. What was he promised in return for his soldiers' lives? His release, perhaps? Mercy? He certainly wasn't shown any. He was handed over to the Black Emerald Clan and sentenced to live by the Clan Council. This – the book makes clear – is the most severe punishment the council had at its disposal.

Merle looks around the little dark cell where she's sitting. Twenty-five years. It's impossible to imagine. And if everything Oberon told her was true: the solitary confinement, the starvation. The chains had started to hurt her wrists after less than a day. What would it have felt like after twenty-five years?

'Now you see how hard they had to work to break me?'

'Darius?'

'Hello, Merle.' She looks up from her book and he's standing right in front of her. Looming. His hair and clothes and eyes so dark in the gloom of the cell that his white skin seems to glow. She has to force her eyes away from his mesmerising face. But when she lowers her eyeline, she finds the dark fabric of his crotch is right in front of her face.

So it's a relief when Darius drops into a crouch in front of her and smiles earnestly. 'You see what they did to me? Do you understand? Forced me to turn traitor. Made me renounce a set of beliefs they'd invented for me. Public humiliation. Sentenced to live. They did everything they could think of to make me suffer. Everything vicious and cruel. They wanted me to suffer forever. Why do you think they were so scared of me?'

His face is so elegantly pretty and perfectly nasty. She hates him. She knows she needs to keep remembering that. She takes a sharp breath and narrows her eyes. 'Because you were a murdering bastard. Because you *are* a murdering bastard. You're killing my father right now.'

'I know. It's very hard for me that that was what I had to do. I am sorry. Even after everything Charles Cobalt helped to do to me I know that now he is just a weakened old man now. I wish there had been another way.'

'There is. Let me go. Give me the antidote and leave them alone.'

'Leave them alone? Maybe I could do that. But leave you alone? Never.'

Again, she has to force herself to look away from him. She looks down at her dirty jeans. 'Why? What do you want with me if it isn't about them?' She pauses as a nasty thought catches her by surprise. 'I'm not a ... not a virgin or anything. If it's that. If that's what you want. Well, I'm not.' And that's it – thinking about Cole wanting to take her virginity, which means thinking about him having sex with her – she's blushing. Hard. She hates the way her skin always betrays her at the most crucial moments. She tries to slow her breathing – an anti-blushing technique she read in a magazine once –

but it's no use. Her face is getting hotter and hotter. And that just embarrasses her even more.

Suddenly – moving quick and sharp – Cole reaches out and catches hold of her chin. He runs the pad of his thumb slowly over her heated cheek. When he speaks his voice is slightly thick. He's very clearly and very suddenly aroused. Not bothering to try and hide it. 'God, oh. I love that you do that.'

She tries to pull away, but his grip on her is incredibly strong. 'Do what? Don't. Stop it.' She puts one palm flat on his chest in an attempt to push him away.

But he doesn't seem to notice her protests. He strokes her cheek again, mesmerised. His touch is deliciously cool where she feels most heated. His voice is dark, slow and heavy. 'I love that you blush. It means I can see your blood. Under your skin. Do you blush anywhere else? Let me see. I want to see you. So beautiful. I want to see your skin, your pink.' He shoves her and she's forced back hard against the wall. He traps her there with his body and starts pulling at her T-shirt, yanking it up.

'No! No! Stop.' Somehow she wrenches herself out of his grip and pulls her T-shirt back down.

Cole meets her eyes and seems to suddenly hear what she's saying. He takes his hands off her and stands up, taking a couple of stumbling steps backwards. He's shaking his head. 'Oh, God, I'm sorry. I'm so sorry. Your blood, it made me . . .' he says, backing away from her. 'It's just so difficult to . . . Oh.'

He bites his plump bottom lip and turns away.

She wants to tell him to wait, but she forces herself not to by scratching at the sore patches the chains made on her wrists.

Day 9

'Is he coming again today?' Merle says, wondering if there is any chance her enquiry sounds casual.

Kristina looks up from where she's clearing away the dinner plates. She's smirking. 'No. He said he was busy today.'

'Oh.' Merle squishes the urge to ask what Cole is busy doing. Trying to find another conversational tack, she says, 'So are you and Oberon all that's left of the Black Emerald Clan now?'

Kristina shakes her head. 'Yeah,' she says. There's no emotion in her voice. But usually, when Kristina speaks, it is all about emoting something.

'So did Darius kill all the rest of them? Why did he keep you and Oberon alive?'

'I really don't know,' says Kristina tightly. 'And much as I'd *love* to spend the evening entertaining myself by trying to guess Darius Cole's motives, I can't help thinking we could find something more fun to do.'

'What? *We* could?' It seems like forever since Merle got to do anything that could be described as 'fun'.

'Well, Darius said I should make sure you don't get bored.'

'Bored? I've been down here nine days!' Merle points at the place on the wall where she's been making scratch marks to count the days. (Almost halfway.) 'Why is he considering my mental health now?'

'Oh, don't be like that. He really is trying to make this OK for you, you know. I think it took him this long to even work out that you might be bored. Vampire minds and humans are . . . different. And he's even more out there than just a normal vamp. He might have jaw-dropping powers of psych, but, really, sometime he misses the little things. Come on.'

Merle realises that Kristina is holding the cell door open for her. As she stands up, her legs start to shake.

Feeling slightly giddy with the freedom, Merle follows Kristina along the narrow corridor outside the cells. She stops outside the last one before the steps to ground level and looks in through the barred window. She beckons Merle over.

Oberon is sitting in a cell much like Merle's. He's manacled and sitting on the wooden bench, slumped up against the wall.

'Is he OK?'

Before Kristina can answer her, Oberon's eyes snap open and he's off the bench and rushing forwards, stopping just short of the door at the limit of his chains. Merle screams and jumps back.

Kristina laughs. 'Don't worry. He's just going a bit crazy because he hasn't had any blood since Darius locked him back in here. You smell like food to him right now.'

Merle steels herself and peers back through the window. Oberon has slumped to his knees on the floor just inside the door. 'Will he die?'

'Already dead, technically. But, no, if he doesn't get any blood he won't die. He'll just get strange. He's already losing it. The only records about what happens to a vampire if you starve them are the ones on Darius. But he was very strong mentally. Oberon seems to be breaking down much more quickly.' Kristina shrugs. She really doesn't seem to care.

'Well, what's going to happen to him?'

'Ah.' Kristina's face lights up. 'That's where you come in. Darius says you should decide if he gets fed today.'

Oberon obviously overheard this because from behind the door his thin voice says, 'Please.'

'What? Why? Why do I have to decide?'

Kristina shrugs. 'Darius thought that would be appropriate after what he did to you.'

Inside the cell Oberon moans, 'Please, Miss Cobalt, I'm sorry. Please have mercy.'

Merle feels queasy. She doesn't want anything to do with Oberon. She certainly doesn't want to hear him begging her for mercy. 'Well it *isn't* appropriate,' she says sharply, sort of holding it together. 'It really, really isn't. If this is what you brought me here to see I'd rather be back in my cell.'

Kristine nods calmly. 'OK. Then he starves. I'm not allowed to feed him unless you say so.'

Merle can't bear it. She remembers how scared she was when she was first brought here. How unsettling it was to be locked in, hungry, thirsty and not even know-ing if she'd been forgotten about. 'Fine,' she says, tightly, 'feed him.'

When Kristina reappears from Oberon's cell – Merle elected to wait outside – she looks a little breathless. She's been a long time.

Merle raises her eyebrows at her, but she just says, 'OK, now follow me,' and begins to lead the way up the steps out of the dungeon.

'What? Where are we going now? '

Kristina smirks back over her shoulder. 'Come on.'

They emerge into the entrance hall. Merle blinks and sways. Kristina leads the way to a huge sweeping flight of red-carpeted stairs. Merle pauses at the bottom. 'Kris-tina? Where are we going?'

Kristina turns. She was already halfway up the first red-carpeted flight. 'Your bedroom.'

'My bedroom?'

'Yeah. You're going up in the world. Darius has decided you can have a room with a window. Although you won't be able to open up the curtains, of course.'

Merle is still at the bottom of the stairs. 'This is an actual room. With a bed.'

'Yeah.'

'And it's not, like, in Darius's own bedroom or next to it or anything.'

'No,' says Kristina, with teasing chastisement in her voice. 'You're on the first floor, same as me. Darius is on the second. But don't be disappointed. The rooms are nicer on the first floor. And Darius can walk down a flight of stairs if he wants to bother you in the night.'

Merle feels that damn blush start and she puts her head down as she follows Kristina up the stairs.

The rooms on the first floor are indeed nice. Very nice. Merle's is turquoise and gold, with frills and fantasia dripping from every lacy surface. She has a real bed, too. A four poster. She drops onto it gratefully. The softness of the mattress – after nine days and eight achy nights on a wooden bench – is almost orgasmic.

Kristina laughs as Merle sighs out loud. 'I'll tell him you're pleased then.'

Merle rolls over onto her stomach, remembering something, and says, 'What were you doing all that time? In that cell with Oberon?'

'What?'

'In the dungeons. You were a long time and there were *noises*.'

Kristina smirks. 'Nothing really. Just giving him his blood.'

'You were just feeding him?'

'Kind of?' Kristina tips her head on one side. 'Look, a girl with your lineage has got to know about Blood Rites, right?'

'My lineage? You mean because of who my parents are? The stuff they taught me about vampires was more about how they're a stinking abhoration.' Merle bites her lip. 'Sorry.'

'S'OK. I know what Cobalt think about vampires. I

know you're a Cobalt.' She shrugs. 'So you don't know about the two sorts of blood?'

'Er, no.'

'You don't know about ... OK, well, there are two types of blood to a vampire. It's like food-blood and sex-blood. Feeding, that's drinking human blood, that's, like, food. Then there's tasting, that's completely different. That's when you take a little of another vampire's blood. It's like sex. *Just* like sex. When you taste the blood of another vampire that's like the orgasmic part of sex.'

'That's, uh, weird.'

Kristina shrugs again. She's the shruggy sort, really. 'Seems normal enough to me.'

'And it can't be with a human. Between a vampire and a human?'

Kristina almost spits her response to this. 'No. It can't. Not ever. Vampires do not perform the Blood Rites on humans. Never.' She looks almost angry to be asked. She jabs a vicious finger at Merle. 'You could have sex with a vampire, with Oberon, say, and he could fuck you, make you come and everything. That could happen. But he wouldn't feel anything much. He'd stay hard no matter what you did. Vampires don't get off on doing it with humans. It's the biggest myth out there. Vampires don't get turned on by humans anymore than you get turned on by looking at a plate of spaghetti Bolognese. Humans are food, other vampires are for sex.' Kristina is shaking. Enraged. Not so shruggy now.

Merle actually shrinks back a little across the bed. A moment ago she was feeling so friendly toward Kristina that she felt guilty telling her how her parents had taught her to think of vampires. Now she's suddenly terrified of her. After all, she is a vampire. A monster. 'Humans are food? Isn't that like a Righteous Power thing?'

Kristina shrugs. 'Righteous Power is illegal now.'

'Even in Darius Cole's house?'

'This isn't Darius Cole's house. This is actually Oberon's house. You should hear him on that subject right now.' She even cracks a smile then but Merle can still see her bristling anger.

Day 10

The next day Kristina brings Merle her breakfast in her new bedroom and asks if she wants to come and torment Oberon again. 'You could find out more about Blood Rites.'

But Merle gives her a firm negative.

Later, when Kristina returns, wantonly dishevelled and flushed, Merle says, almost thoughtlessly, 'So who does Cole perform his Blood Rites with?'

Kristina picks up an apple left over from breakfast. 'Me. Or Oberon sometimes, but mostly me. There's only three of us left here.' Shrug. She brings the apple up to her mouth and sinks her fangs into it.

'So, are you Cole's lover?'

Kristina pulls the punctured apple out of her mouth with an expression of distaste. 'Ew. I really don't know how you can eat these things. Darius doesn't take lovers.'

'But you said yesterday about the Blood Rites. About how vampires need another vampire . . .'

'He does *that* with me. Like I just said. God, does he ever. Fuck, you know. With the psych-powers. Woah. You ever had sex with someone who could read your mind? Like nothing I've ever . . . In fact, what with him and Oberon I'm having to double up on my plasma packs to keep my strength up. But I'm not Darius's lover.' Kristina stops and smiles. A smile that's more resigned than happy. 'Vampires usually bond. Completely. Like a life-mate type of thing. To a vampire a lover means someone exclusive. Someone forever. And, like I just said, Darius doesn't take lovers.'

'Why not?'

'Probably because it would ruin his smouldering locked-in-a-dungeon-for-twenty-five-years-lonely-freak image.'

That night Merle dreams about Darius again. It isn't like the dream she had before – all hyper-real with him appearing to be right there in the room. This dream is far more wispy and loose. She's lying next to him, with him propped up on his elbow looking down at her. She doesn't know where they are, some nameless dreamscape. All she knows, all she is sure of, is that she's in love. In the dream, she is utterly in love with Darius Cole.

Dream Darius runs the backs of his fingers against her cheek. They are deliciously cool against her heated skin. She's blushing. Her face is hot. Darius smiles down at her.

'I love to see your blood under your skin,' he says. His voice sounds like it had the first time she dreamt about him. Like it's coming from somewhere else.

Darius is wearing the same dark clothes as ever. Merle is wearing a revealing froth of a white dress – rather like the one Kristina wears. Darius says, 'I know another way to make your blood rise to the surface.' His voice is soft, muffled and cracking with desire.

His hands are on the hem of her slutty dress. He pushes it up almost to the top of her thighs. She squirms a little at the exposure, but lets him do as he wishes. With her skirts out of the way, Darius strokes the pale flesh where her thighs give way to the planes of her slim boy-hips. She's so aroused. Wet under the lace. Wet inches from his fingertips.

She hears the noise first. Then sees it. Then feels the sting. Then realises that he has just slapped her. Very hard. Looking down her body, she sees a pink mark appear high on her thigh.

But there's someone else in the bedroom.

'Oh,' Darius says, his voice full of weakness and desire, 'you are too beautiful.' And he bends his head and runs his cool tongue over the heated place he has made.

There is someone else right on Merle's bed. But she can't open her eyes. She can't leave the dream. She knows that Darius is going to make love to her.

She sighs under the touch of Darius's tongue.

Someone else. Not someone in the dream. Someone in reality. A weight next to her on the mattress. Someone kneeling there.

Merle opens her eyes. The dream splinters. 'Darius?' she says, still half sleep-headed.

It's very dark in the room, no moonlight with the curtains so tightly closed. Merle can just make out the bed canopy floating above her before someone is on top of her. Holding her down, pain in her neck.

She cries out, but the sound is trapped by a hand on her mouth. She writhes and fights, but whoever is holding her is too strong . . .

Day 11
She opens her eyes. The bedroom is dark. Someone is in the room with her.

She feels something – a pin prick – on her arm and a soft dark voice says, 'You need to sleep, Merle.'

Day 12
She wakes again still in her bed. She tries to sit up, but feels so dizzy she almost immediately collapses back into her pillows. With a grunt she drags herself upright again to sees Darius, sitting across the room in a wing-chair and looking at her.

'Where am I? What happened?'

Darius doesn't say anything. He gets up and walks over to the bed. He takes her chin in his hand and moves her head from side to side. He looks into her eyes one after another. He's never been this close to her before. Her heart is racing. His face is less than an inch from hers. She stares at that wanton bottom lip as he opens her mouth – pulling on her lower jaw with his thumb hooked over her bottom teeth – and looks in there too.

'Darius!' she says, suddenly coming to her senses and pulling away from him.

'Do you feel well?' he says, standing up.

'Yes. I think so. A little dizzy. What happened?'

'Kristina. She nearly snuffed you out. I came by just in time. Luckily you were not at the point where you would have had to drink my blood to survive. So do not fear, you are still human. We didn't have to break the laws against conversions.'

Merle's fingers touch her neck. But there's nothing there although it feels tender.

Darius watches her and says, 'The puncture heals fast. There is a little bruising. That'll go soon. You were very shocked and weakened. I gave you sedatives. You've been sleeping for more than twenty-four hours. It's day twelve now, I expect you're counting.'

'Kristina? Why would she . . .?'

'She is jealous of you,' Darius says in a very plain matter-of-fact way. 'I am sorry. I thought she was fully controlled. She is fearful of me and I didn't think she could tell when I was in her mind watching her. Perhaps she is getting better at controlling her own psych-powers. Or perhaps she was lucky.'

Jealous? She finds it hard to believe that Kristina, who looks like a debauched angel and regularly performs the divine-sounding 'Blood Rites' with Darius, could be jealous of *her* – the girl who spends her time locked up, red-eyed and dowdy. 'Where, where is she?'

'Kristina? In the dungeon. Now Oberon's the one playing jailer. I expect he's having some fun with that.' Darius turns and gestures to the table where Kristina usually puts Merle's food. It's laden with fruit and cheese and bread. 'I have to go now, but there are some things for you. It is important that you eat now. I'll lock you in again. For safety.'

As he turns to leave, Merle says, 'If you weren't in Kristina's mind just then how did you know to come to my room and save me?'

Darius stops and turns a little so he's angled half towards her, half away. 'Because I was in *your* mind. You remember.'

Day 13

Merle is lying on her bed, reading a magazine, when the door bursts open.

Darius stalks in, looking so stern and haughty that she finds herself drawing away from him across the bed. He's dressed a little differently. In a long black frock-coat and black knee boots. He looked much more like a vampire *ought* to look. Formal, even. Formal for him.

Darius stands aside and Oberon strides into the room next. He's towing Kristina, leading her by a rope that is tied around her wrists.

'Anywhere,' Darius says.

Oberon flicks the rope in a way that sort of flings Kristina onto the floor in one corner. Merle flinches, but Kristina doesn't even glance at her.

Darius says, 'You can go.' He's looking at Oberon.

'I'd like to stay,' Oberon says. 'I'd like to see what that bitch gets.'

'You can go,' Darius says.

Oberon says quietly, 'Don't I get to witness the dispensation of justice in my own house?'

Darius turns away from him. 'What do you think, Merle?'

'What?' Merle says, trying to sound cool rather than completely confused and intimidated.

'This is your retribution. Does Oberon get to stay and witness it or should he leave?'

'Actually, Cole, to her, that's *Lord* Oberon of the Black Emerald Clan.' Oberon's voice begins sounding hard and firm but starts to waver as Darius turns to look at him.

'Sometimes I really think it was a big mistake to keep you alive,' Darius whispers.

Oberon smiles. 'Really? You won't do me the mercy of killing me though, will you, Cole? Not after I made you beg for it and refused you so many times. You just don't know how to deal with me.'

The two men face each other off for several heavy moments, then Darius glances at Merle. 'Sorry,' he says, 'change of plan. I've made the decision.' He turns back to Oberon, but not before Merle sees his eyes start glowing, black. 'Get. Out. Now.'

Under Darius's gaze, Oberon weakens visibly. He doesn't even attempt to disobey.

Darius turns his attention to the snivelling Kristina, still cowering in a corner. He starts to walk towards her. She's shaking with fear and staring up at him as he moves closer and reaches out, his palm forwards, his fingers spread.

His hand is inches from her head when Kristina begins to sob, 'No, no, please, Darius. Don't.'

Darius pauses. 'Now, Kristina,' he says, smoothly, 'I need to deep read you to know how to punish you, don't I? I thought you people liked this traditional stuff.'

'No, please, it hurts . . .' Kristina sobs again, shaking

her head and trying to guard herself with her bound hands.

Darius ignores her, swatting her hands aside as he presses his palm firmly against her forehead, his spread fingers cupping her scalp. Kristina stops sobbing and screams in pain. Darius doesn't appear to react to her new distress at all.

He holds Kristina long after her scream has died away. There's a long frozen moment and then Merle sees Darius smile. 'Well, of course,' he says to himself, 'I should have known.'

Darius lets go of Kristina and turns to Merle. Kristina crumples onto the floor like a rag, moaning, 'No, don't, please. Not her.' Darius starts to advance on Merle, his face set.

Merle is terrified but she tries really hard not to humiliate herself by cowering like Kristina. She's still sitting on the bed, her legs stretched out and her back against the wooden headboard. She just sits there as he climbs up onto the bed and draws his body towards her with a cat's sinuous moves. He straddles her legs and reaches out, but he doesn't grab her forehead like with Kristina. Instead he puts one hand on either side of her face, moves in and kisses her.

She holds her breath beneath the touch of his lips. A vampire is kissing her. Darius Cole is kissing her.

And it's amazing.

Darius's cool mouth is familiar somehow. Familiar and arousing. He begins using his tongue and his hands to coax her mouth into opening for him. Very slowly. Savouring each new sensation, each new piece of her lips and the flesh inside her mouth as it is revealed to him. There is no hurry. It's all so controlled. The coldness of his tongue feels a little strange, but not unpleasant. He doesn't smell or taste sour or like rotting flesh. He tastes just like a man. An aroused man.

As he keeps on kissing her, achingly slowly, almost worshipfully, she feels her whole body tauten. Her nipples go hard and super-sensitised. Every hair on her body is up on end. She feels the skin on her face get hot and tight under Darius's hands.

Darius moans softly into her mouth. He loosens his grip on her face and strokes her hot cheeks gently, turning his hands over to use the cool backs of his fingers on her heated skin.

And he's hard. The moment she feels it – the distinct pressure of his hard cock pushing against her thigh – she knows what it is, yet can't really believe it.

Eventually Darius pulls away and she slumps back against the headboard, breathing hard. Darius is still crouched over her on the bed. He turns to speak to Kristina over his shoulder. 'Well, I hope that's taught you a lesson,' he says, his cold voice sounding, for a moment, a little wry and amused. But only for a moment. 'Cross me again, and you can watch me fucking her.'

Kristina – still a whimpering bundle in the corner of the room – wails into her frothy skirts.

Darius turns back to Merle. She's panting. She can't help it. She knows she's wet with arousal – her face isn't the only place that's burning, flushed with blood.

He can read minds. He knows what he's done to me.

Darius gives her a long look of barely contained lust, then slides off the bed and grabs Kristina's rope as he strides out of the room. 'I'll be needing a little of you to finish me now, girl.'

They are both gone before Merle has swallowed the last taste of Darius from her mouth.

Day 14
When Kristina comes in the next morning and plonks down the breakfast tray, Merle is a little surprised. Didn't she try and kill her the other day?

Kristina isn't really her usual chatty self. Her dress seems even more wanton than usual, the neckline sliding off her shoulders which are ringed with bruises and bitemarks. The way she looks at Merle, she seems almost proud of the marks Darius has left all over her. Like she's displaying them.

'He wants to see you in his study,' she says sulkily, as Merle starts to eat. 'Next floor up, third door on the left.'

When Darius calls her in, she opens the large polished oak door into a long elegant room with huge floor to ceiling windows. The room should be flooded with light, but – as with everywhere else in the castle – the curtains are drawn and the lamps are lit. At the far end of the room Darius sits at a large desk, looking far more imposing than the impressive décor. Merle feels self-conscious, fiddling with the hem of her T-shirt, as she walks the endless length of the room to stand before him.

He looks at her for a long moment. 'About yesterday afternoon. I apologise. I shouldn't have done that. You're not here to help me keep Kristina in line.'

'Oh. OK.' She feels herself start to redden. She puts her head down, remembering Darius's usual reaction to her blushing.

'Yes,' he says. His voice sounds even. Perhaps he hasn't noticed? 'Really, I think it would be best if we could just pretend that it never happened. How would that be?'

'That would be, uh ... That would be fine,' she stammers, still not really looking at him and feeling like a fool. She takes a deep breath and forces herself to look up. 'I guess then,' she says lightly, 'that you'll just have to hope that you don't have to make good on your final threat.' She thought that comment would seem jokey, like she didn't think anything of the kiss they'd shared. She regrets saying it instantly.

Darius looks at her. 'My final...? I don't understand. What was my final threat?'

She feels another thrum of blood rushing to her face. She drops his gaze again and looks at the carpet. 'Oh, sorry, nothing.'

'No, Merle. What was my *final threat*?'

She shifts, takes a deep breath and looks up at him again. Her face is practically glowing. 'You told Kristina that if she misbehaved again you'd, uh, fuck me. In front of her.'

Darius's face breaks into a smile. 'Oh, *that*. Don't worry. I really don't think that will be necessary. Do you?'

She blinks. 'If you say so. Um, I mean, no.'

Darius says, 'But that's not why I wanted to see you. You've been here for more than half the term I specified. I was wondering if you wanted to go home.'

'Go home?' she says, still concentrating hard on her breathing and finally feeling her face start to cool.

'Yes,' says Darius. 'Just for a visit, you understand. And the terms remain the same, the terms of my, er...' He scrambles for the word.

'Of your blackmail?' she says.

'If you like.' He smiles, clearly amused. 'OK. The terms of my *blackmail* remain the same. I have arranged for a car to take you to London to see your parents. You will return here in twenty-four hours.' Darius looks back down at the paperwork on his desk, shooing her away. Clearly he's done.

Merle takes a breath. 'Thank you,' she says softly. He shoos her again. Not looking up.

An hour later, she's walking through the corridors of Cobalt. It feels like a dream. Everything is so cool and bright – sunlight! – and clean. So different to the sumptuously-threatening dark of the castle. There are a few people in the foyer who nod hello to her. No one thinks it's odd that she should be there. Cole's attack on her father has been kept deadly secret. No one knows she's meant to be somewhere else.

She uses her swipe card to take the lift to the secure floor. Out of the doors, she finds herself running. She bursts into her father's room so hard she makes her mother scream out loud and drop the book she's reading.

'Oh, darling,' her mother says, turning around, in tears, then rushing to take Merle in her arms. 'It's OK. No one expected you to stay the whole time. We knew he'd make it impossible for you. It was just a trick, darling. Thank God he stuck to his word and actually let you go.'

'No, Mum . . .'

'We've got a squad ready to storm the Black Emerald Castle. They don't know why yet of course, but it's all under control. Now you're back we can take in him tonight. Interrogate him.'

'No. You can't do that. It says in his letter that if we try and take the castle by force he'll destroy the antidote.'

'Oh darling, what choice do we have?'

Merle slows her breathing and looks into her mother's eyes. Appealing for calm. 'No, you don't understand, I'm going back. I haven't given up, Mum. I'm only here because he told me I could come and visit you. I'm going back tomorrow.'

'Oh.' Her mother's face twists.

'I know, Mum. But I'm past halfway already.'

Her mother swallows. When she speaks her voice is taut with emotion. 'Is he – is he treating you well? You look thin. They don't understand food. Is he feeding you?'

'Yes, Mum, it's fine,' she says. 'I have my own room. A very nice room. They bring me good food and magazines and other stuff to read. It's fine. Just a bit boring sometimes. It's like being in a hotel.'

'And he hasn't . . .' Merle's mother looks away from

her, almost as if she can't bring herself to say the words. 'He hasn't *bothered* you? He hasn't done anything to *disturb* you?'

Merle shakes her head, trying not to think about the way she felt when Darius kissed her – that memory suddenly flaring hotly. She bites at her lips and feels those two hot pink spots appear on her cheeks. 'No.'

Her mother pulls her close into an embrace again. 'Oh, darling. I've been sick with worry. I thought we'd never see you alive again.'

Merle nuzzles up close to the smell of her mother and tries to make herself believe that she can stay forever.

Late that evening, Merle watches as her mother falls asleep in her chair. Then she takes her security swipe card from around her neck and goes walking.

She's not sure where she's headed. But when she gets into the lift and sticks her mother's card into the slot a second secure floor appears on the control panel that she's never ever seen before and she knows that has to be the place.

The lift goes down. Down and into the ground. The secret level must be below the basement. When the doors slide open she gets a weird shivery flashback to the castle dungeon, but she steels herself and steps out into the gloom.

Feeling on the walls with flat hands she finds a light switch and flips it. Fluorescent strips flick on, sprinkling the light out to the furthest reaches of the huge room. All the room contains are filing cabinets.

The entire history of Cobalt.

Darius Cole has his own aisle. There's so much information. But she finds a likely looking file about his interrogation – so thick it takes up half a drawer on its own.

In the empty foyer she finds a carrier bag behind the reception desk and slips the file into it. Then, because she doesn't know where else to stash it, she goes out onto the pavement where the blacked-out car Darius provided is still parked and leaves the file with the driver.

Day 15
Merle wakes up on a blanket on the floor and get stiffly to her feet. Her mother is stirring in the chair. Her father is still unconscious in the bed, ashen and sheened with sweat.

'I should go,' she says to her mother – thinking of the file and how she wants to get back to the castle and study it.

'Won't you stay for breakfast?'

'I'd better not. I'm only allowed to be away twenty-four hours. And you know Cole'll be trying to find any loophole he can not to give me the antidote at the end of this.'

'OK,' says her mother, smiling ruefully. 'Take some money from my handbag though. Buy yourself some-thing nice to eat on the way.'

The castle door is answered by a welcoming party of Kristina and Oberon. Merle looks from one creepy smiling face to another. 'Where's Darius?'

Kristina shakes her head. 'Not sure. Like I told you before, he's a busy man.'

Merle feels her heart flip over. There's something disturbing about the way the two of them are looking at her. 'He can't expect me to ... Not you two again. Not after *you* tried to kill me –' she points accusingly at Kristina, then turns to Oberon '– and you tried to, God, I don't even know what you tried to do but it was damn creepy.'

Oberon runs his tongue over his top lip.

She swallows hard, taking a step backwards, further into the sunshine. 'You can't come out here, can you?'

'Out there? Into the daylight? No, Merle, we can't,' Kristina says nastily, 'but you have to come in here, I believe, or the terms of your deal with Darius are broken.'

'What are you going to do with me? When I come in, I mean.'

Kristina smiles. 'What Darius told us to do, of course. Take you back to the dungeon, lock you up, give you some food . . .'

'The dungeon, not my room?'

'Do you know, I don't believe he was specific about that. He did say I was to lock you in though . . .' Kristina's smiling face turns hard as stone.

Day 16

The smallest of mercies is that Merle has been spared the manacles this time.

Neither Oberon or Kristina has done anything in particular to *disturb* her (as her mother would say) but she still feels uneasy. Feels that at any moment Oberon might appear with another twisted bargain.

She doesn't have the file she took from Cobalt. Oberon grabbed the bag from her as she stepped over the threshold. The fact it had been taken from her only made her more desperate to discover its contents.

Day 17

The next day Kristina comes in with the food instead of shoving it through the hatch in the door. She seems quite chatty. More like her usual self. Merle decides to ask her something that she was brooding about the day before. Being back in the dungeon had made her remember.

'Back when I was first brought down here, Darius came down a couple of times and one of those times he said something about this being about me. About how he could leave them alone, meaning my parents, but he could never leave me alone. What do you think he meant by that?' As she's speaking she thinks of Kristina greeting her at the castle door that first evening. *I know who you are, dear.*

Kristina shrugs. 'That just sounds like Darius being Darius to me. Anyway, I don't think I'm really meant to talk to you about that kind of thing.' And she taps her forehead and winks.

'What's that supposed to mean? Darius is in your head. He's using his psych-powers to spy on us?'

'Great,' says Kristina. 'Now you've said that he knows we know. Hi, Darius,' she says. 'Merle, say hi to Darius.'

Merle actually finds herself waving a hand and mouthing 'Hi,' before she stops herself. 'So,' she says to Kristina. 'He does know I'm here then? Locked in the dungeon.'

'Yeah,' says Kristina. 'In fact, I'm meant to move you back to your room right now. It seems there was a misunderstanding about that.'

Day 18

Merle's starting to lose track of time. When she first arrived, counting off the days to 25 had been so important, but now she's starting to drift.

She dreams of Darius again. He's lying next to her on the bed, twirling a razor blade through his fingers and smiling.

When she jolts awake she feels sure someone has been in the room again. And the bedroom door is open.

She pulls on her jeans over her nightshirt and slips out into the silent castle. Thinking she can hear sounds on the stairs, she creeps down into the entrance hall to find one of the doors leading off it standing ajar.

She finds herself in an enormous library. There are books on every vast wall – floor to ceiling and yet more in a gallery above. On a table in the middle of the room a single candle burns.

Next to the candle is the file she took from Cobalt.

She rushes over and opens it. Far too eager to take the file back upstairs, she begins to read it right there.

The first sheaf of papers deals with things she already knows. Background. The story so far. The rise of Darius Cole and Righteous Power. How Cobalt was formed with vampire money to attack the problem with human advantages.

But the next file is very different. It contains minutes of every Cobalt meeting to discuss Darius Cole, detailing the essential problem that Cole was so good at psychic and psychological manipulation that it was dangerous to even be in a room with him. His capture might be relatively simple, but his interrogation appeared impossible. After some searching, Cobalt discovered his vulnerability. Darius Cole had a lover. A human lover. A woman called Magdalena Wright. Magdalena was traced and captured by Cobalt. Darius Cole was told the price of her life was simple. His total surrender.

The next set of minutes is supplemented by a full transcript of Cole's subsequent interrogation. Threatening him with Magdalena's torture, Cobalt forced Cole to reveal the location of his army. The paper gave long and detailed descriptions of the tortures they threatened. How Magdalena's increasingly grisly potential fates were outlined to Cole. It wasn't clear whether any of these were actually carried out or whether Magdalena was even present during Cole's interrogation.

Cole had tried to resist them, claiming to betray his entire army to save one life was wrong. Even the life of his lover. But they promised him his soldiers would die clean and sweet if he co-operated – staked in their sleep. If he didn't Magdalena would suffer for as long as they could make it last.

And then Cole – finally broken – had showed them the locations on the map.

Merle puts down the piece of paper she's reading. She's crying and she senses him behind her. Darius presses his lips to her earlobe and kisses her. She turns around slowly in his arms. He reaches up and touches the place above her cheekbone that is a little damp from her tears. 'Are those for me?' he says.

'Yes.'

'You don't need to cry for me, Merle,' he whispers. 'Not now. Not if you'll come to my bed.'

He leads her back up the stairs. Up past the first floor, along the second floor corridor, past his office and into the very last room. *His bedroom.*

She stops in the doorway. The room is very similar to her own. The ceiling is a little lower, the décor is dove-grey instead of turquoise. The froufrou is rather more under control. But it has a similar layout with a large table set in the tightly curtained bay window and a huge four poster bed. She stares at the bed. At Darius standing right by it.

Not if you'll come to my bed.

'It's OK, Merle,' he says softly. 'You can come in. Nothing will happen to you if you cross my threshold. Nothing bad.'

She holds his eyes. They always looked black before, but now, in the candlelight they seem to be very deep brown. She walks into the room.

Darius says, 'Merle, I am really sorry I haven't been around all that much while you've been here. I don't want you to think it's that I didn't want to be with you.

I did. So very much. But I held myself back. I didn't want to rush things.'

'What things?'

'These things.' He crosses the room to her, takes her face in his hands and touches his lips to hers.

The kiss that follows is even slower than before. Tender and reverent. He uses his tongue to edge her mouth open little by little. She finds her head full of strange images. He's in her mind. She's thinking of him opening her mouth like a flower. And she knows that this isn't really about her mouth at all. The way he is using his tongue and his lips and his teeth to caress and coax her wider and wider open for him is purely a demonstration of a skill that he wants to use on other parts of her body.

When he pulls back from the slow kiss to look at her, she says, 'You really don't like to rush things, do you?' And that comment is enough for her to feel herself colouring.

He's still holding her face. He moans when he sees her start to blush and moves in to lick her warm cheek. He does that very slowly too. Tracing his cool tongue against her flesh. Making lazy swirls.

'But we can't have sex, can we?' she says softly.

He stops moving his tongue on her face and pulls back. 'What? Don't you want to?'

'You can't, though, can you? You can't ... with a human.' She feels her face get even hotter. 'How did you, though, with Magdalena? How could you have had a human lover? How can we ...? Why did you bring me here if we can't?'

He silences her with a single finger to her lips. 'Merle, please, stop. Of course I lay with Magdalena. We were lovers. I gave her pleasure. Giving human women pleasure is a pleasure in itself. I asked you here because I would like very much to give you pleasure, Merle. I feel

I have asked so much of you already. And you have borne it all so well.'

She nods her head. He twists her around in his arms, and guides her across the room to the bed. The sheets smell like him, a scent that is exciting and familiar. He climbs on top of her, positions himself astride her waist and pulls off his shirt.

As she had thought before, his upper body isn't as slight as his slender physique suggests. There is a power in his body. His skin is very pale. But his paleness seems unearthly and exotic. Not a disturbing pastiness of skin that has not seen sun for too long, but a shimmering silveriness that suggests something fantastical. There's just a little dark hair in the upper part of his chest, tapering away to a thin line which disappears into his waistband. She finds her eyes following the little trail, her breath hitching when she looks down at Darius's groin.

He moves over her – the muscles in his arms flexing a little as they take his weight – and ducks into another kiss. His mouth moves faster this time, more strongly. Penetrating. Again making her think of other things.

Did you think he meant to desecrate you?

But she is beyond listening to Oberon's voice in her head. She's in bed with her most delicious nightmare. She struggles out of her T-shirt and bra and Darius's head moves to her small breasts. His sharp teeth graze over them, tweaking and teasing until she can see nothing but sparkling lights behind her tight-squeezed eyes.

He moves further down her body. His slender fingers are on her jeans, unfastening, whisking them away. His mouth is cool, almost cold between her legs, sweeping fizzing sensation into every last sensitive fold.

She bucks in his hands. Her head rolls against the pillows. As he works on her she come achingly close to orgasm time and again, gasping as Darius whisks each potential climax away with a stilling of his tongue. She wonders for a second how he's able to taunt and tantalise her so precisely. Hold her on her rising edge with such precise skill.

Because I'm here with you.

His mind reading doesn't feel like a violation so much as another level of intimacy. Darius moves then, comes up to kiss her. He presses his mouth to hers and she tastes the sweet-stickiness that clings to his stubbled skin. She reaches down to tries to get his fly undone, but she finds herself fumbling. One of his hands takes over, flipping the buttons open while he holds himself over her, supported by one taut arm and a kiss.

When he moves inside her the feel of his cool smoothness sends her spinning, spiralling into overload. She barely feels, barely registers what is happening, even before the walls of her consciousness comes crashing down and she loses herself to the feel of him.

A few small moments of recovery later, she is limp against the pillows. More sated than she thinks she has ever been. Darius is lying beside her.

'Did you feel it too?' she says softly.

'The edges. It is hard to stay in your mind when the sensations are that strong. Perhaps with practice.' He reaches over and places his hand on the flat part of her chest, just below her collar bone. 'All of this part of you flushes when you come. Did you know that? As well as your face.' It's when he says that, with a thickness and a hitch to his voice that she realises – though her haze of satiety – that Darius is still tense. Tight with arousal and desire

'Darius. Do you need...? What do you need?' Deep inside her a traitorous voice says another vampire is what he needs.

'Blood. You.' Darius swallows visibly. 'Will you bleed for me?'

'What? Me?'

'You can say no, of course. Your free choice. Always. But will you? Or, at least, will you consider it? I don't have to bite you. I have some razor blades. I can cut you or you can cut yourself. I don't want to drink, just taste you. Just the tiniest drop would...' He stops talking – he's panting heavily – and looks away.

She looks at him. He's still so aroused, clearly frustrated by it. His hips are rocking slightly. His cock is still hard between his thighs. 'Do you need to? Um, do you *need* the blood, I mean?'

Darius nods. 'To finish? Yes, I do. Just a drop on my tongue, Merle.'

'I really can't do that.'

Darius inhales. 'OK. I understand. I know what you were brought up to think of me.'

'It's not that. It ... I can't let a vampire drink from me. It was bad enough that Kristina tried to ... You can't release any other way?'

Darius shakes his head. His voice is sharp, almost sulky, 'No.'

'What do you normally do?'

'You know. Blood Rites. With Kristina. Or Oberon if she's being really pissy with me.'

'Right, so do you need to go and see Kristina now?'

'What I'd most like to do is to taste you. But if I can't have that then Kristina ... I won't if you don't want me to. But it would be nice not to have to sleep like this.' He looks down at his jutting erection.

'But if it were me. If I did let you use my blood, that would still work? The same as Kristina? She told me it had to be another vampire.'

'Well, they do say that. The vampires. The *other*

vampires. Maybe it is true for them. I really don't know. But I know I can be aroused to completion with human blood. I would very much like to prove that to you.'

She looks at him. Naked and hard and so beautiful. Half an hour ago she wouldn't have thought she would be able to refuse him anything. But this? This is ... 'Darius, I ...'

'You *can* say no,' Darius says again.

She holds his gaze. 'No,' she says. 'I can't do that. It's too strange.' *Too vampire.* 'I'm sorry.'

He nods. 'That's fine. It's OK.'

She bites her lip. 'I think you should go to Kristina now.'

He moves to slip off the bed. Then pauses. 'Would you like to watch me with her? See how it works. It might help you understand.'

Her imagination pulses. Darius in ecstasy. The thought of watching his face as he scales that peak and comes achingly close, his face contorting with need and greed. The thought of hearing him cry out in that shattering moment. Of watching every last one of his barriers come down.

She wants to see that. She wants to give him that. And to do that she has to bleed for him.

She watches him go to Kristina.

Day 19

'Darius, what did you mean that time in the dungeon when you said you could leave my parents alone, but you couldn't leave me alone?'

She's watching him dress. She stayed in his bed over night but he didn't return until after she was sleeping. He paused, fastening his shirt cuffs. 'Ah. I was wondering when you were going to ask me that.'

'Because you heard me ask Kristina?'

'Yes. I am sorry. I was watching her, not you.' Darius

walks back over to the bed. 'And she was right to say she wasn't allowed to talk about it. The truth is mine to tell.'

'So when are you going to tell me?'

'Tomorrow night. Have dinner with me. Let me tell the story properly.'

'Why? Why must I wait until then? Haven't I waited long enough?'

'We both have,' Darius says. 'We both have. But we must not get so close and then rush these things. This must be taken slowly. Trust me. I'm only thinking of you.'

Day 20

Dinner the following evening isn't served in the vast and formal dining hall Merle is kind of expecting, but an intimate little room on the ground floor full of soft inviting furniture. There is a bright fire and enough gold and gilding that everything seems to glitter in the dancing light.

There is a bay window. Probably the most surprising thing in the whole room is that the curtains hanging at the windows are open. It's almost night outside and, in the gathering dark, she can just see the fringe of trees where the castle's wards are placed.

Set in the circular space made by the window is a small table. One place is set for dinner, the food already waiting, hidden by a silver salver. Darius sits at the place opposite. In front of him is a tall stemmed glass. The glass is semi-opaque – a milky white – so the contents look pale pink. Perhaps to spare her the full sight of him drinking blood while she eats.

She takes her place at the table and he leans forward with a smile and lifts the salver. Underneath is an amazing looking meal of salmon with wild rice and spinach. Her stomach leaps. Food while she's been in the castle has never been this exciting.

She picks up her fork and pokes the greens. 'Is there garlic in the spinach? I probably shouldn't eat garlic if we're going to ...' She feels herself starting to blush and stops talking. But this time blushing somehow doesn't seem like such a bad thing.

She looks up at Darius, who smiles and says, 'No garlic.'

'Oh. *Oh!*'

He laughs. 'I'm not sure if it would actually repel me. Most food is not pleasant. But I've never investigated whether garlic is any worse. Some of these things are, well, taken to ridiculous extremes. But to respect the creatures who once ruled this castle, perhaps we should observe these things.' He gestures to the food. 'Please, eat.'

The meal is incredibly good. Merle wonders who cooked it. Perhaps Darius had it brought from a restaurant.

She watches him take a small sip from his glass and then says, 'So why am I here? What do you have to tell me?'

He swallows. 'Merle, when you think about everything you know about me. What you have been told and what you have learnt since coming here, can you think of anything that doesn't make sense?'

'I don't know. I suppose I find it hard to believe that you are the monster I used to think you were.'

'Well, yes. And thank you. But try and think of something more specific.'

'More specific?'

'Merle, you know about Magdalena, don't you? You know that it was through her that they finally managed to subdue me.'

'Yes.'

'And you know she was a human.'

'Yes.'

'You know I had a human lover.'

'Yes. And I suppose that doesn't fit with what Kristina told me. That vampires can't perform Blood Rites with a human. But you said that isn't true. Or isn't true for you.'

'Yes. That's right, but that's not it. Something else, Merle. Doesn't something else strike you about the fact I had a human lover?'

She's holding her fork. When the next thought takes shape in her mind she is so surprised that she drops it, letting it clatter onto her plate. 'You hate humans. You believe in Righteous Power. That's all about killing and enslaving humanity. But why would you want to do that if you were in love with a human?'

His eyes are wild, shining black, reflecting the fire-light. 'Which means?'

'I guess, that you never believed in Righteous Power at all. That, that . . .' her voice swoops from excited whoop to soft realisation. 'That they made it up. That you were framed. Why?'

'Tell me why, Merle?'

'I don't know.'

'What was I doing, Merle? What do I do that the Vampire Clan Council don't like?'

She knows the answer at once, but she still gives a tiny breathless pause before saying so. 'You perform Blood Rites with humans.'

He nods.

'The Vampire Clan Council just said you were advocating Righteous Power because that was so scary to the human government. They just wanted you caught. They offered to fund Cobalt to do it and it looked like they were doing the government a favour. Not only identifying a potential problem but offering an easy way of dealing with it. A cost effective way of dealing with it.' She pauses and looks down at her plate for a moment.

She's not really hungry, suddenly. 'But why didn't my parents see through it? Once they knew about Magdalena. How come they didn't see that it didn't make sense?'

'Perhaps they didn't want to. The Vampire Clan Council were paying them very nicely for destroying me. Perhaps they chose not to look too closely at what they were being told.' He stops and looks right at her, burning her up with the fire reflected in his eyes. She feels the blood rushing; rushing under her skin. He's so beautiful. She'd give him anything at this moment. Even that. More than that. If he asked right now she'd let him slide his fangs into her. Drink her. Drink her to death. 'No one knows who I am, Merle,' he says in a slow cracked voice. 'Or where I came from. Not even me. All I know is that I'm a vampire. According to the Council no vampire siring has been permitted for over a hundred years. But I'm less than forty. These things can be assessed, you know, by tissue analysis. Oberon is hundreds of years old. That's why he smells so sour to you. Vampires *are* immortal, but nothing truly lasts forever. The decay is just very slow.

'All I can remember waking up in a hospital with no idea who I was. I had been burnt by the sun. I don't know how that happened. The name, Darius Cole, was invented for me. Cole is, I assume, some reference to my burns.'

'Ew, vamps are so gross.' She feels like an idiot as soon as she says that. It's nerves. She catches Darius's eye. 'God, sorry.'

'It's OK. I know who you are. And, in a way, you're right. It is gross. The Clan Council chose a name that amused them when they came for me. I believe they have people who alert them to such things.' He takes another drink and continues. 'With no knowledge of who

I was other than the fact that my siring was clearly illegal the Council were unsure what to do with me. I had no line. To a vampire line is everything: it's your status; it's where you live; it's who you love. Without a line I was nothing. It's amazing they didn't stake me on the spot.

'Instead they handed me over to the Red Daggers. That's another of the clans. As vicious and brutal as the Black Emeralds but far less influential. That's probably why they got stuck with me. They didn't explain much to me about what I was and what that meant. I ran away a lot. I met Magdalena in the nearest town.' He pauses and takes another small sip from his glass.

When he sets the glass down, he has blood on his teeth. 'I didn't have much awareness of my psych-powers when I first went to live with the Red Daggers, but as I got more control I realised they were much stronger than anything the vampires around me had. Telepathy is a rare gift and it is very unusual for a vampire to be able to be conscious of another's thoughts for very long. I can stay in a person's head for days. I can read you any time I want if you're somewhere in the castle. I can listen in on Kristina or Oberon at the same time. But, in fact, although my telepathic powers are unprecedented, when I took over the Red Daggers it was mostly through persuasion. I am, it would seem, also very good at persuasion.

'Once I realised that what I was doing with Magdalena was wrong in the eyes of the Council I started to see how fiercely they controlled *everything*. I started to question it all. The rigid structure of the clans, the way who had sired you and when determined every aspect of your life, no matter what your skills might be or who you were before. The way the Council ruled on every aspect of vampire law. The way contact with humans was utterly suppressed. When all of us were human. Once. I might not know who I am but I do know that I was *someone* human just over forty years ago.

'It was almost too easy to show the downtrodden Red Daggers just how the council was oppressing them and ruling their lives. And we took control of two other clans within a month. We decided to hit the Black Emerald next. I was so enamoured of my powers I thought I could even talk the Clan with the most to lose into joining our cause. I thought it was all a matter of persuasion. I was wrong. That ambition lost me everything when I could have just slipped away and made a life with Magdalena. I'm sure that has happened before between a human and a vampire. It must have. They just don't speak of it.' He stops and takes another drink.

'What happened to Magdalena? In the end? Do you know?'

Darius nods.

'Then why don't you go to her? Even if she is old now. I mean, why don't you get her back?'

'That's what I'm trying to do right now.'

'*Right* now?'

'Yes.'

She shakes her head slowly. 'This is the thing you were going to tell me about, isn't it?'

'Yes.'

'Do my parents have her? Is she somewhere at Cobalt? Is that what you want me for? Some kind of trade?'

'I would rather take this slowly.'

'Or is she here? Somewhere in the castle?'

With his glass halfway to his lips, Darius pauses and then throws it across the room. It lands in the fire. Blood splatters in all directions, covering the white hearthrug, the marble fire-surround, the pristine wallpaper. Merle shrinks back. Shocked. But Darius speaks very slowly and calmly, 'I can't tell you. You have to go now, Merle. It is very hard for me to talk to you about this and you're not ready to know everything yet. Please. Another day.'

'But why? What has it got to do with me?'

'Another day. Please.'

Day 21

The next afternoon Merle thinks of the one place where some more of the truth might lie. She didn't finish reading the file she brought from Cobalt. Perhaps it's still in the library.

In fact, the file turns out to be still open on the table where she left it. She picks up the next set of papers. More minutes. Every detail documented in the same dry emotionless style as before. Every devastating fact simply recorded without comment.

After Darius's army was killed and Darius himself handed over to the Black Emerald Clan, Cobalt asked what they should do with Magdalena. Initially, the stone-hearted documents say, Cobalt had though that Magdalena would have to be killed. The knowledge she had of Darius Cole was too dangerous for her to be allowed to live. But then the Black Emerald Clan leader Lord Oberon came to visit Cobalt.

Oberon? Merle checks the papers she's already read. Is this the first time Oberon has been mentioned by name. Further back, amongst the early documents she finds a reference to the Lord of the Black Emerald Clan as the main contact point between Cobalt and the vampires. So Oberon really was Darius's jailer, too.

'And you know just how he likes to treat his prisoners,' says a soft voice behind her.

She turns to see Darius standing in the open doorway. 'Did you . . .? Did you see into my head just then?'

'I can see a lot of what's in your head, Merle.'

'Did you kill the rest of the Black Emerald Clan?'

He nods.

'Why not Oberon?'

'Same reason he didn't kill me. Too good for him.'

'Why didn't you kill Kristina?'

He smiles again, this time more warmly and with a shrug. 'Nothing so sinister there, I just like Kristina. She didn't deserve to die either – but in the opposite way. Besides I needed someone for, well, you know. Blood Rites. And the idea of it just being me and Oberon.' He shudders. It's almost comic.

Merle wonders for a moment. 'Not because she's really Magdalena? Did you somehow turn Magdalena into a vampire and now she's Kristina?'

'Read the paper you're holding, Merle.'

Lord Oberon told Cobalt about the exact nature of Darius's punishment. How he was sentenced to live. According to him, if Magdalena was killed there was a chance her soul would find it's way into another human being. That Darius might one day track her down. That fact would give him hope. He wasn't, Oberon explained, to have any hope of future happiness. The only thing he ought to hope for was death. A death he would never be granted.

As she sets the paper down, tears are pricking at her eyes. 'What did they do to her then?'

Darius just points at the rest of the papers on the table.

Long laborious paragraphs tell her in detail how witches were brought in. Oberon paid them a staggering amount of money for a very complex piece of magic. She struggles to comprehend what she's reading. It seems that Magdalena was killed. Shot by a Cobalt operative. But her soul wasn't allowed to be released into the ether. It was magically stored in a specially constructed glass prism.

Merle lets the paper fall from her fingers and turns to Darius. 'That's just, just weird. She's in a prism? So where is this prism now? Do you know? Are you trying to find it? Can you just break it and then wait for her soul to be reborn in someone else?' As she says these words Merle feels something cold prickling in her heart. There's something else. Something.

'I know where her soul is now. I have managed to acquire its new receptacle.'

'Its new receptacle? What happened to the prism?'

'Storing a soul outside of a body is incredibly and continuously complex. And you know how vampires are about spending money. And about witches. They needed to find another way. The financial strain of keeping Magdalena's soul out of my reach meant they were thinking of shutting down Cobalt to save money. It was only ever meant as a snare for me. But when Cobalt found out about this they countered with a new proposal. The suggestion was that they should put Magdalena's soul inside another human being.'

'But Oberon said they couldn't do that. That then you would have hope of finding her.'

'Cobalt had a unique and devastating idea. Deliberately place the soul into an infant who would be brought up fearful and wary of vampires and, above all, fearful and wary of me. Put her soul in a place where I would never be able to reach it. In a place where, even if I escaped, even if I could stand before her, she would never accept me.'

Merle is holding on to the table's edge. She squeezes a little tighter, looking away from Darius at the swirling patterns on the carpet.

'Say it, Merle,' Darius whispers. 'I know you know. Tell me what they did?'

'Me.' She feels like the word claws itself out of her mouth. 'They put it in me. The baby of Charles and Erin Cobalt. Your conquerors. The world's most famous vampire hunters.' She looks up and bites her bottom lip.

Darius is staring at her. He doesn't speak. She swallows. 'Darius, I have to go to them. My parents. I need to speak to them about this. If I go now will you still let me have the antidote for my father?'

Darius crosses the room to her then, so fast she can't really remember him moving. 'Don't go.' His hands are tight on her upper arms. 'I want to be with you now. It's too soon. You're too vulnerable. They'll try and confuse you.'

She struggles and tries to pull away from his grasp but can't break his grip. He's so strong. Far stronger than Oberon. 'Darius, I have to.'

Darius grips her tighter, stilling her struggles completely. He looks into her eyes. 'Merle, you must not. You will not go now. You will go to your room and rest. Perhaps you will be ready to go in the morning. You must take this slowly.'

Darius's eyes look pure black. Not a hint of warm brown. His grip is painful 'OK,' she says finally, feeling nothing but relief at giving in to him, 'OK. But I will go first thing tomorrow morning.'

'We'll see.'

Day 22

Merle wakes up early and slips out of bed. When she remembers the day before in the library and Darius's ink-black eyes and calm low voice ordering her to stay she feels slightly light-headed and confused. She's sure Darius would be able to stop her again if he caught her leaving.

She's outside the castle, walking away towards the tree line, when she hears the front door of the castle open behind her. She turns and Darius stands just inside the doorway. 'Merle!'

She knows she's out of his reach, standing in bright sunlight. 'I have to go Darius.'

'No, Merle, wait. I have something for you.' He holds up a small parcel wrapped in canvas. She shakes her head, she knows that if she goes back to the castle doorway he'll be able to drag her inside. What with his psych-powers and his strength, the sunlight is the only weapon she has against him. Merle shakes her head and turns away from him, starting to run.

She has no money. Hitchhiking is something she'd always considered dangerous, but now, after nearly a whole month living in a vampire castle, it seems like nothing. It takes a few hours to get to London and almost as long again to get into Westminster. But eventually she's walking through the corridors of Cobalt again, buzzing with confusion and close to exhausted tears.

Her mother rushes over when she appears in the doorway, embracing her and muttering the same platitudes into her hair as before. How it was no problem that she couldn't make it all the way, that Darius Cole would have primed her to fail, that they would storm the castle and overwhelm him.

She pulls back from the embrace. 'No, Mum. I'm not here for that. I'm here to talk to you, because I know. Because he told me what you did.'

Her mother's face goes white. 'Whatever he's told you ...'

'No. Don't. Just listen to me. I just need to know the truth. Please.' Merle explains everything Darius told her as fast as she can, stunning her mother into reluctant silence with her explosive burst of speech. Talking and talking until she dissolves into gasps and tears.

Her mother grabs her by the shoulders and pulls her into a forceful embrace. 'It's not true. Darling, none of it. This is what he does. It's a game to him.' Merle's mother strokes her hair. 'Darling, it's us. We're your parents. You know that. Cole is doing things to you. Nasty things. He's using his psych-powers on you. Come home with me. I can show you your baby pictures. Pictures of me when I was pregnant. It wasn't until two years after Cole was imprisoned.'

'And Magdalena Wright was killed?'

Her mother looks a little uncomfortable

Merle pulls away from her so she can look at her properly. 'Magdalena Wright? Is she real?'

Her mother swallows. 'Yes. At least, there was a woman. She was important to him and that is how we captured him in the end. I don't know who she was.'

'Did you kill her?'

'She was killed.'

'Was her soul put in a prism?'

'What? No. We don't do things like that here. We don't mess with that kind of stuff. Cobalt is funded by vampire money. We don't touch witchcraft. Can't you see what he's doing? This is his revenge. We know he wants revenge on your father and me. Look at what he's already done.' Her mother waves a hand to her unconscious ashen father. 'And what better way to punish us than to take you away? Destroy your love for us. Oh, I should have known. Sweetheart, remember what you knew about him. Before. He is the master of this type of deception. Think about how he's spun this story to you. Hints and secrets. I bet he made it seem as if you were uncovering the truth for yourself when all along he was controlling every part of the web of lies he was spinning for you.'

Merle stares at her mother's face, her mind racing. It could be true. He could have constructed this entire thing, fed the information to her piece by piece. She sits down on the chair. She feels like she's losing her mind.

Darius's words echo in her head. You're too vulnerable. They'll try and confuse you.

'I'll kill him myself.' Merle turns to the sound of the familiar, strong dark tone. Her father.

'Dad!' Merle jumps up. He's sitting up in bed. Still grey and weak looking, but with something of his usual imposing charisma back.

'Erin,' he barks, 'pass me my clothes. I'll go and stake that sucker myself.'

Her mother rushes to the bedside. 'Charles! No! Please, you're very ill.'

But Merle's father is already swatting the pads of the monitoring equipment from his body as if they were irritating insects.

'Dad,' Merle says gingerly, 'you can't. This is about me.'

'No it isn't, Merle. This is nothing to do with you. He's only using you because he knows that the thing that would hurt us the most –' He freezes. He stays rigid for a second, then slumps back onto the bed and starts jerking wildly around.

'He's arresting,' Merle's mother shouts, grabbing a trolley that holds a large machine and knocking Merle out of the way as she rushes back with it. She places two large metal plates on Merle's father's chest. Merle just watches in horror.

When her mother turns to her, having shocked her father's heart back to life, Merle says, 'I'm going back. Right now. I'll kill Cole and bring back the antidote.'

Moments later, as she emerges onto the street, she has her mother's handbag in one hand and a Cobalt-issue wooden stake in the other.

Kristina opens the castle door. Merle pushes straight past her. 'Where is he?'

'I don't know if he's taking visitors,' Kristina says weakly.

Merle raises her stake. Kristina's eyes go wide. 'Where. Is. He?'

'His study.'

'Thank you,' Merle says, starting up the stairs. Half-way up she pauses and turns. 'And don't you dare follow me.'

'Yes, ma'am.'

In Darius's study, Merle runs the length of the room. Darius smiles and gets up, walking around his desk to meet her. He doesn't seem to notice her anger, even when she's almost on top of him, forcing him back against the desk, pressing the stake to his heart.

'You've been running,' he whispers. 'You're exerted and excited. I can see it in your skin. You look so beautiful.' He raises a hand and moves to touch her cheek.

'Don't,' she spits, 'don't touch me.'

Darius stills his hand a fraction before it makes contact. He looks down at the stake. 'Are you really going to use that thing, Magdalena? Is that what you want? Why don't you lift my clothing out of the way? Make me feel it against my skin.' His voice throbs with arousal.

'I'm going to kill you, you bastard.'

'Yes,' Darius sighs, doing what he had suggested she do herself and pulling up his sweater so the point of the stake presses against his bare chest. He makes a sound like a bitten off moan when it makes contact. 'I used to beg them for this, Magdalena.'

'Who?'

'The Black Emerald Clan. They would usually keep torturing me until I begged them for the stake.' He pauses and covers her shaking hands on the stake with his own. 'They would have me place it against my own chest. Just like this. It amused them to see me that desperate for death. Especially when they laughed and refused to administer the blows to drive it home. How much easier it would have been to bear if I'd known that when death finally did come, it would be you that brought it.'

Merle looks into his dark eyes, holds them and tries to keep thinking of her father, convulsing in that machine-enshrined bed at Cobalt. 'It was wrong, what you did. No matter what happened to you. My parents didn't torture you, the Black Emerald Clan did. Why did you attack my parents and not them?'

'I did attack the clan. They're all dead, remember. Not that your parents weren't equally responsible in their own way. But I had no choice, Magdalena. I had to go through your parents to get to you.' He takes his hands off the stake and cups her face. 'I promised I'd come for you. I promised *you*.'

She looks at him. The pain in his eyes goes deep, deep down. Maybe he really does believe she's Magdalena. Maybe he's insane. It wouldn't really be that surprising after what had been done to him. She drops the stake and pulls away from him.

He catches her wrist. 'Come to my bed, Magdalena. Please. Come to my bed and bleed for me.'

Merle pulls her hand free and runs.

She's still breathing heavily when she gets to her own room on the floor below. On the table in the window – the one where her food is usually left – is a small canvas-wrapped parcel. She recognises it as the one Darius was carrying when he called to her from the doorway as she was leaving.

She unwraps it.

Inside is a small stoppered bottle containing a gold-coloured liquid that sparkles in the light. The bottle is labelled *Charles Cobalt Antidote*.

Darius isn't in his study. Merle goes to his bedroom.

She stands in the doorway for a second. Darius is

sitting at a small table by the window, writing in a journal. She holds up the bottle as she walks across the room to him. 'This is the antidote.'

'I know.'

'You were trying to give it to me when I left.'

'I know.'

'But if you'd given me this I might never have come back.'

'I know.'

She inhales sharply. Darius is close enough that if she reached out she'd be able to touch him. 'Is that true, Darius? This isn't a game? They told me you were playing mind games with me.'

'This isn't a game.'

'This is real?'

'This is real.'

She looks at him. For a long time she can't think what to say. And then, sudden and sure, she finds the perfect words. 'I think, I'd prefer it if you did the cutting. I'm not sure if I could cut myself.'

Darius goes pale. He stares into her eyes. 'Now you have to promise that you're not the one playing games.'

'I'm not, Darius. I know it. Maybe it's the only thing I know for sure right now. But I know I want to bleed for you.' She pauses for a moment to trace her bottom lip with her teeth. 'I want to see you come.'

Darius doesn't say anything else. He gets up and goes and opens the small top drawer of his bedside cabinet. A second later he turns around holding a tiny silver object. A razor blade. Merle swallows.

'You want me to do the cutting?' Darius says softly.

'Yes.'

Darius makes a soft little aroused noise. 'With the razor? It's up to you. If you prefer I could bite you.'

'If you bite me is it different? For you, I mean?'

'A little. The sensations are rather more intense for me. That way.'

She nods. 'Maybe next time then. I think the razor blade would be easier to accept, right now.'

'I understand.' Darius raises his hand, holding up the blade between his fingers as if he were showing it to her. 'Where?'

'What?'

'Where may I cut you?'

She closes her eyes. 'Cut me where you used to cut her.' Then she looks right at him. Deep inside. 'Where you used to cut me.'

They're standing so close to each other and yet Darius manages to move in and close the gap further. 'There were many places,' he whispers. 'Inside your thigh. Just above your breast. And then, there was this. I think this was your favourite.' Darius flickers the blade against her bottom lip. The pain is instantaneous and gone. Hardly pain at all. And then she notices a slight damp feeling on her lip and licks at it. Blood. The razor blade makes a tiny *ching* as it hits the floor and in Darius's eyes she can see he is almost incapacitated with arousal.

Moving with a dreamy underwater kind of slowness he reaches out and runs the pad of his ring finger over her bloodied lip. Then he pulls his hand away and turns it around, staring at the redness there. Very, very softly he says, 'Magdalena.'

He locks his eyes with hers as he pushes the finger into his mouth and slowly draws it out again. The sight of that alone is making her start to burn between her legs.

He pauses with the tip of his finger still in his mouth. She realises he's waiting. Waiting for her to indicate to him that she's OK. OK with him having her blood in his mouth. She reaches out, moves his hand gently from his mouth and kisses him.

He gasps, so overcome he barely kisses her back for a moment. She takes a step backwards, bringing him with her, holding him in her arms until she can feel the bed behind her. She lets herself fall backwards with Darius on top of her.

He groans again as his weight crushes her body down into the mattress and then he uses the position to drive himself harder down on her broken lip. Worrying the wound with his tongue. Delicately coaxing it open with his trademark skill and precision. Pain spangles across her mouth with each new exploration of his tongue. She finds she is bucking her hips up under him. Unable to think of much beyond the sensation.

Darius raises his head from her mouth. 'I'm going to bite you now. I have to.'

She sits up as he moves off the bed to the floor and kneels by her feet. He unbuttons her jeans, waiting while she kicks them away. He removes her underwear too and his sweater, then takes hold of her left leg with two cool hands, turns it outwards a little, and sinks his teeth into the thin skin of her inner thigh, just below the pouty lips of her cunt.

Just the fact his mouth is *there* is overwhelming. But the feel of the bite, the penetration, of him inside her – in a more intimate way than she would have ever thought possible, is beyond anything she's ever felt in her life. It transcends any pain; moves through it into crystalline ecstasy.

He moves back from the bite, the lower part of his face bloodstained and beautiful, and smiles up at her. Again he says, 'Magdalena.'

Ducking his head back down, he starts moving between lapping at the wound and sweeping his tongue over her clit. In her mind she sees how he must be covering her cunt in blood. Mixing it with her scents. When she thinks of how the swirling cocktail of frictionless musky slickness and sticky metallic scarlet must be over-whelming his senses, it almost feels like she can read *his* mind.

His tongue brings her over and over to her edge, just as before, but this time he quells her orgasms by spiking the sensations with sharp slivers of pain as he slips his mouth away to bite at her again. He goes through this cycle over and over, until she is delirious, fallen back on the bed, beyond herself.

Darius rises from the floor, sudden and majestic. He moves himself onto her. He's already naked and he slips inside, his cold hard cock adding a new layer of sensation to the mix of heat and blood and pain and pleasure.

As he begins to thrust inside her, he takes her face in his hands and rolls her head gently to one side. There is an instant – a flash of clarity in the mass of overwhelm-ing sensation – when she sees his fangs, whiter and longer than ever before. And then his mouth is on her neck sinking deep, deeper, and she is coming and so is he.

Blood Rites. Letting him bite her. Making him come. Inviting him in. It is everything she'd imagined it would be in a life growing up with vampires – with Darius Cole – as the ultimate totem of the forbidden.

Day 23
Late the following afternoon, after many, many recrea-tions of that first set of Blood Rites, Merle finally makes it back to her own bedroom, tottering and swaying down the corridor like she is aboard a ship on the high seas.

In the bathroom washing her face, she feels a sudden thrill as she glances in the mirror and sees the multi-layered wound on her neck. It's low enough in the crook of her shoulder that an ordinary shirt will cover it. She tries several from her case until she finds the best one, and then lies down on her bed.

She drops into sleep. The moment of unconsciousness seems fleeting, but when she opens her eyes again, in answer to a knock on the door, it feels like night.

'Hmm? Yes?'

The door opens and Kristina appears carrying a tray piled with bread, cheese and fruit. She feels her stomach jump for joy.

Kristina sets the tray down on the bed and returns her smile. 'And that's not all,' Kristina says happily. She leaves the room and comes back moments later with a second tray holding a teapot, milk jug, sugar bowl and cup and saucer. As she sets this second tray down on the bed Kristina says, 'Darius said it was vital I learnt how to make tea properly. He says tea is to humans what blood is to vampires.'

Merle feels herself blush. 'Maybe not quite.' She runs her tongue over the scab on her lip.

Kristina gives a little laugh as she starts to pour. 'Well, I guess, I do remember being human. Just about. And drinking tea, and, well, hmm...' Kristina passes Merle a warm cup. 'But I think I've got it so at least you'll have some nice tea for your final two days here.'

Merle pauses mid-sip. 'Oh.' She'd completely forgotten that she's so near the end. 'Actually,' she says slowly, 'I might stay a little longer.'

'What? Why?'

'There are still some things I need to work out. With Darius.'

Kristina catches Merle's eye with an expression that makes her feel instantly on guard. 'Merle, what has he told you? You do know you can't trust him.'

'No. It's not like that. I do trust him.'

'You know he has incredible psych-powers, don't you? You remember you saw that thing he did to me – ripped my thoughts right out of my head? And don't think that wasn't set up. Getting me to try and kill you so he could 'punish' me like that. It was probably all for you. You can't even begin to imagine how his brain works. Some people say he isn't even a vampire. Or he's some kind of super-powered version. No one knows what he really is or where he came from. He *says* he doesn't know. But why trust him? The only thing we know for sure about him is that he's dangerous. And he is controlling everything. Everything. He has all your reactions planned out before you even know what they are.' Kristina pauses and her gaze fixes on Merle's lower lip. 'Oh, God, he hasn't taken you to his bed, has he? And bled you? Merle, he's playing with you. You have to resist him. Just hold out for the antidote and get out.'

Merle shakes her head. 'He's already given me the antidote.'

'Then leave! Look, Merle, if you won't do it for your own sake, do it for his. You're no good for him. While you're here, while he's performing Blood Rites with you, he's marked for death. The Clan Council will take this castle back and stake him. If Cobalt doesn't do it first.'

Merle swallows. 'You're only saying it because you want him for yourself.'

Kristina's shoulder rise and fall. 'If that's what you . . . OK, fine. You know, I thought you might say that. Look, Merle, I have an idea. I have something in my room I can give you. It's a draft that can block his psych-powers temporarily. I've been saving it for emergencies. It can't stop his manipulation but it can block the telepathy. And it will help you see him more clearly.'

'I do see him clearly.'

Kristina stands up and her eyes suddenly flash. She points to her forehead and then raises her eyes to the ceiling. 'Let's talk later,' she says brightly. 'Perhaps tomorrow night.'

Day 24

Merle wakes back in Darius's bed. Great red spidering shapes of her blood are staining the linen everywhere. She feels light-headed. Darius is crouched over her, nude and holding an apple in his hand.

'Take care, Magdalena. Don't sit up yet. Eat. I don't want to deplete you completely.'

She grasps the apple gratefully and takes a large bite. She's ravenous. But as she eats, she can't help staring at Darius's beautiful naked body.

'You can't still want more from me, Magdalena,' he says. But his voice is thick and heavy with desire.

She sits up and kisses him, her mouth still full of apple flesh, but he pulls back, wiping his mouth with his hand, his features wrinkling in disgust. 'You taste of food,' he says. 'Let me make you taste of something far sweeter.' And he's already digging in his drawer for a fresh razor blade.

That evening Merle excuses herself.

She's been naked all day and her clothes feel alien as she pulls them over her skin. She goes down a flight of stairs and then wanders down the corridor looking for Kristina's room. Three doors down from her own, her knock is met with a cry of 'Come in'.

Kristina's room is a mess. But underneath the flurry of clothes and bed sheets and what appeared to be ripped up soft toys is a room as smartly sumptuous as Merle's own. Kristina sits on the bed, holding a glass of black liquid in her hand. She grins at Merle.

Merle stares at the content of the glass. 'Is that it? Is that the draft?'

Kristina nods. 'Well it's not my night cap, is it?'

Merle starts to cross to the bed. 'And if I drink it . . .'

'You'll find it easier to see through his lies. It'll keep

him out of your head. What he's done by persuasion, well, that can't be undone, but where he's twisted your mind deliberately to entice you to believe his lies. That'll go.'

Merle reaches out and takes the glass. She pauses. 'I don't know.'

Kristina holds her gaze. 'If everything he says is true, you'll still be his after you've drunk it.'

Merle inhales and raises the glass to her lips. But just as it touches them she freezes. Her hand suddenly jerks and she throws the glass across the room. It smashes against the wall. Confused, she whirls around to see Darius standing in the doorway. He is across the room before she's even properly registered him, diving onto the bed, pining Kristina down, pulling out a stake. Merle blinks, looking again at the black liquid dripping down the wall. She's still astounded at how easily he took control of her body. She's never seen him do anything like that. What is he? His powers are frightening.

On the bed, Kristina is screaming, terrified as Darius holds the stake to her heart. 'No, no, no.'

Darius looks up at Merle. 'You can't trust her,' he says, 'she slipping from my control.' He turns back to Kristina. 'Aren't you?'

'Merle, make him stop,' Kristina screams. 'Tell him. He'll listen to you.'

'No,' Darius snaps, '*she'll* listen to *you*. Tell her. Tell her what you just tried to give her.'

Kristina starts sobbing, beginning again her chorus of, 'No, no, no. Darius, please. I saved you from them, Darius. Without me . . .'

'Tell her,' he snaps, interrupting her. 'What did you just try and make her drink.'

'Death,' sobs Kristina.

'Death?'

'Death,' says Darius. 'Poison. It's poisonous to humans. Black Emeralds like Kristina and Oberon drink it like a liqueur. They find it amusing. Don't you?'

Kristina – still sobbing – nods.

Darius lowers his mouth to Kristina's ear. 'You remember what I promised you your next punishment would be?'

Kristina nods again.

'Well, we've moved a long way past that now.' He lifts the stake.

'No, Darius, not me. Never me. I love you.'

Darius lifts the stake higher above Kristina's heaving chest, poised to strike.

'No!' Merle is shaking as hard as either of the vampires.

Darius pauses, but he turns on her with livid eyes. 'She tried to kill you, Merle. For the second time. What am I to do? Keep on forgiving her until she finally manages it?'

Merle looks at Kristina's terrified face. 'I just, just want to know why. What did I ever . . .?' she walks over to the bed and sit down next to where Kristina is lying, pinned under Darius's thighs. 'Please, Kristina, why?'

Kristina narrows her eyes. 'You know why.'

'Because you're in love with him? Because you're jealous?'

Kristina nods.

'But you know that he doesn't love you, right?'

'He should,' Kristina says, her voice cracking to more tears. 'He's just some filthy feral thing and I *saved* him.'

'How did you save him?'

'I brought him blood. Oberon was starving him. It helped to control his psych-powers to limit the amount of blood he got. But he looked so wretched. I brought him some extra plasma packs. I didn't know then what it would do. But that's how he broke loose. Because of me. And he killed everyone. And now I don't have anything – anyone – left except him. And he doesn't even care.'

Kristina stops talking and rolls her face away. Merle looks up at Darius. 'Come on,' she says to him, 'let's leave her. You don't need to punish her. You've already punished her enough.'

'No I haven't,' Darius says and he thrusts the stake right into Kristina's screaming chest.

In bed, Merle says, 'Where is Oberon?'

'In the dungeon. I know I ought to kill him too. But it's so hard to give him the peace he denied me.'

The coolness in Darius's voice makes Merle shiver. 'Has he been down there long?'

'About ten days. I shut him down there for making Kristina put you back in the cells. I don't know why I even keep letting him out. I just get rather overwhelmed sometimes by the reality of him being down there suffering as I did ... And I let him out again, until he tries something.' Darius shrugs, looking strangely sheepish.

'If you can't kill him Darius, I will.'

'Oh, Magdalena,' Darius says, rolling over on top of her and dipping his head to open up one of the wounds on her neck.

Day 25

Merle rolls over in Darius's arms. The curtains are drawn as always, but it feels like morning.

Darius is awake, looking at her. 'You can leave whenever you want. You don't have to wait until six o'clock.'

'Do I have to leave?'

Darius smiles. 'No. You know that. Do you want to stay?'

Merle smiles back. 'Maybe a little longer. And there was something I told you I'd do.'

'Of course.' Darius runs a cold finger over her collar bone. 'I do have some things to do today, too. I would love to lie with you all day, of course, bleed you, taste you, see if I can find a part of my dead body that hasn't yet made you flush pink and come, but . . .' He stops and grazes his plump bottom lips with his teeth.

Merle puts her hand on his cheek and moves to kiss him. 'Perhaps later.'

A little later, down in the dungeon, Merle peers through the barred window into Oberon's cell. He's manacled and lying on the floor staring at the ceiling.

Ten days without blood.

Merle draws back the bolts and steps into the cell. Oberon lifts his head. Lord Oberon of the Black Emerald Clan. The man who arranged it all.

After she's closed the door behind her, Merle keeps her back pressed against it. She knows the exact limit of Oberon's chains very well. He won't be able to reach her where she stands.

'What do you want, Miss Cobalt?'

'I have something for you, Oberon. Food.'

'Food?' Oberon snorts.

Out of her pocket Merle pulls one of Darius's razor blades. 'Well if you're not hungry.'

'Oh.' Oberon's eyes go wide. He starts to get to his feet.

'You can get off the floor,' Merle says gently, 'but then I want you to sit down on the bench. You remember how it goes. You have to earn your food down here.'

'You want me to kiss you?' he says as he sits down, grinning, almost high – on nothing but the promise of her blood. This was going to be too easy.

'No. No kisses. Remember the other time. I want you to answer my questions. I want to know the truth.'

Oberon smiles. 'You know, in the end, that's often all

humans want from vampires. Funny. We do know how to make you dizzy so many ways, don't we?'

Merle holds up her left hand. With the razor blade she snicks the pad of her thumb and turns her hand a little so Oberon can see the wound. 'You know, I'm sure there's a huge stash of blood – what did Kristina call them? Plasma packs – somewhere in this castle – but, I thought this might be more effective. You still like it fresh best of all, don't you? Vamps? I remember my mum telling me about how vamps sometimes kidnap people for a little of the warm stuff then do a mind wipe before they send them back. Very occasionally the mind wipes don't take – that's when Cobalt hears about them.'

Merle tilts her wrist so the blood from her thumb starts to run down her arm. 'You ready to talk yet?'

'You really think I'm going to tell you the truth?'

'Actually, yeah. You've been starved down here, haven't you? Makes it much harder for you to spin me tales, doesn't it?'

'Sounds like you got a few psych-powers there your-self, missy.'

'Are you going to tell me the truth, or not?'

Oberon leans over and spits on the floor. When he looks up his face is defiant. 'If you want the truth, why don't you go and ask Cole. He seems very keen that everyone knows his side of the story.'

'He does, doesn't he? Except I'm not sure he really knows the truth. He only really knows what you told him, doesn't he? And why would you tell him the truth? You're a vampire. All his information about what was done to Magdalena really came from you. If anyone has the real answers you do.' A splatter of Merle's blood hits the floor. Oberon's eyes go wide looking at it. Merle waits for him to look back at her. 'Did Cole really believe in Righteous Power?'

Oberon looks sullen for a moment. 'No,' he says

quietly. 'No. He was just a trouble maker. He had no line and nothing to lose. He said he wanted the Clan Council reorganised, more contact between vampires and humans, Clan leaders elected, that sort of thing. I doubt he knew about Righteous Power, probably never even heard of it, feral thing like him. But you'll never convince the Clan Council of that. It'll be his word against mine. Darius Cole is a legend. My legend. And every last vampire that heard him speak joined his cause, and every one of them was killed. There's no one left to say what his doctrine really was, but it wasn't Righteous Power.'

Merle nods. 'And was he performing Blood Rites with humans?'

'Oh, yes. Well, with one human.'

'Magdalena. The woman you had killed. The woman whose soul you trapped in a glass prism.'

Oberon's eyes flash like he's suddenly pleased about something. 'Oh no. That part's not true.'

Merle swallows. She knows she's getting close. But close to what? The truth. The truth that she isn't Magdalena at all? 'Talk to me, Oberon, or you can rot here. Starved into insanity. I mean it.' Another red splat fell onto the dirty floor.

'I am telling you the truth,' Oberon says softly. 'You're right. I can't manipulate you right now. I'm too weak. I can't see in your mind, you're just a blood sack to me right now so you might as well listen. I did not put Cole's creature's soul into a prism. Of course I didn't! Have you any idea how much that would *cost*? Why does everyone think old vampires have unlimited resources? Covering the running of your parents stupid Cobalt operation was bad enough – but then a soul prison on top! If I'd really done that I'd have been ruined. I'm 300 years old; everything is so bloody expensive these days.'

'Oh for God's sake. It's called inflation and I don't see

you vamps complaining about it when it works in your advantage. You're all richer than gods.'

Oberon spits onto the floor again. His juices must really be flowing. 'I would never have had to have bought witchcraft in. Vampires and witches, never a good mix. And I had already spent enough on Cole. So I...'

'Oh,' says Merle, her stomach flipping over with the realisation of what Oberon is saying. 'I get it. It was a trick. A vampire mind trick. You just made him *think* you had her soul. So he wouldn't have hope, right? That's the point.'

Oberon nods. 'That's how vampires operate. It's all games. It's all lies. It's not what you can do as much as what you can make people think you can do. Everyone believed I had Magdalena Wright's soul trapped in a glass prism, and that knowledge destroyed all Cole's hopes as surely as if I had really done it.'

'So why did you change your plan. I mean, why tell him you'd put the soul in me?'

'Because, even with his brain starved of blood he was still a cunning creature. Even when he was rolling around on the floor of that cell naked, filthy and deranged, he worked out, or found out, what keeping that soul secure would have been costing me. He realised I wouldn't be able to afford it forever. He started to get hopeful. Started to believe that one day I would have to release her.'

'So then you came up with the idea of me. Of telling him you'd put her soul in me.'

'Not exactly. Cobalt came up with that one. I thought if I shut down Cobalt Cole would think I was serious about his woman's prison. When I told your parents – mummy and daddy – they basically sold me their first-born child. You. As a receptacle for Magdalena's soul. They didn't even want to have children until this little problem came along. They were both too committed to making money. No wonder they had such an affinity with vamps. Nice people. But it was their idea to conceive a child, place the soul there, and then raise that child to hate and despise vampires. And to hate and despise Cole most of all.'

Merle puts her hand on the cell door behind her for balance. 'My parents suggested it!'

'You can't blame them. They were desperate. Cobalt was a cushy number and they knew it. I owned them. That nice house you grew up in? That fancy office building just off Whitehall? Who do you think pays for all that? Me. Well, the Black Emerald Clan.' He leans forward on the bench. 'Want to know something really funny? Guess who's been rubber stamping all of Cobalt's expenses for the last two years, since he took this place over?' Oberon's eyes rolled to the ceiling.

'Never mind that.' Merle's shaking, Oberon might be too weak to lie to her, but his truth was still devastating. 'So you fooled Cobalt along with everyone else. They think it's all true, too. They think you really did put her soul into their child. Into me!'

'Yes.' Oberon looks impatient. 'Your parents think it's true, Cole thinks it's true. The only people who know it isn't true are in this cell.'

'So what really happened to Magdalena's soul?'

Oberon shrugs. 'Whatever you believe happens to the soul when someone dies. She was shot. She's dead, that's all I know. I'm sure when you tell him he'll start trying to find her.'

'Oh.' Merle feels her heart drop straight through her body as she realises the truth in what Oberon is saying. She isn't Magdalena. She isn't Darius's lover.

She pulls the stake out of the back of the waistband of her jeans and stakes Oberon before he's finished laughing at her. She's never staked a vampire before. It's surprisingly easy.

Merle slides the bolts of the cell door closed and turns around, Darius is standing right behind her, right up close in the tiny corridor. She starts. 'Darius, are you OK? I thought you were busy.'

'I was. But I thought I'd come and check on you. Did you do it?'

'Yes.' Merle swallows. Oberon's dead. Which means she's the only one left now who knows the truth. 'You weren't in my mind when I was in there with Oberon?'

'No.' Darius smiles, a little confused. 'Why? Were you doing something I wouldn't like, Magdalena?' He catches Merle's left wrist and lifts her bloody hand.

'Darius, I . . .' Merle's voice trails away. She isn't Magdalena. But that's her secret. She doesn't have to tell him. But he can read her mind. How can she keep a secret from him? There's a look in his eyes. Something dark and comforting. Unless it wasn't a secret. Unless he'd known all along. 'You know, don't you? You know I'm not . . . Not her.'

'I know. And, yes, I've always known. Oberon isn't half as clever as he thinks he is.' He reaches out touches a wisp of hair that's stuck to her cheek. 'She's dead. They killed her because of me. As for where her soul is now. Gone into the ether to find another place to rest. Who knows, maybe you *are* her reborn.'

'It'd be a billion to one chance if I actually was . . .'

'But she brought me to you. Her story. My love for her. Something in what was done to me and the lies I was told drew me to you. Only to you. And when I look on you I feel something that I only ever felt before when I looked on her. Maybe . . .' He looks intently at her. 'Maybe there is some part of her. Somehow . . .'

'Darius . . .' Merle's voice trails away.

Darius brings her bloody hand to his mouth and licks at her thumb with his cool tongue. 'Let me get that for you, Magdalena.'

Visit the Black Lace website at
www.black-lace-books.com

FIND OUT THE LATEST INFORMATION AND TAKE ADVANTAGE OF OUR FANTASTIC FREE BOOK OFFER! ALSO VISIT THE SITE FOR . . .

- All Black Lace titles currently available and how to order online
- Great new offers
- Writers' guidelines
- Author interviews
- An erotica newsletter
- Features
- Cool links

BLACK LACE — THE LEADING IMPRINT OF WOMEN'S SEXY FICTION

TAKING YOUR EROTIC READING PLEASURE TO NEW HORIZONS

LOOK OUT FOR THE ALL-NEW BLACK LACE BOOKS – AVAILABLE NOW!

All books priced £7.99 in the UK. Please note publication dates apply to the UK only. For other territories, please contact your retailer.

SPLIT
Kristina Lloyd
ISBN 978 0 352 34154 9

A visit to Heddlestone, a remote village in the Yorkshire moors, changes librarian Kate Carter's life. The place has an eerie yet erotic charge and, when Kate is later offered a job in its puppet museum, she flees London and her boyfriend in order to take it.

Jake, the strange and beautiful curator and puppeteer, draws her into his secluded sensual world, and before long she's sharing his bed, going deeper into new and at times frightening explorations of love and lust. But Kate is also seduced by Eddie, Jake's brother, and his wild Ukrainian wife, and she becomes tangled in a second dark relationship. Split between the two men, Kate moves closer to uncovering the truth behind the secrets of Heddlestone, ever sensing danger but not knowing whether the greatest threat comes from ghosts or reality.

WILD KINGDOM
Deanna Ashford
ISBN 978 0 352 33549 4

Salacious cruelties abound as war rages in the mythical kingdom of
Kabra. Prince Tarn is struggling to drive out the invading army while his
bethrothed – the beautiful Rianna – has fled the fighting with the
mysterious Baroness Crissana.

But the baroness is a fearsome and depraved woman, and once
they're out of the danger zone she takes Rianna prisoner. Her plan is to
present her as a plaything to her warlord half-brother, Ragnor. In order
to rescue his sweetheart, Prince Tarn needs to join forces with his old
enemy, Sarin, whose capacity for perverse delights knows no civilised
bounds.

Coming in December 2007

THE SILVER CROWN
Mathilde Madden
ISBN 978 0 352 34157 0

Every full moon, Iris kills werewolves. It's what she's good at. What she's
trained for. She's never imagined doing anything else . . . until she falls in
love with one. And being a professional werewolf hunter and dating a
werewolf poses a serious conflict of interests. To add to her problems, a
group of witches decides she is the chosen one – destined to save
humanity from the wolves at the door – while her new boss, Blake, who
just happens to be her ex-husband, is hell-bent on sabotaging her new
relationship. All Iris wants is to snuggle up with her alpha wolf and be
left alone. He might turn into a monster once a month, but in a lot of
ways Iris does too.

MINX
Megan Blythe
ISBN 978 0 352 33638 5

Miss Amy Pringle is pert, spoilt and spirited when she arrives at Lancaster Hall to pursue her engagement to Lord Fitzroy, eldest son of the Earl and heir to a fortune. The Earl is not impressed with this young upstart and sets out to break her spirit through a series of painful and humiliating ordeals.

The trouble for him is that she enjoys every one of his 'punishments' and creates havoc at the Hall, provoking and infuriating the stuffy Earl at every opportunity while indulging in all manner of naughtiness below the stairs. The young Lord remains aloof, however, and, in order to win his affections, Amy sets about seducing his well-endowed but dim brother, Bubb. When she is discovered in bed with Bubb and one of the servant girls, how will father and son react?

Next collection of novellas coming in February 2008

POSSESSION: THREE PARANORMAL TALES OF SHAPE-SHIFTING AND POSSESSION FROM BLACK LACE
Mathilde Madden, Madelynne Ellis, Anne Tourney
ISBN 978 0 352 34164 8

Falling Dancer: Kelda has two jobs: full-time bartender, part-time exorcist. She meets vengeful spirits and misguided demons wherever she goes. She wishes the spirit world would leave her alone so she could have a relationship that lasted longer than 24 hours, but, when she's contacted by a sexy musician who wants her to solve the mystery of his girlfriend's disappearance, she can't help getting involved . . .

The Silver Chains: Alfie Friday is a werewolf. For seven years he has controlled his curse carefully by locking himself in a cage every full moon. But now he's changing when it isn't full moon. His girlfriend Misty travels to South America to try and find a way of controlling Alfie's changes, but discovers the key to the problem lies in Oxford. The place it all began for Alfie and the place he has vowed never to return to.

Broken Angel: After stealing a copy of an ancient manuscript, Blaze Makaresh finds himself being hunted down by a gang of youkai – demons who infiltrate human society in order to satisfy their hunger for sex and flesh. When Talon, an elitist society of demon-hunters, come to his aid, he's soon enmeshed with the beautiful Asha, and the dawning of an age-old prophecy.

Black Lace Booklist

Information is correct at time of printing. To avoid disappointment, check availability before ordering. Go to www.black-lace-books.com. All books are priced £7.99 unless another price is given.

BLACK LACE BOOKS WITH A CONTEMPORARY SETTING

☐ THE SOCIETY OF SIN Sian Lacey Taylder ISBN 978 0 352 34080 1
☐ UNDRESSING THE DEVIL Angel Strand ISBN 978 0 352 33938 6

BLACK LACE BOOKS WITH A PARANORMAL THEME

☐ BRIGHT FIRE Maya Hess ISBN 978 0 352 34104 4
☐ BURNING BRIGHT Janine Ashbless ISBN 978 0 352 34085 6
☐ CRUEL ENCHANTMENT Janine Ashbless ISBN 978 0 352 33483 1
☐ DIVINE TORMENT Janine Ashbless ISBN 978 0 352 33719 1
☐ FLOOD Anna Clare ISBN 978 0 352 34094 8
☐ GOTHIC BLUE Portia Da Costa ISBN 978 0 352 33075 8
☐ THE PRIDE Edie Bingham ISBN 978 0 352 33997 3

BLACK LACE ANTHOLOGIES

☐ BLACK LACE QUICKIES 1 Various ISBN 978 0 352 34126 6 £2.99
☐ BLACK LACE QUICKIES 2 Various ISBN 978 0 352 34127 3 £2.99
☐ BLACK LACE QUICKIES 3 Various ISBN 978 0 352 34128 0 £2.99
☐ BLACK LACE QUICKIES 4 Various ISBN 978 0 352 34129 7 £2.99
☐ MORE WICKED WORDS Various ISBN 978 0 352 33487 9 £6.99
☐ WICKED WORDS 3 Various ISBN 978 0 352 33522 7 £6.99
☐ WICKED WORDS 4 Various ISBN 978 0 352 33603 3 £6.99
☐ WICKED WORDS 5 Various ISBN 978 0 352 33642 2 £6.99
☐ WICKED WORDS 6 Various ISBN 978 0 352 33690 3 £6.99
☐ WICKED WORDS 7 Various ISBN 978 0 352 33743 6 £6.99
☐ WICKED WORDS 8 Various ISBN 978 0 352 33787 0 £6.99
☐ WICKED WORDS 9 Various ISBN 978 0 352 33860 0
☐ WICKED WORDS 10 Various ISBN 978 0 352 33893 8
☐ THE BEST OF BLACK LACE 2 Various ISBN 978 0 352 33718 4
☐ WICKED WORDS: SEX IN THE OFFICE Various ISBN 978 0 352 33944 7
☐ WICKED WORDS: SEX AT THE SPORTS CLUB ISBN 978 0 352 33991 1
     Various
☐ WICKED WORDS: SEX ON HOLIDAY Various ISBN 978 0 352 33961 4
☐ WICKED WORDS: SEX IN UNIFORM Various ISBN 978 0 352 34002 3
☐ WICKED WORDS: SEX IN THE KITCHEN Various ISBN 978 0 352 34018 4
☐ WICKED WORDS: SEX ON THE MOVE Various ISBN 978 0 352 34034 4
☐ WICKED WORDS: SEX AND MUSIC Various ISBN 978 0 352 34061 0
☐ WICKED WORDS: SEX AND SHOPPING Various ISBN 978 0 352 34076 4

To find out the latest information about Black Lace titles, check out the website: www.black-lace-books.com or send for a booklist with complete synopses by writing to:

> Black Lace Booklist, Virgin Books Ltd
> Thames Wharf Studios
> Rainville Road
> London W6 9HA

Please include an SAE of decent size. Please note only British stamps are valid.

Our privacy policy
We will not disclose information you supply us to any other parties. We will not disclose any information which identifies you personally to any person without your express consent.

From time to time we may send out information about Black Lace books and special offers. Please tick here if you do <u>not</u> wish to receive Black Lace information.   ☐

Please send me the books I have ticked above.

Name ....

Address ....

....

....

....

Post Code ....

Send to: Virgin Books Cash Sales, Thames Wharf Studios, Rainville Road, London W6 9HA.

US customers: for prices and details of how to order books for delivery by mail, call 888-330-8477.

Please enclose a cheque or postal order, made payable to Virgin Books Ltd, to the value of the books you have ordered plus postage and packing costs as follows:

UK and BFPO – £1.00 for the first book, 50p for each subsequent book.

Overseas (including Republic of Ireland) – £2.00 for the first book, £1.00 for each subsequent book.

If you would prefer to pay by VISA, ACCESS/MASTERCARD, DINERS CLUB, AMEX or SWITCH, please write your card number and expiry date here:

....

Signature ....

Please allow up to 28 days for delivery.